Second Chance

NORTHWEST COUNTER-TERRORISM TASKFORCE BOOK 2

Lisa Phillips

Chapter 1

The second he opened the door, Haley Franks slammed into it. She used the force of her weight, coupled with the surprise, to shove her way in.

Gun up.

Instead of shooting him, which would've been pretty satisfying, Haley used a double-hand grip on her Sig to sideswipe the gun he held. Then she slammed the butt into Yuri's chin. She'd have gone for the temple, but he was taller up close.

Yuri stumbled back.

Haley kicked the door shut. "We need to talk."

He brought his gun up again, but she hit it with a round house. It went off. Shot a hole clean through the '90s artwork on his wall. Then the gun skittered to the floor across the room and she kicked him again, square in the sternum.

He fell to the floor, and it was a good three seconds before he managed to breathe.

"Like I said." She settled into a wide stance, gun loose. Glad she'd pulled her hair into a ponytail.

There was no way to get around the fact this guy was going to see her face. But that was the point. Yuri needed to understand this was personal. She was wading in and nothing was going to stop her from finding out what happened to Ana.

Not even this cop.

He looked up at her from the floor. A muscle in his abnormally square jaw flexed. Yuri Kartov had been with Portland Police Department for four years. He'd been investigated by internal affairs twice, but no charges were ever filed. Still, everyone knew he was dirty. They just couldn't figure out precisely where the link was between him and the Russian mob.

Haley didn't much care about that.

She pulled a cell phone from her left back pocket and hit the home button with her thumb. No code. She'd taken that off since she had found it in the woods outside of the city. It was Ana's phone. And the only thing on there now was her friend's picture.

She showed Yuri the screen. "This is Ana. She disappeared a few weeks ago."

Haley let that sink in for him. Watched his eyes flare with recognition and...something else.

Yes, she'd given away her weakness—the fact she cared about her friend—but she'd also let him know that this was all desperation. That could be good or bad for him, depending on what he wanted to do with it. On the other hand, she had nothing but the need to find Ana.

She'd gotten out of the Navy a month ago and spent the time since trying to track down Ana. Four weeks of trying to get ahold of her friend. Then using her skills to track Ana's phone to the forest in the middle of nowhere. Not somewhere Ana would have gone for fun, preferring shopping malls to hiking trails.

Haley was the outdoorsy one. Though, she'd been rethinking that. It might've just been a byproduct of Navy life. She'd worked for years in military intelligence. Amassing data. Finding links, filing reports, and generally organizing the crap out of the stuff that came across her desk in the commander's office. Then there was the time she'd jerry-rigged the copier to get it to quit spitting out black pages.

Interrogation wasn't really her forte. But she was willing to give it a try.

Yuri's gray eyes looked up at her. "You think I know this..?" He referred to Ana in a Russian word that Haley was going to have to Google—one she didn't think meant anything good.

"I don't know. Do you know her?"

The fact he might have kidnapped Ana had occurred to her. Or, he'd been with her and things had gone too far. Maybe he'd killed her. Maybe it was an accident.

Or an overdose.

She wasn't about to repeat herself, asking if he knew Ana. He was the last person to have seen her best friend alive. Or at least one of the last people.

Grief pricked hot tears in her eyes. Ana wasn't dead. She couldn't be.

Haley tilted the cell in front of her. "This is Ana's phone." One she'd traipsed through the forest to find, following the GPS history. Haley had prayed for a miracle...for something. And then she'd found it right before the battery died.

"She texted you, set up a meeting. It was one of the last things she ever did. I want to know what you were meeting for."

His mouth curled up on one side, but there was something in his eyes. He wasn't quite so confident in himself. All pretense was gone now, his Russian heritage bleeding through in his tone even though she'd heard him speak with an American accent.

He planted his boots on the threadbare carpet and stood. He leaned his hips on the slip-covered couch, one of those ill-fitting ones where the owner didn't care to readjust it.

She lifted her gun so her aim was on his center mass. Was she going to kill a cop in his own home? No. At least, she sincerely hoped that wasn't what this was going to come to. But still, he didn't need to know that. He had to think she was prepared to go to *any* lengths.

Even murder.

She said, "I think you're going to tell me what was between you and Ana and what you know about her disappearance."

He said nothing, just stared at her in a way that made her wonder if he was debating internally. If maybe he *wanted* to tell her what he knew.

"I have evidence that proves you're guilty of dealing drugs." She paused for a second. "What do you think your captain is going to say when I bring that to him?"

"So you think…what? I killed your friend?" He took a tiny step toward her.

"How should I know?" She took a tiny step of her own. Backward, to maintain the distance between them.

"They sent you to kill me?"

Did who…what?

He was still coming toward her.

Haley said, "Stop moving. I will shoot you." She had her finger on the trigger, a round in the chamber. One squeeze and this cop, pretending to be a good guy, wouldn't be a gray area anymore. He would be nothing but a stain on his nasty carpet.

The skin around his eyes twitched, but not with humor. "Some kind of superhero, vigilante person? Like on TV? Cops don't like that." He took another tiny step.

Hers brought her back in contact with the wall beside the door.

"If you're not going to pull that trigger," he said. "Then you'll have to come with me."

"That's not gonna happen." She would shoot him.

She might have to.

The gun was new to her, but it had a colorful history. She'd paid way too much in cash for something that couldn't be traced back to her. It could, however, be linked to a murder three weeks ago. Someone had killed a Mexican gang member in a shooting that had, as yet, been unsolved.

It would look like a simple retaliation. Or another hit. Some connection between Yuri, the dead Hispanic man and the killer. Or perhaps Yuri *had* been the killer.

The fact was, Haley had prepared for this. She'd assumed he would answer the door armed. She had concluded that she might have to kill him in order to get away. But she wanted answers. She wanted to look him in the eyes and ask him where her friend was.

She lifted the gun an inch, pointed right at his heart. "What was Ana into?"

Her friend had always lived on the wild side. Not even renting a house and having a steady job had calmed Ana. She'd wanted it all. Live free, have fun. Work just enough to keep her head above water.

Yuri grinned. "You don't even know, do you?"

And then he launched himself at her.

. . .

NCIS Special Agent Niall O'Caran raced across the front lawn and down the side of the house. The gate was latched but unlocked. He shoved it open so hard the vinyl slammed against the fence with a crack. He didn't wait around to see how broken it was. He just raced down the side of the house. Mostly praying there wasn't a mean dog in the yard. And also that the woman inside didn't get herself killed.

What was she thinking?

Yellow light spilled out of the side window. He peered around the frame in time to see Yuri slam the woman into his coffee table. It splintered underneath her.

Niall winced. Seriously. What *was* she thinking? Never mind that she was going to blow his whole case by confronting the Russian like this. He was supposed to be doing surveillance, finding out why every time he asked questions about Western Oregon Research College Scholarships, Yuri's name seemed to come up. It made next to no sense that a possibly mafia-tied police officer was connected to a local college. The whole thing was bizarre. Enough that no other police and federal agency even wanted to be bothered by it.

Enter Niall.

Well, more like his boss. Director Victoria Bramlyn took up cases nobody wanted. Or cases everyone else fought over. Their jurisdiction was a creatively-defined gray area, mostly—he figured—so Victoria could sweep up whatever she wanted for them to work on.

This case? Probably nothing but busywork for Niall to keep occupied with. All because he'd chosen his family over his team on the last case. Delayed—or attempted to delay—two of his teammates going after their suspect. It wasn't like he'd actually done what those people had tried to blackmail him into doing. What he had done was to protect his sister and his niece.

Still. Probation sucked.

Yuri thought he was an untouchable cop. He thought the badge afforded him rights he wouldn't have been privy to otherwise. Most of which turned Niall's stomach. His looking into Yuri's life didn't have much to do with the man's predilections, thank goodness. This was about college scholarships.

But this woman, whoever she was, evidently wasn't too worried about it. Over the surveillance feed, he'd listened to their entire conversation. Her friend was missing. That was all she cared about. No matter that Yuri went through women like a kid at the carnival.

The woman rolled off the splintered coffee table.

Yuri kicked at her but missed. She jackknifed to a stand and rushed at him, using her shoulder and the force of her momentum to hit Yuri in a tackle that knocked the wind out of him. She was fighting for her life. Too bad he looked like he was having fun. Playing with her.

Niall should go in there and help before Yuri did something stupid. Like kill her.

He took a step toward the back of the house, his gaze still fixed on their brawl. She landed a solid kick in Yuri's stomach. He grabbed her foot. She let him swing it out, followed with the other one and kicked him in the head.

Huh.

She landed on the floor. *Ouch.* They rolled, a tangle of limbs as they each grappled for dominance. Yuri was taller than her. The woman had been trained—and in more than the dirty fighting styles the cop knew. Police holds and nasty tricks were being pitted up against a serious level of martial arts skills and something else…

She used a Navy move.

Niall pulled out his phone. He lifted it to the window and took a burst of images until he got one that was a good shot of her face. Then he sent the image to Talia.

He might be a Navy cop, but he was attached to a counter-terrorism task force that operated in the northwest. Based out of Portland, Oregon, they traveled all over. Washington, Idaho, Montana, Nevada. Utah. Even Wyoming and Colorado sometimes. Wherever the winds of criminal activity blew them. Anything that could be construed as terrorism. Which, these days, was basically anything if you worded it right.

And yeah, that was bitterness ringing through, but he couldn't help it. Moving his whole family to a different state had been exhausting. On top of *that,* his sister wasn't happy. His niece kept giving him sideways looks like she doubted his sanity. Everyone on the team thought he'd betrayed them.

Sure, they didn't say it out loud. But he knew what they were thinking.

He stowed his phone back in his pocket. Would Talia even bother running the search on this woman's image for him? Maybe she'd just ignore his email. Even though the woman was an NSA analyst, as well as the nosiest person he'd ever met.

Niall watched the woman twist and punch Yuri in the stomach. "Where is Ana?" Blood had collected in her nose and at the corner of her mouth. One cheek was flushed red. Still, she moved like she would keep fighting and never give up.

Yuri's answer was to laugh. Like their fighting was fun for him. Then he stumbled but still managed to catch her. They both went down.

Niall winced. Both of them would have a collection of bruises tomorrow.

The woman rolled out of his grip and got to her feet. She should just run out the front door. Get clear of this guy and split town. Anywhere out of reach of a cop with Russian mob ties. Which kind of meant southern hemisphere. Still, there were plenty of nice places to choose from.

Places to disappear to.

But she didn't run. She stood there, staring down at Yuri. Both of them breathing hard. "I'm not going to let this go until I find her."

She took one step back and then turned.

Walked out the front door, as cool as anything. No worries. No fear.

This woman was going to get herself killed. Niall wanted to know who she was, not to mention where some friend of hers who hadn't called her back had disappeared to. Could be anything. And not a single one of those options he thought of was good. He'd seen too much to be optimistic about anything.

Niall shifted to leave, feeling much older than his thirty-four years. He probably looked it, but thankfully none of the team was babysitting the task force office with him so they weren't seeing it. Everyone was off on assignments. Working on their open cases.

He got saddled with answering the phone and this busywork assignment. Busting a dirty Russian cop and trying to nail down the particulars of a bunch of fishy college scholarships. However those two were connected.

"Yeah." The Russian's voice was muffled behind the glass. "She was here, asking questions."

Niall turned back to the window.

Yuri held a flip phone to his ear. Not the cell he used for personal calls, the one Niall had a warrant for. This phone he'd never seen.

Unregistered.

Untraceable.

Probably both, which meant he was going to have to get into Yuri's house—again—in order to find it.

"We have to take her out." Yuri listened for a second then spoke again, his accent thick. "Because it's our only choice. She's going to ask wrong questions. Draw too much attention and we will be blamed. We'll never get paid." He sucked in a breath.

Niall watched his hands shake as adrenaline bled off. He was still on the floor, surrounded by the destruction left over after the fight. Couch flipped onto its back. Shattered coffee table. Broken lamp.

Yuri said, "*Da*. That's what I'm saying. We have to take her out." His teeth flashed. "Permanently."

Cold settled deep in the pit of Niall's empty stomach.

They were going to kill that woman.

Chapter 2

Haley kept her back straight and tried her best to walk as normally as possible. Meanwhile, her entire body screamed.

She headed straight for the coffee pot, grabbed the biggest mug her brother owned and filled it nearly to the brim with the steaming black nectar of life. She carried it two steps to the sink and added cold water. Had to pour some out. Added some more cold.

All the while she could feel his big-brother stare on her back. Haley turned and surveyed the bare floors, bare walls and sparse furniture of the dining and living rooms while she sipped her coffee. Open plan was her favorite.

Her brother was still staring at her. "What's wrong with you?"

She lowered the mug only enough to say, "Nothing."

Her brother's snort told her what he thought of that. "What'd we talk about?"

Haley wrinkled her nose as she tried to remember the pact they'd made as teens. "No lies."

"No lies." He leaned his big body against the other side of the kitchen island, which currently had no countertop. He looked at her with those huge brown eyes she'd never been able to say no to. Especially that time he'd asked if she'd snuck out to meet her boyfriend the night before. That was a long time ago now, more than ten years.

He'd always been able to pin her with that knowing look. The one that made her want to spill every secret. Those dark eyes of his were the foundation of the "look." These days the whole thing was augmented by a deep-set, purple scar that ran from the top of his head on the left side almost down to his eyebrow. As though someone had tried to split his temple open.

Corporal Isaac Franks, USMC, had barely escaped that IED attack with his head still attached to his shoulders. These days he wore a beanie or ball cap everywhere. Except when he was with her.

She wanted to squirm but forced herself to stand fast. "I'm not a child," she pointed out. Like that had ever been an issue. "And you're not the parent." Their father lived in Virginia.

"Like that's ever stopped me."

"True."

"If it didn't work," he said, "I'd give up trying. So maybe you should think about that."

Haley sipped her coffee.

"Coward."

She choked on a mouthful, but managed to swallow without dribbling on her NAVY T-shirt. She swiped at the corner of her mouth. "So what's on the docket for today?"

"You're painting the walls above the stairs. I'm doing the upstairs hallway." The "look" was back.

Haley didn't want to ask why that expression was on his face again. She upturned the empty mug in the sink. "Sounds good."

The sooner they were done with fixing up this house, the better. Isaac could take a few days off. Get a break from the intense pace needed to transform his latest dump into a pristine home with a for sale sign in the yard. Bank the profit. Relax while he searched for the next one.

As far as therapy went, it seemed to be working for him. Though the fact he was holed up inside and working for weeks while he got a house ready bothered her. He needed to get out. Meet someone nice. But the question was whether he even wanted to entertain the possibility of something better in his life. No, he didn't. He was too busy working and nagging her to do something constructive with *her* life.

In case he hadn't noticed, she *was* doing something.

Haley did the prep work, then poured paint in the tray. She dipped the roller in and got right to work on the walls. He'd put her on the stairs while he did the second floor hallway because she was steadier on her feet, and he still had issues with balance. Didn't stop him from riding his motorcycle, though.

She stretched to the top of the wall, up on her tiptoes, and pressed the roller up as far as she could reach. Pain ripped through her side.

She bit back the cry, pushed breath out between her clenched teeth, and lowered the roller.

"I knew it."

She dipped the roller again and coated it with paint.

"Got yourself into some trouble."

At the top of the stairs, he leaned his weight against the wall like he had all the time in the world. "You were walking funny this morning."

And yet he'd sent her to paint, even though bathroom cabinets were on the schedule for this week. Haley rolled paint up the wall, not going as far as she had before. The twinge in her side was manageable.

"Don't suppose you're going to show me."

Nope.

"Or tell me what you got up to last night?" He paused. "Went looking for Ana. Who'd you find?"

"The last person to see her alive."

"Who?"

She dipped the roller again.

At the top of the stairs, Isaac sighed. "Ana was a lost cause. I get that you want to know what happened to her, but it's not going to change the fact she's gone."

"I know that."

"Too late to save her."

"I know that." She bit back the tone she wanted to use on him. It wasn't Isaac's fault, and she was trying not to be the kind of person who took out their frustration on someone who held no blame. That was why fighting with that cop last night had been so satisfying.

Not to mention the satisfaction of leaving him on his butt on the floor looking worse off than she felt. Even this morning.

"You have a job interview on Friday."

She whirled around, flicking paint on the wood of the stairs.

"Local company, private security and investigations. You're after a job as support staff. Research, stuff like that. Pays well enough you'll be able to afford a nicer apartment than the dump you're living in now."

He'd drawn the line at her living in the houses he was in the process of flipping, which was no different than what he did. Between jobs he either crashed on her couch, bunked at a Marine buddy's, or stayed in a hotel out of town.

"It's at two. On Friday. Don't be late."

"Yes, sir."

"Don't get smart with me, petty officer."

He left her staring at the space where he'd stood, a smile playing on her mouth. This was the first time something he said had birthed that reaction in weeks. Maybe even months. Was it her fault that she was perfectly content right here? Mostly content, anyway. He seemed to think her helping him was a bad thing. He called it a "waste of her skills."

The *former corporal* was only good enough to do construction? Or so he seemed to think. She had her own opinion about the fact he only wanted to live his life off the grid, never meeting anyone he didn't already know.

The *former petty officer* apparently needed to continue using the skills she'd gained in Navy Intelligence and get a *real* job. But it wasn't going to stop there. The second she found gainful employment, he was going to be on her about moving. Then finding a relationship. Then it would be about marriage. Having a family.

It was never going to end.

And despite how nice that might sound in some far-off dream future, it wasn't her reality right now.

She called out, "I don't even know if I want that job." Not even knowing if he was going to hear her.

The reply she got back was an electronic voice with a British accent. "*Phone two connected.*"

Isaac had turned on the Bluetooth speaker he'd connected to his phone. A couple of seconds later he hit play, blasting Christian hip hop. Discussion over.

Haley sighed. Apparently she had an interview on Friday. Which meant three days to figure out what was going on, where Ana had disappeared to. What that cop had to do with it. All those naval intelligence skills she'd put to use had failed her so far. They hadn't helped find Ana.

Which meant she needed a new plan.

As satisfying as beating on that cop had been, especially knowing he was dirty, it hadn't actually gained her anything.

She was never going to get this done before that interview. Before her life got sucked up with hourly work that had no flexibility for taking personal time to search for a wayward friend.

A woman who'd succumbed to drug addiction and a party lifestyle with no boundaries.

A path she just as easily could have also gone down. Mostly Haley figured the military had saved her life. At least it had given her somewhere to direct her intensity. Only why was that not working in her favor to find Ana?

Haley had to face the fact she needed some help.

. . .

"Hassim, right?" Niall shook the guy's hand.

He nodded. A limp grip. "Bukhari."

"Thanks for talking to me, Mr. Bukhari. I appreciate it."

Hassim settled into the folding chair opposite Niall. This was the career counselor's office of Western Oregon Research College. Small. Mostly medical research students. Niall was still trying to figure out their history.

DARPA had funded a lab here, but that funding had been cut five years ago. These days the lab was still up and running. Where was the money coming from? There had been rumors there was a new recreational drug being created here, though the board members he'd spoken to swore that was all theory. Experiments. No funds for actual testing.

He took a sip of his coffee.

So much of terrorism was paid for by other crime. Money from drugs was used to fund terror operations—purchasing materials to make bombs. Recruiting and training operatives. It was often impossible to distinguish between all the crimes, they were so interwoven.

Was that happening here in Portland? Niall didn't want to believe it was just because the college brought in students from overseas. He wasn't prejudiced. Just cautious. And he was going to suspend judgment until he had evidence.

Kind of like what had happened with that woman last night.

Talia still hadn't replied to his email. He had no idea if she was looking up who the woman was—or ignoring him completely. Which meant he'd have to do some research of his own when he got back to the office.

Niall looked at the student's file. "Says you've been here for three semesters. You have a student visa, correct?"

Hassim nodded. A frown drew his dark brows together. "My sister is a student at Harvard. I came here."

"And what is it you're working on? Anything interesting?" Like he was simply curious about the student's latest project.

Hassim stared for a moment then seemed to decide the question was benign enough. "I work with a substance similar to what was LSD. We're looking at ways to affect brain chemistry enough to aid those who've suffered trauma. Like dulling the impact of PTSD."

"By sending someone on a trip?"

Hassim shook his head. "It's a low dose and it's been augmented. What we're using bears little similarity to LSD. We've broken down the components, figured out how it works, and now we're trying to use it to help others."

"A noble cause." Like other illegal substances people bought anyway because they "helped." Maybe they did, and maybe they didn't. But unregulated substances could do a lot of damage. Who knew what the side effects were? Or the long term problems that would arise.

"It's research," Hassim said. "Sometimes the benefits aren't what we anticipate at all. We won't know until all tests have been concluded."

Niall nodded his head slowly, as though he cared about the outcome. All he wanted was for his probation to be lifted. For things to go back to normal. If doing this meant earning back the trust of his team, he would see this case through. Find out what that Russian cop had going on with ties to the college and its work.

He said, "Have you had anyone show up asking about what you're doing? Maybe someone interested in the finished product, offering to buy it from you?"

"The only person asking questions here is you."

"What about the product?"

"We are not making drugs, Special Agent." Hassim shifted back in his chair. "That is all you need to know."

Maybe. Maybe not. He pulled a photo from the paper file he'd brought. "Have you ever seen this man?"

Yuri Kartov posed in his uniform.

Hassim sighed. "I don't have much dealings with the police."

"I'd like to take you all up on the offer of a tour of the lab now."

Hassim tucked the chair back where Niall had pulled it over from by the wall. "Find someone else to show you around. I have work to do."

The Syrian student strode out, his lab coat flapping around him. Niall leaned back in his chair and blew out a breath. He was tired. Pushing hard on this case had gotten him nothing but exhausted so far.

He looked at the time on his cell phone and saw there was a missed call from Patricia. Probably her daughter, Siobhan, wanting to know if he was bringing donuts home this morning. He hadn't done that in a few weeks.

When his career was on track again, things would get back to normal. He could take a dozen assorted home to his niece where he lived in the guest room. Spend the day ferrying her to basketball, then the movies. Hang out like they used to. The way Niall and Patricia's extended family of aunts and uncles and cousins had never done with them. Because they were too caught up in the family business.

Portland was a long way from Boston and the stronghold the Irish had on that city. They'd moved away as soon as they could. Determined to change their family, to make a new life for themselves. Patricia hadn't told him she was pregnant until they crossed into the midwest. Seattle had eventually been home. Now it was Portland.

He got his tour of the lab from a student, along with the press-kit speech about what they were doing. Then Niall drove back to the office. He called Talia a couple of times on the way, but she never picked up. He decided to get on her nerves by actually leaving a voicemail.

When the tone sounded, he said, "I need a reply to that email. There's a hit out on this woman, probably from the Russian mob. And if they succeed and she turns up dead, then guess whose head that's going to land on? Because it won't just be mine." He pushed out a breath. "Call me back."

Watching a woman get kicked and punched—and valiantly fight back—had affected him. Not that he was comparing her to his sister or his niece. Siobhan, which was pronounced *Shu-vawn*, and her mother weren't even the self-defense types, though both were active. He lived in the third bedroom and stuck around as much as he could to keep them safe.

Even when his job threatened their lives.

17

That was what family did. They looked out for each other.

What they didn't do was drag them into illegal activity and turf wars that spilled blood. None of it proven, of course. Niall had been asked about his family history when he'd become a Navy cop. He'd told them everything they wanted to know—and assumed most of that was passed on to the FBI.

Since then, things had been quiet. Though he had a Google alert on his father's and uncle's names. If they ever got arrested, he wanted to know.

Niall parked in the marked space behind the red brick building that housed the office for the Northwest Counter-Terrorism Task Force. No one walking past would ever know that was what it was.

He rounded the front corner to the main door.

In the alcove, laying on the front step, was a body. For a second, Niall thought it was a homeless guy. Definitely not a woman. It crossed his mind, though. For a second he wondered if the hit had been carried out, and they'd dumped her here. But it wasn't her, it was Yuri Kartov.

Niall had a dead cop on his doorstep.

This was going to be difficult to explain.

Chapter 3

The pounding on her front door woke her. Haley shifted and realized she'd fallen asleep on her couch. On the TV screen, Netflix was asking if she was still watching.

She hit the power button on the remote and dropped it to the cushion, then ambled to the front door.

A look through the peep hole showed two men in suits and overcoats. Mob guys...or cops. Neither of which she especially wanted to talk to right now.

She twisted the handle and opened the door until the chain pulled taut. "Can I help you?"

"Detective Mason." He flashed a badge. Bald head, two days of scruff on his chin. "This is Detective Brower. Can we come in for a moment?"

Haley shut the door, unlatched the chain and then stepped back, holding the door wide. They wandered into her foyer. Mason said, "Can we sit?"

She nodded. He took the armchair her brother sat in when they hung out here. Haley reclaimed her spot on the couch. The other detective stood by the TV unit Isaac had found at a yard sale.

"What's this about?" She focused on the man sitting.

He studied her for a second before he spoke. "I'd like to ask about any interactions you've had with an officer on our force, Yuri Kartov."

Everything in her stilled. They had to have seen it. "What about him?"

Had he made some kind of complaint against her after what happened last night? Could he really justify getting her in trouble, considering she had evidence against him? There was no way he'd get out of that fight as the victor. If he thought he could get away with it, maybe he *was* filing charges against her.

"Can you tell me the last time you saw him?"

"Last night."

"And where was this?"

"At his house."

"And the nature of your relationship?"

"I'd never met him before last night," she said, honestly. "And aside from one conversation, we have no relationship."

He studied her as he absorbed that, as though assessing her statement, probably in the context of whatever he knew. Or whatever Yuri had said about her.

Detective Mason said, "And that bruise on your cheekbone?"

"As I said, Officer Kartov and I had a *conversation*." She couldn't deny it. There was no way they were going to believe otherwise. Considering how they both looked, it was obvious they'd been in a fight. Why try to hide the fact?

"I see."

Did he? She highly doubted that, unless he was fully aware that Kartov had been a dirty cop with ties to the Russian mob. She couldn't figure out how those ties had been established. Yuri hadn't owed anyone money. He didn't have any family link. Maybe it was friendship that had developed into brotherhood. A family chosen, one he'd pledged loyalty toward even before he joined the police academy.

In fact, it might have been the reason *why* he joined the force and become a cop. The Russian mob's inside man in the Portland Police Department. One of them, at least.

Before Mason could ask, she offered him the information. "A friend of mine recently went missing. I've filed a police report but nothing has been found yet, and it's been weeks."

"And you believe Officer Kartov knew something? Or, perhaps, that the police department was not investigating your *friend*'s disappearance to your level of satisfaction, and you felt the need to vent that frustration on one of our officers late last night. In his home."

Mason continued, "Perhaps it went too far. You were in the military, so you've been trained in hand-to-hand fighting styles."

"I worked behind a desk." That didn't mean she wasn't deadly when the situation warranted. But Haley much preferred to fight against the new threats in this world. Computer-based attacks. Cyber warfare was the new front line, and America was behind the curve every time new technology was invented. Defense was paramount or the regular citizens of this country would continue to be vulnerable.

She needed to ask this company she was interviewing with on Friday what they were doing about that. Maybe it would be something she could get on board with—the only way she was going to take a job that kept her from helping Isaac.

"Why Officer Kartov?" Mason tipped his head to the side. "Is there a reason you chose him for your...conversation? He wasn't listed on the police report you filed about Ana Emerson."

He'd read it. This guy had done his homework on her and everything she was up to. He might have even pulled her military file and read that too.

"I found Ana's phone. Yuri was the last person who spoke to her."

"And you didn't think to include this in your report?"

She shook her head. "I didn't find the phone until a few days ago." And she'd filed the report more than two weeks ago.

"I see."

Did he?

"What is this about?" She glanced at the other detective, then back to Mason. "Why are you asking me about this now?"

"Can you tell me where you were between the hours of 3 a.m. and 7 a.m. this morning?"

"At three I was asleep. At six, I was already up and at my brother's house," she said. "We're fixing it up togeth—"

"Can he verify this?"

"I can give you his information."

"That would be good." Mason's lips pressed together for a second.

"Really, what is this about?"

"Officer Yuri Kartov was found dead earlier today."

Her eyes widened. She couldn't stop the reaction. Not when there was pure surprise. Did they think she…Did they come here to… "My brother can verify my whereabouts."

"But you were at home during some of that time. Alone."

"Yes." Of course she'd been alone. It wasn't like she'd gotten into a fight and then found someone to bring home to her apartment and cozy up to for the rest of the night. She'd been sore, and she was *not* that kind of person. Honor ran through her. If she didn't have her own sense of right or wrong, things would get out of control. And that was something she could not handle.

"Our job is to dig into Officer Kartov's life. To find out who might have killed him."

"Well, it wasn't me." She needed to say it. She *had* to say it.

Detective Mason nodded slowly, like he was trying to decide something. "We will be in touch."

"Of course."

He stood then, and Haley opened her front door for them. "I would advise you against leaving town."

She nodded, unable to say anything else. Fear rang like a gong, colliding with that streak of honor. Admittedly, she'd come down hard on Yuri, desperate to find out what happened to Ana. Was that going to come back to bite her?

She'd looked into his life and still had the information she'd discovered. Did these guys want to know that Yuri was dirty now that he was dead? Maybe the Russians had killed him, for whatever reasons they had.

Cops hated people who ended the life of one of their own. Maybe this was a warning from these two detectives. A warning that her entire life was about to be turned upside down as they looked into why Yuri was killed and who had done it.

All Haley could think was thank goodness she hadn't gone ahead and planted those bugs in his house.

. . .

Niall slammed the car door and looked up at the apartment where Haley Franks lived. He hadn't gotten a reply from Talia. What he had received was a file sent to him from an untraceable email account. Was that from Talia? He had no idea.

The woman was part of his team. They all had work emails and work phones. It wasn't like she needed to use subterfuge just to get him what he needed. And who else would've sent it to him?

So either their computer tech was bored and wanted the challenge of maintaining an untraceable account, or she didn't want him to know for certain it was her who'd sent it. Then again, maybe she didn't want someone else to know. The last option was that someone entirely unrelated to this whole situation—as far as he knew—had sent him the information. Just to be helpful.

The "helpful" option was also the scariest. Considering they had to know he was looking into Haley. And if that was the case, then what else did they know?

If it was Talia, maybe Victoria hadn't wanted her to help him. But he figured the NSA analyst couldn't keep from giving him the information he needed. She wouldn't want him to go in blind, whether or not she had authorization from their director.

But that wasn't his biggest concern in the next half hour. Haley Franks, formerly Petty Officer Haley Franks, Naval Intelligence, had higher security clearance than he did. Though, not higher than his director, Victoria Bramlyn. Her brother had served with distinction and been honorably discharged with a Purple Heart. Isaac Franks was off the grid, and Haley—who had more savings in her portfolio than Niall could amass in ten years—was living here. In a rundown apartment in a rundown neighborhood, smack dab in the middle of the rundown section of Portland. Emphasis on the smack.

What was she doing here?

Niall stopped at the bottom of the stairs to her second floor apartment. Two men walked down. Cheap suits, straight off the rack in some department store—because he bought his at the same place—headed right for him. Gold shields on their belts. Both had a duty weapon under their left arm.

"Gentlemen."

"Special Agent O'Caran." Whatever that tone was, it dripped off the man's words.

Niall didn't know if the detective didn't like him, specifically, or if he had a problem with the Navy in general. Or maybe he was unhappy with the fact Yuri's body had been dumped on federal turf. Then there was the fact he'd had to explain to the cop about the surveillance equipment in the police officer's house—and the federal warrant to put it there.

Niall said, "Thought you guys were done for the day."

He shifted to the side while they stepped off the bottom of the stairs onto the cracked sidewalk.

Detective Mason shrugged one shoulder of his cheap suit. "Figured it wouldn't hurt to wrap a couple of things up before we clocked out."

Except that he had specifically told Niall they were done for the day and were going to work more on the case tomorrow. Not that they might potentially speak with the prime suspect tonight.

Brower flipped it back on Niall. "How about you? Figured you federal types need your beauty sleep."

Niall said, "Not as much as you'd think."

"I can see that."

For real? Now they were insulting the way he looked? "It's been a long week, what can I say. Not every day a dead cop is left on your doorstep, know what I mean?"

They didn't, but that wasn't the point. They'd already questioned him about the fact one of their own had been delivered to him. What that might mean. Like Niall was supposed to have the first clue of a possible link between his research into the awarded scholarships and the cop turning up dead. Yes, he'd been running surveillance on the Russian. The guy had been linked to the college, but Niall hadn't been able to figure out how.

He eventually had to relent and admit to these two that he had no idea what the murder was about.

Niall said, "She say anything I need to know?" He motioned to the top of the stairs and the petty officer's apartment. The woman had a hit out on her. Presumably one that had been taken up by the Russians. Niall had no idea if the wheels were already in motion on it now that Yuri was dead. Usually hits couldn't be called back once the order was given.

Did these guys know? He needed Talia to look into them next. Maybe they had Russian connections also. Were they keeping this whole investigation under the radar, standing back to see what shook out before deciding what to report to their captain? It was a tough line to walk, looking above board and squeaky clean at the police department while also catering to whoever handed them cash under the table.

Mason scratched at his chin. "Not much. She says she didn't kill him but had words with him last night about a missing friend of hers."

"Whatever that was about," Brower said with a smile on his face, "I figure Kartov got his licks in. She looked pretty messed up."

Niall had been suspicious of the speed of their response time when he'd called in the dead body. These two had shown up quickly after he'd called in Yuri Kartov's murder. He said, "I'll see if I can get her to share more."

He'd been about to say he'd ask if she saw anyone by Yuri's house last night, but the only other person there had been him. She hadn't seen him. Still, it wouldn't be a good idea to put the idea in these guys' heads.

He said, "And I'll get you those files."

They wanted access to everything he'd amassed during his surveillance of Kartov. And Niall was going to be sure to hand deliver that right to their office. Maybe even into the hands of their captain. Just to be safe.

Mason eyed him. "Don't go leaving town."

"You think you're gonna find something in this that points to me?"

"Who knows?"

They passed him. Brower clipped Niall's shoulder with his own in a completely juvenile move. Niall could've grabbed the guy's gun he got so close. But he let the guy shove him, and he just stood there. Shame Victoria didn't see it. She'd have been impressed by the clear evidence of his restraint.

He gritted his teeth together so hard it was a wonder they didn't crack. When they were away from earshot, he blew out a breath. These guys were going to cause him some serious problems. Enough he knew they would disrupt his attempts to figure out the connection between the Russians and the college. Scholarships and the mob? It made no sense.

Trying to launder money, maybe. Funding scholarships to give international students a leg up. Or trying to bring in people they thought would benefit whatever they were up to. Getting someone a student visa was probably easier than a lot of other ways in.

He trotted up the stairs, wondering what Haley Franks knew about all that. Maybe something she didn't even know she knew. He'd have to figure out the right questions to ask her.

Halfway up, he heard a door slam. Haley's front door. At the top, he saw her on the far side of the foyer space between the four apartment front doors. She turned and caught sight of him. Fear washed over her face, and then she disappeared down the other side of the stairs so fast she nearly stumbled. She was running.

Chapter 4

Haley stumbled on the bottom step but kept going. Keys in her hand. She shifted them so two poked out between her fingers. If she was a target like that dead Russian cop, then she wasn't just going to stand around and let the killer get her next.

She glanced back and saw the guy in pursuit.

First it was two shady detectives she didn't trust farther than she'd be able to flip either of them on their backs. Though she figured it was unlikely they'd give her that opening, even if the dead cop had done it. Now this guy? Jeans. Dark jacket. Tight brown hair.

Piercing blue eyes.

It was a cliché, but boy was it true. Didn't matter that he'd be the stuff of a made-for-TV romance. She wasn't interested. It was a shame, though. Why was it always the good-looking ones?

And that was only from one flash of his face as she headed for the back stairs, toward where she parked her car in its assigned spot. She wanted to stop. To turn back. The pull to him was that strong. It almost overtook her need for self-preservation, as he was probably there to kill her.

Haley raced down the sidewalk to her car so fast she nearly slammed into the front panel. His boots hit the pavement at a run. He was chasing her.

She fumbled with the keys.

"Stop."

The keys fell to the floor. Haley lifted her gun from inside her purse and whirled around to point it at him.

Blue-eyed guy shot her a look. The gun on his hip stayed in its holster. "You're gonna shoot me?"

They both knew she wouldn't. Not just because those two cops would be over here seconds after she did.

"Who are you?" It came out breathy. She cleared her throat. "What do you want?"

"Badge." He lifted two fingers and slid them around back, to his pocket. She let him because his gun was on the other side. Unless he had another weapon back there?

But a badge? That meant he was some kind of...

"NCIS."

Haley blinked. "A little far from port, aren't you?"

His lips twitched. "Special Agent Niall O'Caran."

She didn't know that name. "And the fact you're following me?"

"We need to talk, Petty Officer Franks." He flipped the wallet containing his badge closed. "But you're gonna put that weapon away first."

Haley stared at him for a second before she lowered it.

"You have reason to believe you need to defend yourself?"

"Yes," she said.

"You think whoever killed Yuri Kartov is going to kill you next?"

How did he know that? Though given he knew her name and rank, maybe she shouldn't be surprised.

"What all did they tell you?"

She relayed what the two detectives had said about the dead cop. "I don't think they even cared about Ana. They just wanted to know about the last time I saw Yuri." It had occurred to her that they might use the information to make a case against *her*. The last thing her brother needed was for her to go to prison for the murder of a cop.

Haley stowed her gun back in her purse.

"Thanks."

She nodded. "What does all this have to do with you?"

"Kartov was left on the front doorstep of my office."

"He had issues with NCIS?"

"I'm attached to a different operation," he said. "It's complicated, but no one is supposed to know where it's at. We're…under the radar as far as federal agencies go."

And yet he was telling her? Though he'd basically told her nothing. Certainly not what it was, or where it was located. "Were you investigating Kartov?"

"What makes you think that?"

She shrugged, way too jittery now that the rush of adrenaline was dissipating. "Why else drag you into this?"

"That's what I've been wondering." He glanced aside. "Do you want to go somewhere, get a cup of coffee? We could talk it over and see if we can't figure out the answers."

"You think I want any part of this?"

"I think you want to know what happened to your friend."

"How do you—"

"I was at the house," he said. "When you talked to Yuri."

She opened her mouth, thought twice and shut it. Who cared why? She needed to find Ana, he was right about that. If she never knew what had happened to her friend, it would torture her. She wouldn't be able to tell Ana's parents what she'd found. There would be no rest for them unless she could provide that closure. No rest for her. No peace.

A memory of her mother standing at the kitchen sink flashed through her mind. She'd walked in the door from school to find her mom dumping pills down the drain. Water running. Motor from the disposal whirring. One of those rare good days when she'd tried to turn her life around.

Haley shook her head.

"What?"

"Nothing." She swiped her keys from the ground. "I have to go."

Where to, she didn't know. What if he could help her figure out what happened to Ana? Was it worth it to learn the answers?

"Your life is in danger."

She clicked the locks on her car and glanced back over her shoulder. "The cop's death has nothing to do with me."

She didn't like the look on his face at all.

"Yuri called a hit on you before he was killed. I have no idea the state of play on that. Your life could very well be in imminent danger."

"I can take care of myself."

"I don't doubt that." He paused for a second. "Remember, I was there last night—I saw how you held your own." He shrugged in concession, "And I've read your file."

How much about her did he think he knew? Instead of slapping him, she concentrated on not dropping her keys again. She flung her car door open and almost hit him in the stomach with it. "Fine. You know about me."

Pretty much everything, given the pitying look on his face. Most people in the Navy knew her family name. As much as her father had tried to squash the rumors, they'd run rampant. Some were just overblown insinuations. Others were eerily close to the actual truth.

"You already know what you need to know, I guess." Haley climbed in her driver's seat while he stood there, still eyeing her with that look. Ugh. It was so close to her Isaac's disapproving older brother stare that she wanted to give this guy Isaac's number. They should be best friends or something.

What a nightmare that would be.

A bad enough idea that she almost chuckled over it. Almost. Her life was in danger? Let them come. She wasn't going to leave Ana's disappearance alone. What she *was* going to do was go nowhere near this dead cop thing.

And that included the NCIS Special Agent. Niall O'Caran. What kind of name was that anyway? *Do you want to go somewhere, get a cup of coffee?* Nothing good would come of "coffee," even though she was practically gasping for a mug of it.

"Petty Officer Franks." His voice rang with authority.

We could talk it over. See if we can figure out the answers.

Haley actually paused before she shut the door, even though she wanted to kick herself for it. She looked up at the agent. Why did she want to take him up on his offer? She would only end up saying too much, incriminating herself and then getting arrested.

If he'd been there during her "talk" with Yuri, then he already knew more than she wanted him to.

He said, "Be careful."

There was more. She was sure of it. Special Agent Niall O'Caran was going to show up again before this was over. There would be more talking. She could read it on his face.

She turned her engine on, then shut the door. Mr. NCIS Agent stood at the curb while she backed out of the space and then threw her car in drive. She turned toward the complex entrance, hardly knowing where she was even fleeing to.

She wanted to blow through the stop sign out of sheer frustration but tapped the brake instead.

Nothing happened.

Haley shoved her foot against the brake again.

And then went flying through the intersection.

. . .

Niall watched her drive off. He had to wonder if this friend of hers—Ana—knew the answers to his questions. Perhaps Ana had the information as to what the Russians' business was with the college. Then again, maybe she was dead. Or she'd been kidnapped. Though if whoever was behind this was the one who had killed Yuri Kartov, then it was unlikely they'd have killed a cop to cover up an abduction.

The missing woman no one except Haley seemed to care about.

More likely was the fact Kartov had been silenced permanently. Dumped outside his office as a warning because of what he knew. People that got too close ended up dead. Give up the investigation, stop trying to get information. They wanted Niall to back off from the college scholarships thing.

It was the only case he was working on.

Which meant there *was* a link between Kartov and the students. But what was it?

He should call the student he'd spoken with this morning, Hassim Bukhari. He needed to tell Hassim to watch his back. Niall wasn't sure the student was actually in danger, but he should warn him—just in case.

Niall rolled his shoulders, wishing for a shower. It had been a long day, and he still had to get home. Now that he'd seen her up close, he was going to be thinking about her, a fact he had to face and deal with. Pushing the attraction aside wasn't going to do him any favors.

She was beautiful—and scared. That long, dark brown hair. So dark it almost looked black. She'd secured it all on the crown of her head, strands sticking out every which way. Her eyes were dark. Black like the night sky. He hoped she hadn't thought he was staring at her like a weirdo. Going up against her fear, coupled with that streak of legendary Franks stubbornness, perplexed him. Even the authority behind his badge hadn't made her want to sit down with him and talk through this.

Niall turned to head back to his car when he heard it.

The crash of metal against concrete. Everything in him flinched. Before Niall registered it, his feet were moving. He ran down the street to the exit where she'd headed. Her brake lights were lit up, her car sticking halfway out of a building. Some kind of storefront, or business. He didn't concentrate on the sign long enough to figure that out.

He squeezed between cement bricks of the façade and sheetrock, ignored the pipes that jabbed into his sides, and got to the driver's door. Through the window he saw her slumped over the airbag.

Niall pulled the door open and checked her pulse. It thumped under his fingertips, just as stubborn in its beat as she was. He pulled out his cell phone, dialed 911, identified himself, and asked for an ambulance.

Hopefully those two detectives wouldn't turn around and head back. He didn't exactly want to deal with them. They might've even been the ones who had done this. It was his job to be skeptical.

"Haley." He crouched in the space between the door and her seat, and shifted her face out of the airbag. "Haley, can you hear me?"

She moaned. Maybe it was for the best that she wasn't waking up fully. No doubt she was in a lot of pain. He touched her shoulder. "Hang on. An ambulance is on its way."

First up were a uniformed officer and his trainee, a guy who didn't even know about the Naval Criminal Investigative Service. An explanation that would be only slightly less complicated than who Niall was, and why he was here. Shortly after came the ambulance and two female EMTs.

While they looked after her, Niall laid down on his back and crawled under the car.

"Special Agent…" The officer paused.

Niall answered, "O'Caran," and crawled back out. "You're gonna want forensics to look over this car."

The training officer lifted his chin. "That right?"

Niall said, "Her brake line was cut."

The trainee shifted, then caught himself. From his stance, Niall figured he wanted to look under the car and see for himself. The officer in charge nodded. "Take a look." Then he turned back to Niall. "This have to do with something you're working on?"

Niall explained about the dead officer and the two detectives.

"So it's about Kartov?"

He nodded. "Looks like she might know something that could point to Kartov's killer."

After all, why cut her brake line?

Haley called out then, sitting up. "I do not!" More of a wail, really.

Niall moved to her and stood over the EMT, who was touching a wet rag to her nose. "There's a reason Kartov wanted you silenced. Probably the same reason he was killed. Someone didn't want him talking, and someone obviously doesn't want you talking either."

She opened her mouth to argue again, but didn't say anything.

"I'll meet you at the hospital. We can talk about it more there, but the bottom line is you need protection. Something about your interest in your friend's disappearance has caught the attention of the wrong person."

She shut her mouth and glared at him.

He said, "Good choice."

That didn't resolve the glaring issue, though, because she kept making that face. Neither did it fix any of their problems. "Looks like you're stuck with me for the time being."

"I don't need your help."

The EMT with her glanced at Niall then looked back at Haley. "Pretty sure I'd let him watch my back. If you know what I mean." She shifted to look at the training officer. "Uh, no offense, Alanson."

He chuckled. "None taken."

The EMT helped Haley out of the car. She gingerly walked to the ambulance herself and was helped inside. All the while completely ignoring the fact he was standing right there waiting for her to...what? Admit she needed help? Like that was even part of it. She didn't exactly need to give him permission to watch out for her.

"Petty Officer Franks." It came out far sharper than he intended. When she looked over, he gave her a small smile to soften his look. He did that with Siobhan when he didn't want to come across as mad at her. Niall said, "Is there anyone you want me to call for you?"

She shook her head and patted her purse, tucked on her lap. "I'm fine."

That wasn't true. But he got what she meant. This woman was going to stubbornly refuse his help. The last thing she wanted to admit is that her own life was in danger. This was all about her friend, and she would repeat that mantra to herself until she got the answer she wanted.

Not just any answer.

Haley wasn't going to stop until she was satisfied.

The EMT shut the doors and the ambulance drove off.

He'd read her file. He'd read her psych evals even. Her personality type was something he understood, because he lived it every day of his life. His own need to protect the people he cared about had meant betraying his team. Niall had put family above the case they'd been working on.

Now that he was relegated to probation he'd had time to think on it how it all went down. The reason he'd been benched by Victoria. And if he were honest with himself, he'd do the exact same thing every time. Maybe some minor variations. But the fact was, he'd been backed against a wall. A place no man worth his salt ever wanted to be.

Forced to make one of two bad choices. And he still stood by the decision he'd had to make at that moment.

Niall finished up talking with the officers on scene and then made his way back to his car. It was the early hours of the morning when he entered the hospital and asked for Haley at the front desk.

"And you are?"

Niall flashed his badge. "NCIS." And gave the lady his name.

The receptionist typed Haley's name into the computer. "Huh."

"What?"

"Says here she was never even admitted. After the initial exam, she declined anything further. Against medical advice, the patient left."

Chapter 5

The mug clanged against the coffee table. Haley was pretty sure she yelped as she sat up, coming awake quickly. All that military training, teaching her to be up and ready to move on a second's warning. Apparently it was going to come in handy now that someone was looking to kill her.

"Why do you look like you were hit by a truck?"

She took the mug from the table and sipped, ignoring her brother's death stare. He had brought her a cup of coffee. He couldn't be *that* mad. She winced. "Wow, that's strong."

"I like it thicker sometimes." Isaac sat in the ratty recliner he refused to throw out. Or clean. "Wanna tell me why you're here, looking like that?" He motioned to her face.

Haley lifted her fingers and touched the bandage covering her nose. Winced. "Someone cut my brake line."

"And you didn't call me? I'd have picked you up instead of you showing up here at whatever hour and breaking in. You're lucky I didn't wake up and shoot you."

He had been moaning pretty loudly in his sleep. That was why she'd stayed downstairs instead of heading up and sleeping in the bathtub like she'd planned. Bare floor wasn't something she appreciated, so she'd crashed on the couch. Still, she'd felt bad enough that comfort won out over safety.

Haley pushed back hair from her face and told him about Yuri. Then about the two detectives and the Navy cop.

"Ana." His face didn't give anything away. No surprise. No fear. Not even a little astonishment. There was a distinct tone, though.

Haley didn't confirm or deny this had anything to do with her friend. Though, she was probably kidding herself about that. She shifted on the couch. Not because of what he thought about her life choices or anything, she was just realizing she still wore her clothes from yesterday. Either she was going to have to go to a store and buy something else to wear, or she'd have to actually go home and change.

Face the real world.

And the fact someone might be trying to kill her.

"You should've told me." His jaw clenched. "You should have *called me* from the hospital."

Haley pressed her lips together.

"How did you get back here?"

"Two cabs. Then I walked."

"Pay cash?"

She nodded.

"Sure you didn't miss a career in the CIA?" One of his eyebrows lifted for a second. "Travel the world. Save all kinds of people."

"I'm no good at that." And boy did it hurt to admit she'd have been no good when other people's lives were on the line. Haley was good behind a desk. Information. Computers. Money. Satellite images. Not real life. Otherwise she'd know where Ana was by now.

He said, "Yeah." She knew that tone. "After all, you couldn't save me from getting blown up."

"You know what I mean."

She'd been assigned to the base in Bremerton, close to Seattle, during Isaac's deployment. As soon as she'd found out what happened, she kept up with the latest information. Read every report that came in. She'd flown to Germany and met his plane when they'd transferred him for continuing medical treatment. Those had been some of the hardest hours and days of her life.

Harder even than the days leading up to their mom's death.

"You need to give this up."

Haley said nothing.

"Ana is gone."

"We don't know what happened to her." Haley's voice broke. "I don't know if she's dead or alive, or why she hasn't called. She could be a prisoner somewhere and needs our help."

Isaac sighed. "Maybe she doesn't wanna be found."

"She would never have left without at least telling me."

"Because you were her 'sober sister.'"

"Yes." That was the arrangement they'd had back in the day. Now that she was out of the Navy, she didn't know what their relationship was. She just knew she hadn't found Ana yet. "I couldn't save her. I couldn't stop her from living that life, but I wasn't just going to stand by and let her get killed by it."

"So you're the stupid patrol?" He shook his head. "Good to know, in case I'm thinking of being an idiot. You'll be here to protect me from myself."

"Isaa—"

He stood up, waving off what she'd been about to say. "Just good to know." He straightened, pinning her with a stare. "Considering we evidently all need a babysitter, and you're primed for the job."

Haley got up. "She was taking drugs!"

"So it was your job to make that safe for her? Well, guess what? It's *not* safe. She should have quit."

Her head pounded, concentrated in the broken cartilage of her nose. "I tried to get her into treatment. She wouldn't listen."

"It was her life. She was gonna do whatever she wanted."

"So I shouldn't have tried to stop her? What kind of friend would I have been then?"

He lifted both hands, palms up. "Oh, I don't know. The kind who stays out of *other people's business*?"

She'd heard that tone before. "I don't babysit *you*. I'm trying to help your business."

"Oh, so you think destroying your career by living in a dump so you can throw money my way is 'helping?'" He lifted his fingers and made quote marks in the air.

Haley hated it when people did that. It was so patronizing. "Why is helping you a bad thing? And finding Ana? She could need help. She could be—" Her voice broke.

"Dead?" he said. "Maybe the world would be a better place if she *was*."

Haley moved to slap him.

At the last second he grabbed her wrist. Before she made contact with his cheek, he used his grip to shove her arm back down. "Don't even think about it."

"So I should just leave Ana to her fate because she asked for it?" Haley said. "And leave you to yours? Go live a life that's going to be *so great* without you guys around to drag me down. Is that it?"

What did he want her to do? If she was the one who'd disappeared—only her phone found, no trace of her anywhere—she would want there to be someone in her life who stopped at nothing to find out what had happened to her. She and Ana had been great friends once. Maybe that was years ago now, before life had come between them. But she'd tried.

That was all she was doing now.

Trying.

Isaac leaned down so his face was in hers. "Yes. I want you to *go and live your life*."

She shoved him back, two hands flat on his chest. One giant push with all her frustration behind it. And he let her.

"And then find a guy who doesn't mind that you get physical when you're mad."

"Isaa—"

"Make sure you put your kids in karate. They'll learn how to channel it instead of ending up with bleeding hearts, trying to fix everyone else's problems because you couldn't fix Mom's."

Haley's chest burned. "Don't—"

"I'm going out." He strode to the hall and swiped his motorcycle helmet off the floor. Then he pocketed his wallet and the flip phone she made him carry all the time. Just in case. Not just when he remembered to take it. Little things she'd managed to persuade him to do so she had peace of mind.

Looking after him.

Isaac flung the front door open and pulled up short. "Are you the Navy cop?"

It took a second, then a familiar voice said, "That I am."

"Good," her brother said. "Try to talk some sense into her while she's busy getting herself killed. I'm done."

Then he stepped out. A few seconds later his motorcycle roared to life. The sound moved down the driveway, then down the street.

Niall stepped inside. "Nice guy, your brother. He saw combat?"

Of course, Isaac hadn't been wearing his helmet. Or a ball cap, or beanie. He'd stood there talking to Niall, mad enough that the guy had seen his scar. He hadn't even realized. Or cared.

Haley flopped down on the couch and started crying.

. . .

About an hour later, Niall went upstairs and knocked on the bathroom door. "Breakfast is ready."

Haley called back. "I'll be right out."

He trailed back to the kitchen and started plating what he'd made. The freezer had been stocked with those hash browns you laid out on a sheet pan and baked until crispy. They were basically a core tenet of Niall's rules for what the "good life" looked like. Brother and sister duo Isaac and Haley also had bacon and eggs in the fridge.

He'd made enough so that if her brother showed up again there would be some for him too. Niall wasn't sure if he would. But just in case.

He waited until she wandered back into the kitchen and lifted a clean mug. "More coffee?"

She nodded absently, taking in the plates piled up with food. "You made all this?"

"My niece and I make a huge breakfast on Saturdays. It's usually close to lunch by the time we're all up and moving, so I suppose it's more like brunch. Doesn't matter if we make French toast or casserole. There's *always* bacon with it." He grinned and turned, holding out her mug.

Haley took it. "Your niece?"

"I live with her and my sister." He set the plates on the breakfast bar and sat beside her on a ripped leather-topped bar stool. "It's not exactly like when we lived together growing up, but it's also not far from it. Except there are two of them on their periods now."

Haley's eyes widened.

"I'm not supposed to talk about shark week? I try to take out-of-town assignments to avoid it."

A laugh bubbled up. Wet hair and no makeup. Haley looked gentler right now than he'd seen from her so far. They hadn't officially met. Not really. But they were past the point he'd have introduced himself. She felt like more than an acquaintance, and yet most of what he knew about her he'd read in her file.

One brother, recipient of a Purple Heart.

Deceased mother.

Their father a Rear Admiral on the special counsel to the President.

And here she was, in a rundown house on the west coast. Living in a shabby apartment. Working with her brother. Trying to find her friend.

Targeted.

"I won't let anything happen to you."

"Why do you think I care about me?" She tapped her thumb on the side of her fork. "I just want to know what happened to Ana."

"And Isaac thinks that's a bad thing?"

She rolled her eyes. "Isaac thinks…whatever Isaac thinks. Sometimes I have no idea what that big brother speak means."

"Maybe you should write it down, go compare notes with my sister."

"Maybe I will." She stuck a mouthful of cheesy egg in. When she'd swallowed she said, "This is really good."

"I'm glad."

"Thank you for running that bath for me. I guess I didn't even know I needed to relax like that."

He shrugged. "Either you want to get yourself together, or you want to keep crying. Either way, I figure the bath can muffle the sound."

She cracked a smile.

"Works for the hormonal women who live in my house anyway."

The smile bloomed into gentle laughter.

"That, and chocolate ice cream."

She groaned. "That might be better than bacon."

Niall gasped, as though that was a deep travesty. An insult to bacon.

Haley laughed again. She took a few more bites, and he finished his meal. "How did you find me?"

"I have a friend," he said, though Talia was more accurately a team member. "She has NSA credentials."

"Ah."

"Still," Niall said. "This house was purchased by a company. Took some digging to link it to your brother."

"It's not a secret. But he does like privacy."

"I can understand that." He fingered the handle of his almost-empty mug. "When Patricia and I moved across the country, we kept things quiet for a long time. Took jobs where we got paid under the table, rented an apartment where the manager didn't ask for ID."

"Hiding?"

"We have a...rough family back in Boston. It was worth our while to stay off their radar, at least for the first few years. So we got settled. Built up some cash to get a better place so my niece could grow up somewhere without fear of going outside."

Haley nodded. "You took care of each other."

"Sometimes that's all we have. That drive to take care of the people we love. To make sure their lives are good so far as it's in our power to make them that way." He shifted slightly to face her. "I'm guessing that's what you've been trying to do for your friend Ana."

He'd also read in her file about her mother. This deep-seated need in her to get answers about her friend probably stemmed from that, though most of what he'd gathered had been ideas. Conclusions he'd been able to draw from what had been reported. The Rear Admiral had done a stellar job of explaining away his wife's death as an "illness." She'd been found dead and the cause was listed as heart failure, despite the cocktail of substances in her system.

Haley said, "I called the hospitals first. Then the morgue. I asked about anyone unidentified, like maybe she'd been in an accident, and then maybe a coma. Or if there was some Jane Doe whose ID they didn't have." Haley swallowed. "Her parents don't care. I figure they think she's dead in a ditch, and they don't have to worry about her anymore. But what if she's not?"

Her bottom lip quivered. "I wanted to give them answers. Like I was looking into this for them, not me." She shook her head, the sheen of tears in her eyes. "I think I was kidding myself about a lot of things."

Niall wanted to lay his hand on her shoulder and offer some comfort that was more than a bath and a meal. That draw hadn't lessened, not even with her hair wet and down and no makeup on her face. She had a fresh bandage on her nose. Bruises under her eyes. This Haley was...honest. She wasn't forced to be tough no matter what came up against her. She didn't have to put on a pretense for cops, or the brother she was trying to protect.

Niall was no one to her, and she didn't have to pretend. Which was both a good and a bad thing, though he would stick with the good. What he wanted from her was something honest that would preferably lead to a result on this case.

Attraction wasn't something he needed to entertain right now. He should focus on getting off probation before he let a beautiful woman distract him. Still, for the time being it would make things much more pleasant having good company.

Haley set her fork down. "I want to go back to the spot where I found Ana's phone." She opened the lid of a laptop on the counter and found a map of the area online.

It wasn't close to anything.

She clicked a satellite image, but there was literally nothing there except trees.

"You think there's something worth seeing?"

Haley hopped off the stool. She faced him, lifting her chin. He'd seen that look on his sister and his niece's faces. She wasn't going to back down. "Yes. I do."

Get her out of town for the day? Search the woods?

He liked hiking.

"Okay, let's go."

"That's it?"

Niall shrugged. "You'd rather I dragged my heels? Argued?"

"I guess not."

"Should we leave your brother a note?"

"Leftovers in the microwave?"

He nodded. She wrote on a couple of sticky notes. They were out together, but she didn't say where they were going.

Niall drove his car, and they parked at a lot used by hikers. Snowshoers in winter. People walking dogs, or riding mountain bikes. He was glad he'd put on jeans this morning and changed into tennis shoes while sitting on the lip of the trunk of his car.

"It's about two miles up the trail." She glanced around, the fresh bandage on her nose making her look far too vulnerable.

"What is it?" He knew what he felt, but he wanted to know where her instincts were at. Someone had tried to kill, or at least injure, her. Did she have the same itchy feeling he couldn't seem to shake?

She bit her lip. "I guess I'm just antsy after yesterday."

He stood and shut the trunk. "I'm coming with you."

"I know you are." She shifted her stance. "It's just...thanks."

Niall clicked the locks on his car before she could decide she wanted to head out solo. "Let's go."

The quicker he got moving, the farther they could both get from the source of this niggling feeling on the back of his neck.

Chapter 6

"Crunchy or smooth peanut butter?"

Haley glanced back at Niall following her on the trail. Boy the guy really liked his food, didn't he? "Crunchy, I guess."

He made a face. As if the fact her stance on the subject wasn't vehement enough astounded him.

Before he could call her on her insufficiencies, she said, "Mexican food or Chinese?"

"Mexican." Like that was obvious.

Haley turned back to the trail in front of her.

"Uh-oh."

"Mexican is fine."

Behind her, he stifled a laugh. "Oh, the many issues when a woman tells you *it's fine.*"

"Hamburger or hotdog?"

"Depends if your grill is gas or charcoal."

"Exactly," Haley said, inordinately pleased. And why did she care so much? Seriously, this guy was hanging around her because of his case. Not because he wanted to get to know her. She was just distracting herself from the swelling in her face…and the fact someone had cut her brake line.

He thought she was in danger. In fact, he'd stressed multiple times that she should be careful going anywhere. That they were only out here because he had a gun, and there was no one around. It had made her feel a little better that he'd approved of her going to her brother's house, considering how under the radar Isaac lived.

But he'd found her there. Niall clearly had access to some pretty well-buried information. Whoever dug it up had managed to figure out that was where she might go. Pretty good guess, considering that was exactly where she'd been.

If Niall could find her at her brother's house, that meant whoever tried to kill her could as well.

Haley patted her pockets. She had her ID and some cash. A gun tucked in the back of her belt. Two phones—hers and Ana's. Hers was a burner, something she and her brother agreed on. She wasn't sure about Ana's.

She could be tracked.

Found.

Killed.

Terror sat like sour milk in her stomach. She tried to breathe in fresh air and swallow down the feeling so that it didn't creep up to her throat. Isaac thought she should leave Ana's disappearance alone now and that things had gone too far. But she had protection, didn't she? Niall was here, for whatever reason.

She figured it was mostly about solving his own case than it was about making sure she survived the investigation. She'd been waiting for him to start grilling her about what she knew of Yuri. But maybe he had the answers he needed for now.

Or she was his chief suspect and that was why he'd stuck with her. Waiting for her to slip up. Though, that didn't account for the breakfast. Or the casual conversation. Like they were getting to know each other. Maybe even building some kind of friendship.

That was the only reason she didn't wonder if he'd driven her out here to kill her himself. Still, she didn't know him.

Haley shuddered. She pushed aside those thoughts and went back to the idea of breakfast.

It couldn't be more than friendship. Not when she had so much going on in her life—helping Isaac and finding Ana. Relationships weren't something she'd ever intentionally invited into her life. Especially not in the military.

She'd never actually gone looking for a guy to "complete" her. Haley wasn't sure that was how it worked. Still, sometimes things developed. A couple of times she'd found herself spending more time with a guy. Then inevitably it would end. They would move on, and she'd be alone again.

She hardly wanted to go through all that with Niall, who lived with his sister and his niece. Niall, who made her breakfast. Who'd run her a bath for goodness' sake. He wasn't the kind of man you casually brought into your life...and then casually let go.

That would be too much of a shame.

It was better to be friends. Stay friends. How many people could she say had been her friend for years? People drifted in and out of her life, here for a season and then gone. Ana was one of the few who had hung on for years. Maybe that was why she was so driven to find her. She cared deeply about her friend. It was just human decency—especially when no one else was prepared to take the time.

And maybe that was the core of it.

That deep down, Haley was scared something would happen to her...and no one would care. Which was nuts, considering the fact that, of course, Isaac would care. Her father would grieve alone, in silence. Her brother would actually do something about it.

Could she do something about Ana's disappearance?

If she did find her friend and help her, then maybe it would feel like—for once—she had actually succeeded in doing the right thing.

Like Niall, keeping an eye on her. He was here to make sure nothing happened to her. Was he trying to do the right thing in the same way?

She glanced back at him, climbing the hill behind her. He shot her a polite smile. This could all just be about making reparations for something he'd done.

The phone in her pocket buzzed.

Haley pulled up short. Probably Isaac checking in, making sure they were both okay. He did that once he'd cooled off. She slid the phone out. No. Not Isaac. This was Ana's phone.

It vibrated again.

"Niall."

"What is it?" He crossed the two steps between them and looked down at the screen.

"It's connecting." Notifications beeped, one after each other in a string. They lit up the screen like a grocery list. The phone vibrated over and over. Notifications popped up, a string of them. Alert. Alert.

Click for rewards.

Your friends miss you.

Don't forget to check in!

One time offer, click now!

She read each one aloud, then looked up. "What is this?"

"Looks like an app on her phone."

Haley left the notifications there and swiped through. "It says PerkLife. That's the name of the app." Her phone didn't even have apps. "I've never heard of it."

He pulled out his phone and swiped the screen, then put it to his ear. "Yeah, it's me." Niall's call had connected.

Haley wandered around a few steps, trying to figure out why the phone had suddenly connected now. It had been charged. Turned on. Proximity to something had triggered the influx of notifications.

Geographical proximity?

She'd never heard of an app doing that. The whole point of phones was connection, regardless of where you were. But perhaps this was dependent on location. What other theory made any sense?

Haley looked at the app's registration details, trying to find out who the people at "PerkLife" were. It seemed to be about rewards, but over a sort of social media platform.

"What?" Niall shifted.

Haley looked over.

"What do you mean, you can't see me?"

. . .

"Where are you?"

"Talia, I need you to access the phone," Niall said. "There should be three at my location." He explained about the app and the rush of notifications. "I need you to figure out what it is and why it just started blowing up right now."

Silence.

"Talia." He was getting frustrated.

"That is so weird."

Niall glanced at Haley, back to being deep in her own thoughts. She'd seemed almost sick with worry over her friend. Understandable, even considering Ana had likely been her own worst enemy. Self-sabotage was hard to combat in someone else. He'd seen too many people destroyed because of their own choices. Drugs were especially hard to get out from under the grip of. Anyone who managed to get clean and stay clean deserved respect. That was a hard fight.

"I see the phones. I think." Talia paused. "What I don't see, is you."

Niall frowned. "What does that mean?"

The woman was an NSA analyst, a computer wizz. One of those kid prodigy hackers who signed on with the government they'd penetrated instead of serving years in prison. The fact Talia was a curvy African American bombshell, like the heyday of Hollywood movies, made it all the better. No one expected her to be busy accessing a black door into their server from a device tucked into her giant gold purse. Her entrance into any space was the perfect distraction. All eyes were always on her.

Almost made Niall feel sorry for them. But if they were going to underestimate her, that was their problem.

The other woman on the team, Dakota Pierce, was also a force to be reckoned with. Native American blood and a fierce spirit. She was all fighter and couldn't be more different than Talia, though the two seemed to be friends nonetheless. Dakota had recently fallen for a DEA agent who was now part of their team. They worked cases together—or as "together" as they could be. Josh had asked her to marry him, but they hadn't yet said their vows.

Victoria was their boss. One of those power players from Washington.

Salvador Alvarez was a Marshal. Every bit a backwoods tracker, except that he hunted people, not game.

But none of them were here now. It was him and Haley, and Niall had to figure out this scholarship thing so he could get off probation.

He could hear Talia clicking keys.

"Wanna fill in the rest of the class?"

She sighed. "There's nothing there. And that goes for you, too."

"But you can see the phones at my location from your satellite…or whatever you're looking at."

"Right," she said.

Okay, so that wasn't it, but he didn't know that technology stuff enough to have a clue what her problem was. And she knew better than to try and explain it to him. He could do enough to get by, but don't start talking about servers and firewalls and all that, or he was lost. Mostly it seemed that people who knew about technology solved the problems they had by turning whatever device it was off and then back on again. Didn't seem all that high-tech if you asked him.

Niall said, "So can you access Ana's phone and see what that app is?"

"Click the home button on your phone twice."

"My phone?"

Niall waved Haley over. He did what Talia asked on his phone, then said, "Done."

"I know." Keys clicked in the background, her long nails tapping the plastic.

His phone screen flashed and turned black. Green text scrolled across the screen, line after line. A string of code. "What are you doing to my phone?"

"Making it realize its full potential." Her voice sounded distant, like she was suddenly farther away than she'd been before. Because of whatever she was doing through his phone on her end?

Okay, so her abilities with technology were pretty scary.

"What is it?" Haley whispered to him. She'd barely finished speaking when his phone screen flashed again.

Talia said, "Hold them back-to-back, like transferring pictures between two Samsung phones."

Niall had heard about that from Siobhan, but he'd never done it. Haley held Ana's phone out, and he touched his to it. They buzzed simultaneously.

"Whoa."

Niall grinned. "That's Talia for you."

"Huh." The word came through the phone line. "You can let go now."

He did and put his own phone on speaker. "What is it?"

"I'll keep you posted on the app. You have a call coming in, and you're gonna want to take that." She paused a second. "Good luck."

The line went dead.

Haley said, "What was—"

His phone started ringing. "Sorry." Niall answered it. "Special Agent O'Caran."

"It's Director Bramlyn."

Victoria wanted to talk to him? Niall said, "Yes, ma'am. How are you?"

"Why would that be relevant? Tell me about the phone you found."

"Wasn't me that found it." He told her everything, while Haley stood there and stared at him. All these women in his life. Not for the first time, he considered getting a new job. But changing occupations just because he was constantly surrounded by women didn't sound like an upstanding idea. He needed a better reason than that to upend his life—and his family.

They'd suffered enough in Boston. Now, for years, things had actually settled down. Then he messed up at work, and they'd moved to Portland to get away from the memories of having their house invaded. He was reluctant to make them endure more change.

Victoria said, "You're adding protection detail to your resume now?"

Did she want him to explain all of it while Haley was standing there? "It's given us a new lead with this phone, as well as the installed app that just blew up."

"I'll have Talia keep me in the loop on that." Victoria was silent for a second, then said, "And your opinion as to why this cop was left on our doorstep?"

"Some kind of statement," Niall said. "Or indicating it's our job to clean up the trash."

"On a local issue?"

"It appears that way. It's the first time we've been part of something that is Portland-based." And he wasn't all that excited to be caught in the middle of it. Usually one of them staffed the office. They did it on rotation, and priority was given to whoever was the most injured or in need of downtime.

"We know for sure this has a wider scope."

"How's that?" Niall asked.

"The money behind those scholarships has been funneled through some of the same businesses whose funds were used to receive the money Clare Norton paid for that VX gas."

"Seriously?" That was huge. And they hadn't told him that when they'd sent him to the college to investigate. He'd thought it was busywork, and yet it turned out to be an integral part of their ongoing investigation into whoever was behind that VX.

Clare Norton had her own agenda with it. But still, the fact she'd received direction from someone else was also clear. Now it was clear here too. Money funded through the research college. And how did that connect to Ana and her disappearance?

"Find out what's going on there." Victoria hung up without even waiting for a response. Didn't need one, or didn't want one.

Niall sighed and stowed his phone in his jacket.

"That did not make me want to go to the interview I have on Friday." She shot him a smile, slightly negated by the bandage on her nose. "I just need to convince my brother to take me on as a partner in his home renovation business."

Niall opened his mouth to respond when shots rang out.

Haley dove to the ground and grunted on impact.

Niall had his gun out a second later. He crouched close to her. Who was shooting at—

The next bullet hit him in the arm.

Chapter 7

Haley saw him get shot. Niall hit the ground. She rolled and came up to a seated position with her gun pointed at the source of the shots. She fired even before she spotted a target. It wouldn't do to have both of them injured.

The shots rang out, exploding in her ears even as the sound blasted out from her weapon.

She saw the flash and heard answering shots. A bullet whizzed past her head, entirely too close for comfort. She could count on one hand the number of gunfights she'd been in during her lifetime, even with her military service. People had their individual skill sets. Hers was collating data. It was how she'd come up with Yuri Kartov's dirty side business. It didn't exactly help her be bulletproof.

Niall groaned and shifted on the grass beside the trail.

In the distance, someone moved. Haley caught the flash of a dark jacket between pine trees and tracked the person. Friend or foe? Was the gunman running toward them, or away? She hardly wanted to fire her gun and wind up hitting a random innocent person out for a run.

The dark jacket guy was circling. Was he heading back in their direction?

Whether or not he was intending to cut them off, they needed to get out of here so Niall could get his arm seen to.

She turned to him. "Gotta move."

"Copy that." He spoke through gritted teeth and clambered to his feet.

She headed for the trail. "If we run, we can get ahead of him. We should get you out of here, where you can get that looked at." She glanced at him as they started moving. "How bad is it?"

"Knocked me on my butt, but I think it's just a graze."

She nodded, moving faster than a walk but not running. Doing that on a trail like this meant one of them was going to get a twisted ankle. And that would make getting out of here extremely difficult.

The gunman stepped onto the trail ahead of them.

She gasped. "Detective Brower."

Niall shoved her off the trail, into the trees. Shots rang out. He'd reacted quickly and saved her life.

He motioned at her. "Run." And then turned to fire back at the cop.

A tree branch slapped at her face. Niall's footsteps shifted leaves and cracked branches as he brought up the rear, right behind her. So close she could feel him move.

She wasn't alone. If she did die, he would be here.

The realization imbued her limbs with strength she didn't know she had. All the aches and pains of the past few days dissipated and she ran, gun still held in one hand.

A downed tree up ahead gave her an idea.

Haley ran to it and jumped over. She dropped down on the far side and turned just as Niall followed her over. Taking cover behind the moss-covered trunk, Haley braced her arms on it and fired three shots at the man in pursuit.

Brower yelped.

Had she shot him?

His body fell to the ground. Then she heard a pain-filled, "She hit me. Get them!"

"There's another one." Haley spun around to look in every direction. Mason was out there. Or someone else, a different partner. Maybe Mason didn't even know what the now injured Brower was into. One partner dirty, the other completely in the dark, unknowing that everything they were working on was a part of Brower's side business.

Was Brower the one who'd cut her brake line?

Before she could wonder further about this whole crazy situation, Niall grabbed her forearm. "To the west. Run."

She didn't have time to glance over. He tugged on her and pulled her along with him as they raced between trees.

Shots were fired.

She ducked her head and kept going, every breath a sharp inhale. Her lungs burned. Legs shook. Her heart pounded under the bandage on her nose. How long could they keep up this pace? She had no idea where they were even going.

"Mason," Niall muttered the name. He'd been shot and was probably in pain, bleeding profusely.

A sob welled up in her throat.

What was so wrong about wanting to lie low, or wanting to work behind a desk? Perfectly reasonable people worked behind desks, and they were successful. The world could be changed from behind a desk. Or with a handshake across a table.

Doing construction.

Okay, so she was losing her marbles. They were running from gunfire after all.

More shots rang out. Niall changed directions, which sent them farther to the southeast. What would they find there? More miles of wooded hills with no trails, probably. They'd left the hiking behind, along with the worn path. This was more like an overgrown uninhabited wasteland. The trees owned this land.

And animals.

Would they run into a bear? She hoped not.

More bizarre thoughts. Like the idea they were being herded in a specific direction.

Haley stumbled. Corralled.

Targeted.

Sent...where?

"Stop."

He didn't.

Haley tugged on his arm. "We have to stop."

53

"If we stop, we get killed." He kept tugging her along. "I'm out of bullets already."

"I think I have a couple left." She'd lost count but given how many times she'd fired, it wasn't going to be many.

"To the right."

She angled again, per his instruction. He'd bitten off the command without as much authority as before. He was getting tired. The pain was becoming too big to ignore. Her head throbbed now, all the blood pooling in the areas where she had injuries. This should have been a nice hike. Now she was running for her life with an injured federal agent.

"Can't you call your friend again, get us some backup?"

He said, "They'll never get here in time."

She figured even local cops wouldn't be able to get all the way out here. A helicopter couldn't land with the trees so close together. A park ranger, maybe? Even if she could get a team of them, that would take time to assemble. And how did they explain two police detectives were trying to kill them? No one would believe it.

They'd think that Haley and Niall were the criminals.

Niall stumbled. She grabbed his arm this time. "We have to keep going."

He nodded, and they ran on. Slower now that exhaustion was setting in.

Another shot rang out. Not closer than before, but still nearer to them than she'd have liked. Close enough to maybe hit one of them. The other would never be able to get away. Both Haley and Niall would end up dead or bleeding to death out here.

Help us. The whispered prayer was nothing but a plea. A reflex born of the knowledge that they were likely about to die. They were out of options.

The edge came up in front of them before she even registered what she was seeing. A drop off. A cliff.

She started to slow.

Shots rang out.

Haley let out the scream. Fear, plain and simple. What was wrong with acknowledging it? This was the end.

They were going over the edge.

Niall tripped. She landed beside him and their momentum started her roll. She picked up speed, shoulder-over-shoulder as she rolled down the side of the mountain they'd climbed.

All thought eclipsed by what was happening to her.

Haley's arm was pinned for a second and her body rolled over her wrist. Twisted it enough that she cried out.

Niall grunted.

Haley splashed into ice cold water and everything went black.

. . .

Niall heard a low noise as he came awake. It took a second to realize it was him moaning. He blinked against the cloudy sky and tried to figure out what just happened.

The smallest shift sent pain screaming through his arm. Like race cars off the starting line. He hissed out a breath, unable to keep it from escaping as a groan, and sat up.

Blood had dampened the jacket over his arm. A bullet hole. He reached to feel the outside of his arm. A wide shot. Hole in his jacket, gash in his skin. Not far enough in that it shattered his shoulder blade. That wasn't something he wanted to experience, thank you very much. Still, his arm was basically useless right now.

He looked around at the trees and the dirt surrounding him. "Haley?" His voice came out breathy and too quiet. He sucked in a breath and yelled, "Haley!"

When she didn't answer, he tried to locate his gun. No sign of it. He'd been out of bullets, so it wouldn't help anyway. But losing it wasn't good. It was a federal agent's assigned weapon, not something that any hiker should find out here.

Where was he, anyway?

At the base of a hill. One he'd rolled down until he came to a stop. The knot on the back of his head didn't feel too good. He stood up, going slowly to fight the way the world swam when he got to his feet.

Phone.

Gun.

He located his cell and checked it. Sent a text to Talia and updated her on the situation. Cops had shot at them. Then he kept looking. Haley. His gun.

He found his weapon first, on the dirt not far from where he'd ended up. Niall slid it back in his holster and zipped up his jacket. It was freezing, and the damp in the afternoon air had settled into everything so that he shivered against it.

Where was she?

"Haley, where are you?"

He kept calling out as he tromped between trees and over upturned logs. He crossed what was probably a deer trail, but couldn't be sure. Up ahead he could hear a stream. When he got to it, he realized it was more of a river.

Niall saw something lying on the bank and rushed over. Her gun.

He stared at it in his hand before tucking it in the back of his belt. Then he stared at the water. It ran from left to right. Moving fast enough that if she'd fallen in then she would be downstream. Maybe as much as a mile away already.

His phone buzzed with a text.

State police twenty minutes out. Alvarez 2hrs.

Backup was coming. How the state police were going to make it to him in only twenty minutes was something he wanted to puzzle out, but that would take time from finding Haley. He started moving downstream. Alvarez couldn't be too far away from Portland if he could get here in that time. Pulled from whatever assignment he was on and flown in. Or he was in the Oregon backwoods and that was the length of time it would take him to walk here.

Hours and hours of endless walking.

Niall didn't stop moving, but he halted the train of thoughts that circled through his head. He couldn't lose focus. He had to find Haley. Keep an eye out for those detectives. He replied to Talia so she knew he was still conscious, then set off again. Half a mile later he saw something. Niall picked up his pace to a trot and headed for it.

Haley, pale and soaked, lay half-in and half-out of the water.

His knees sank into the dirt, and he touched frozen fingers to her neck. A pulse. She wasn't going to last much longer in this state. Maybe not even until the state police showed up. He grabbed his phone, fingers slipping on the buttons as he typed frantically.

Haley needs. Ambulance.

He couldn't get more out than that, and he didn't have time to fix it before he hit SEND. Talia would understand. What he needed was to get moving, knowing they were on their way to meet him.

Niall lifted her up to a seated position, got her arm in place, and then bit down on his back teeth. This was going to seriously hurt. He got his feet under him and moaned as he made his way back to standing with Haley draped over one shoulder. Holding onto her with the arm that didn't have the bullet hole in it. He grabbed a handful of her belt to keep her steady and started walking.

Each step wobbled until he locked his knees in turn. Left. Right. He was practically stumbling, legs shaking. He blocked out all thought and the screaming pain and followed the bank of the river. Heading the same direction it flowed so that Talia would know where he'd be going. She would get help. Someone who could take care of Haley, and make sure she made it out of this alive.

What other option did he have? Build a fire, make a shelter, and wait it out? He wouldn't make much progress before they got there. Better to meet them part way.

His phone buzzed again.

Two o'clock. Half a mile.

Direction and distance. He wanted to drop the phone, but forced his arm to bend. Far enough to stow it back in his pocket. Then he continued on. Sweat beaded on his forehead. He was probably bright red, his skin felt so clammy. Legs still shaking.

He fought through the discomfort the way he had when Siobhan laid down back-to-back on him while he did push-ups. It had been years since they'd done it. Something they shared, seeing how many he could do before his arms gave out. He was going to buy that girl a cupcake even though it was forever ago now.

Niall swayed on the next step and had to lean against the closest tree. Haley shifted. Probably uncomfortable propped with her stomach against his shoulder.

He took a breath then heard something over the roar in his ears. To the left, someone was moving through the trees.

Two men. The detectives?

One called out to the other; a solid American accent—not one of the detectives. "Where is it?"

"Keep going."

"There's a river here. You want me to swim?"

"It's that way."

Neither was Russian, that was for sure. Niall didn't look to see where the guy was pointing. He had no intention of giving away his position if he could help it. Instead, he stood completely still.

"We're right on top of it."

They were looking for something.

"He's going to be pretty happy we found it. Maybe he'll give us one of the girls. We can celebrate."

"That all you think about?"

"Yes," the first one said. "Now find that phone."

"Whatever. Just don't splash me."

Of course, Ana's phone had connected suddenly. A product of this particular geographical location. Maybe. Talia would have to figure all that out. Right now he needed to get Haley far from these guys.

"Got it!"

"Great. Let's—"

Haley moaned.

She shifted against his shoulder, and Niall winced. He couldn't run with her. These guys had guns, and he was basically standing in plain sight with an unconscious woman over one shoulder.

"Hey!" One of the men splashed into the water, heading right for him.

Niall turned to run, but there was nowhere to go. No way would he be able to get himself or Haley there, even if he had the chance.

"I'll shoot you!" The man ran around him and came into view in front. Black fatigues. T-shirts and protective vests. "Hands up."

Niall lifted his free hand. "I'm—" Pain tore through his arm and one knee gave out. He sank down, depositing Haley on the ground. She rolled over, face up. Still unconscious.

The man's eyes widened. "Looks like we found more than just a phone." He glanced at his friend. "Looks like we found the meddling girl, too."

Chapter 8

Haley didn't open her eyes. Her entire body was frozen, and she highly doubted she'd be able to move much of anything if she had to.

She'd regained consciousness hearing voices and stayed quiet just in case. It was hard to keep her eyes from opening. The need to see what was going on around her was driving her mad. That urge to maintain control over her circumstances.

Her fingers and toes were completely numb. Her hair felt like a lump of frozen crystals. Ice on her head. Hypothermia was probably here, or close.

"We'll get a bonus for this."

The second man said, "Should we kill them both, or kill him and take her to the lab?"

"The lab?" The first one shifted fast, rustling his clothes. There was a dull thud.

"Ow. What? They'll be dead anyway. Or they won't be able to tell anyone. What's the big deal?"

"I've told you to keep your mouth shut." He took a breath. "Shoot that one."

Haley laid still, waiting.

"Hold up." That was Niall. "You don't want to do this."

"Pretty sure I do," the man replied.

"I'm a federal agent. You wanna know what will happen if I'm killed? Then go ahead and shoot me, but people know where I am. And when I don't report in, they're going to come looking for me." Niall paused.

She was impressed that he managed to keep his voice steady. She would probably be crying for them to let her go. He said, "You want a team of agents tromping through these woods with scent dogs? I wonder what they'll find."

He was good. She figured he might actually be able to talk their way out of this. Though, the alternative to dying was visiting this "lab," and that was not somewhere she especially wanted to be taken. Too many scary movies played in her head. Victims. Experiments.

What were they hiding out here?

And what did it have to do with Ana? Her friend's phone had been found not far from here. Was this lab place the reason she was missing?

Haley cracked her eyes open. She prayed her head was angled in the direction that would allow her to see something. She didn't want to have to turn just to look.

"You think we care about federal agents?" The second man sounded like he wanted to believe his own words but didn't quite. Nothing but bravado. At least, she hoped so.

"We get rid of your bodies," the first one said, "and no one will find anything. Take you to the lab. Kill you there and use the incinerator."

Sickness rolled through her stomach as she saw them. Two guys stood over her and Niall. Was that what they'd done with Ana? Her heart cried out. She kept the sound from emerging out of her mouth. They knew her. They wanted her dead or captured.

Niall was willing to stand up to them. She was so grateful for that, but how would it get them out of here? He had no bullets. She had no gun.

Her fingers shifted even before she thought about picking something up. A rock. Something hard she could fling at one of them. A distraction so she could go for his weapon. She would have to move fast. Get the projectile in the air and then get herself up. She prayed hard, asking for help. Her entire body was stiff with cold. It was possible she wasn't going to be able to move at all.

Niall was crouched. He would have to react just as quickly as she did. Her fingers found something. Haley sat up. She swung her arm toward the guy at the same time. Her arm felt like a branch, snapped in two. She cried out, using frustration to add strength to her throw.

The pistol she'd grabbed and tossed hit him in the face.

The gun in his hand went off, the trigger squeezed out of surprise. The bullet kicked up dirt as it embedded in the grass.

Niall launched himself at the second man. She forced herself to stand but moved too slowly. He brought the gun around. Haley saw it moving in slow motion. She knew what was coming, and she wasn't ready for it.

She didn't want to die.

She was headed right for the gun, her body rebelling the entire way. A split second before he pulled the trigger something flashed like a spark in his front pocket. He reached for it. The distraction was sufficient enough she could swipe at his gun.

He dropped it and cried out.

The pocket of his jeans flickered. He was on fire. The gunman slapped at it to fight the flames against his skin. His cell phone. It was alight.

Haley didn't have time to stop and say a prayer of thanks. Her body ready to collapse, she swiped up his gun and put a bullet in his head. It was the last bit of strength she had. The only small movement her frozen fingers could make.

Another gun went off.

Niall and his guy both jerked. Who had been shot? She moved her guy's gun up so it covered Niall, but she had no shot. There was nowhere she could aim without hitting him in the process. Unless she moved around him.

The guy fell back and landed on the dirt with a gunshot wound low in his stomach. Niall had a hold on the second man's weapon.

A rush of movement brought her attention to the forest around them. Scores of cops in uniform rushed over, yelling.

Hands up.

Drop those weapons.

Haley's legs collapsed, and she found herself sitting on the ground again. The gun fell from her hand. She heard Niall call to them from a distance but couldn't tell half of what they were saying.

"Ma'am?" One of the officers, state police, crouched in front of her. He took up the gunman's weapon with his free hand and touched her shoulder. "Geez, you're freezing. Can I get some blankets over here?"

She flinched.

"Sorry. I shouldn't have yelled."

She wanted to say it was okay but it wasn't, and she didn't have the strength to speak anyway. They'd come through this. Another piece of the puzzle had fallen into place. But what did it mean? The gunmen were dead. The detectives were gone. They couldn't find out what "the lab" was right now. Would she ever learn what had happened to Ana?

A single ice-cold tear ran from the corner of her eye down her cheek.

She saw Niall glance at her, mid-conversation with some guy in a uniform. She couldn't tell him she was all right. She wasn't. For some reason she didn't want to start lying to him, falling back on pretense where there was no strength left to fight.

The state police officer with her settled a blanket around her shoulders. Beyond him, beside the dead body of the man she had killed, was Ana's phone. He fussed with the blanket, tucking it snug around her. Over his shoulder, another state police officer crouched.

The phone was out of view for a second. Then the officer who'd crouched by the body stood up.

The phone was gone.

. . .

Niall turned back to the conversation he'd been having with a sergeant from the state police.

"That's some story."

"I know." What was more astounding than his twisted explanation of what was going on here was the fact he was pretty sure Talia had exploded that guy's phone. Without that, Haley would be dead right now. It was purely a product of the favor of God that he was alive.

He would have to tell Patricia about that. She liked to hear those stories. Not so much the part where his life had been in danger, more the bit where he'd been saved. Protected. Exactly what she prayed for every day. Interspersed with pleading for his immortal soul.

Religion had been too tied up in the life they'd led growing up in Boston. A time when church attendance was about being "seen" instead of actual faith. Family reputation had been everything—theirs worst of all. He knew what his father had done every other day of the week. How he'd thought that one visit to the house of God made up for that, was something Niall had never understood.

Patricia had held on to her faith, while Niall figured he'd never had much to begin with. Otherwise he'd have been able to see it beyond his father's actions. But he couldn't reason out why his dad thought doing one thing, yet saying something else, was okay.

Breaking legs and then turning around and breaking bread.

Still, he'd tell her about this. She'd believe maybe there was hope for him yet. Niall wasn't so sure.

He pulled out his phone and sent Talia a text.

Thanks.

The reply came quickly.

You're welcome.

Some of the racing adrenaline faded. Niall took a breath and looked around. Just in time to see Haley's eyes roll back in her head.

"Hey—"

He didn't even finish before the officer with her hauled her up into his arms. "I could use some help!"

"O'Caran."

Niall spun to see Alvarez striding toward him. He turned back and watched the officer carry Haley over to where medical personnel walked toward him. Niall's legs itched to go after her. They'd stuck together this far. He should finish what he'd started and make sure she was well taken care of.

"Hold up, brother."

He turned to Alvarez, feeling the frown still on his face.

"Talia told me, but I didn't believe it until I saw it now." Alvarez rocked back on his boot heels. "You're sweet on her."

"We met like two days ago." Actually only last night, considering the first night he'd watched her fight but hadn't spoken to her.

"You don't think I've never been sweet on a woman I saw across a room before?"

Niall said, "What happens at the honky tonk should *stay* at the honky tonk."

Alvarez barked a laugh. Several state police guys turned to look. Niall had to admit it was a sight. Gruff, skinny as a rake. The man looked like he'd been tracking grizzly bears in the Montana backwoods for the last month. And he didn't smell much better than that.

Niall stuck his hand out. "Thanks for coming." He didn't add, "brother" in his reply, because it was implied. He'd had a brother, a long time ago. Much older than him, Niall hadn't known the man well before he was killed.

Now Alvarez was the closest thing he had to a male sibling. And while they couldn't be more different, it still worked. Respect had been earned and didn't seem to have been eradicated by what Niall had done to get himself benched on probation.

Alvarez shook it. "Sure you don't want to drag your feet on this? Stop me from doing my job?"

"I'm sure there aren't armed men at my house right now, holding guns to my sister's and my niece's heads."

"No," Alvarez muttered. "Cause they're out here, shooting at you."

"Another day, another bad guy?"

"Something like that." He actually cracked a half-smile.

Niall didn't find any of this amusing. "She could've died." He had to take a second and tamp down some of the rage. "They shot me. They would've killed her."

"You need to get that seen to."

So Alvarez could take over? "This is *my* case."

"I'm going to assume that's the pain talking, because I don't want *your* case." Alvarez folded slender arms across his chest. "Figured you could use a hand, though. Unless you don't want help."

He was going to make Niall say it. "I want help."

"Good." Alvarez slapped him on the shoulder. The side where Niall had been shot.

He squeezed his eyes shut. The pain flashed lightning across the back of his eyelids and pushed out a low breath.

"Seriously. Go get that seen to. You look like you're gonna hurl."

Niall waited for his breakfast to settle back down then opened his eyes. He took a few breaths of fresh air, but there was gunpowder and blood on the wind. If Alvarez was here, that meant Victoria had called him in to assist. Niall had to be more focused now than he'd been so far, otherwise his colleague would make the arrest, and he would never get off probation.

Alvarez would totally hog the glory for himself.

Niall strode toward where they'd taken Haley. She wasn't going to walk out of the hospital this time, and not because he didn't think she was up to it. Once she woke up, she would totally attempt to bail. She would hide out again and keep going at this until she figured it out. He needed to stick with her, so they could do this together. She wasn't out of danger.

In fact, he was more convinced now than ever that there was a target on her back.

Alvarez peered down to look at the body. He was going to follow the brass trace shell casings and bullet striations until he found the owner of the guns supplied to these two dead men.

Niall pulled out his phone and kept walking, ignoring the shake in his legs. He dialed Talia's number.

"You okay?"

"Alvarez is here."

She said, "That isn't what I asked you."

Niall frowned. "I'm headed to the hospital. Graze on my arm."

She was silent for a second, then she said, "And Haley?"

"Hypothermia from falling in the river. Probably a few bruises to add to the ones she already had."

Talia muttered under her breath. It sounded like, "For goodness' sake," but he couldn't be sure. "Make sure she's okay."

"I will." His thoughts caught up with his mouth. "Is she something to you?"

"No, of course not. I've never met her." She sighed. "Okay, so I pulled her file. Between her mother and her brother, let's just say the woman could use some happy. That good enough for you?"

"I agree with you." Niall added, "I met her brother this morning."

"He as cute as his picture?"

"Uh…" How was he supposed to know how to answer that?

"Never mind. What do you want?"

Any other time, Niall would have chuckled. "It's good to be back in the fold."

"Don't tell Victoria that."

"Too soon?"

"The jury is still out. But I'm here," she said. "And Alvarez is there."

"True." He needed to move this along. "Anything on your satellite images about a lab?" He kept his voice low as he moved toward the state police vehicles. They'd parked two miles from where he and Haley had been, and Niall was almost there.

"To go with the parking lot that doesn't exist?" She paused. "You really have the state police there?"

"Quarter mile in front of me. Four SUVs."

"That is *so* weird."

"What?"

"It's like when thieves loop the security footage—which is ridiculous by the way—and no one sees them steal the jewels. Someone looped satellite images. Which is next to impossible unless..."

"Couldn't you see my phone before?"

"That's disappeared as well now. No one is anywhere near you." Talia made a frustrated noise. "Not even you."

Niall turned in a full circle, at least thirty cops wandered the area. They all had phones. Or at least, he figured they did.

"Nothing?"

"Not. One. Thing."

What was going on here?

Chapter 9

"He picked up the phone, and then he was gone."

Isaac sat forward on the uncomfortable hospital chair, a ball cap backward on his head to cover his scar. He'd discarded his leather jacket. "But you don't know it was a guy, right?"

Haley clutched the edges of the blanket. "It was definitely a state police officer who took Ana's phone."

They'd covered her in pre-warmed blankets and now she was snuggly. Inside, where she remembered the feel of that water, she was still cold. Maybe she would always be cold.

Her brother got up and moved closer. He settled his weight on one hip on the edge of her bed. "You okay?"

She nodded.

"Freaked me out when you called me. Said that you fell in a frozen river. Wasn't the Navy cop supposed to be protecting you?"

"He got shot."

"That's supposed to make me feel better? You got shot *at*. And he's a cop."

Haley shook her head. "Niall is…"

"Niall? That's his name?" Her brother snorted.

"He's Irish, I think." She frowned at her brother. "Don't be a jerk. He's a good guy."

"And the state police aren't? Guess which ones I trust. And it's not the federal agent, sweet talking you into a field trip that nearly ended up with both of you dead."

That might have been the most talking she'd heard out of him in years. Especially considering what teenage-Isaac had been like. She loved her brother, but conversation wasn't one of his favorite things.

"You know I'm right."

Haley made a face. "He isn't a sweet talker."

No, that wasn't true. He'd said nice things. He'd also made her breakfast after he'd gotten her to take a bath. All because she'd been crying and inconsolable. Next to a hug from someone who cared deeply about her, it was the best thing.

"And you'd know whether or not he's playing you?" Isaac paused. "Seems like we've been here before."

"In the hospital with hypothermia?"

"Not funny." His lips mashed into a thin line.

"Sorry."

"I meant you reeling from a guy."

"It's not like that. This was about Ana."

"And yet they knew who you were," he said. "They *specifically* knew who you were."

Yes, she'd told him about the gunmen's reaction to her. There was no point in keeping it a secret since she figured as soon as Niall showed up he was going to tell her brother everything. Not that she was trying to control the narrative, but…okay, so her brother would freak out. More.

She was totally going to do exactly that. Intelligence wasn't just about who knew what. It was also about how information was disseminated, and *when*. That was almost as important as the rest of it. Timing could make or break the success of an operation.

"At this point," she began, "I'm relatively sure Niall is the only one I actually can trust."

"You're using the voice."

"What?"

He stared at her. "The voice where you're trying to convince yourself almost as much as you're trying to convince me."

"I can't trust the cops. I can't trust the state police. I can't trust regular folks walking on the street." She paused. "That leaves you and Niall. What else do you want me to do?"

"Go to Europe. For a month."

She opened her mouth to speak. Her brain raced through the pros and cons of his idea. She had always wanted to go to the English countryside. And the Italian coast. But Ana's disappearance was still unexplained, and how would she find out what had happened to her friend while she was on vacation? No one else was looking for Ana.

"Don't answer that." He waved away what she was about to say—she didn't even know what that was. Then he sighed. "Maybe I'll go."

"What are you talking about?"

"Nothing."

Yeah. It wasn't nothing. "I'm not going to tell you not to worry," she said. He would worry, and there was every reason for him to, but she had to say it anyway. "Niall and his team can protect me while we figure out what happened to Ana."

He didn't need to voice what he was thinking out loud. It was written across his face.

Haley said, "She isn't dead."

His voice was soft. "You don't know that." Probably because he wanted to ease her gently into the idea. Still, it sounded way too much like he was attempting to placate her.

She didn't want to be placated. "If she is dead, then I want to know. Why am I the only one who cares? Why am I the only one who's looking?" Okay, so Niall was also after answers as well. But not in the same way.

He'd told her about his investigation into college scholarships. What that had to do with Ana, the Russians, corrupt police officers and this "lab" one of them had mentioned, she didn't know. Maybe it all tied together. Maybe it didn't.

Would she wind up getting killed before she could find out?

There was a shuffle at the door. Isaac jumped to his feet but wound up stumbling into the chair. He landed sideways as the door opened.

A blonde in a nurse's uniform came in, a smile on her face. She looked at Isaac, who grunted and shifted his weight and mostly just tried to pretend that he hadn't fallen. Then she looked at Haley and her expression faltered. "Is everything okay?"

Isaac hissed like he was in pain and stood. "Yeah, babe. Everything's fine."

In a split second she tried to gauge both their body language while she gaped. "You…" Was this new? Was it good? Who was this woman? Was she nice?

His face whipped around to hers and said something before she had a chance. "Don't be a dork."

Haley shoved the   questions from her mind and grinned so wide it was almost painful. She laid a hand on her chest and tried to look insulted. "Would I do that?"

The nurse giggled.

"Yes." His dark eyes stared thunder at her. "You would."

She shifted to the woman and stuck her hand out. "I'm Haley."

The nurse came close enough to clasp Haley's hand. Confident but still a little nervous. Strong grip, not limp or so strong she'd break Haley's bones. "Blair." Nice. A little "cheerleader" vibe going on, but she had a good job.

Isaac said, "Haley."

"What?"

He ran his hands down his face which dislodged his hat. He pulled it off and slapped it against his leg. He didn't put it back on his head, though. Just sat there with the scar in full view.

Very interesting.

"I didn't mean to barge in," Blair said. "I just heard you were up here." She glanced at Isaac, then back at Haley. "I'm on break, so I figured I'd come and say hi. Make sure you were okay." Her gaze settled on Haley. She was more nervous than she wanted to let on.

"I'm okay." Haley said, "It's really nice to meet you."

Isaac coughed. It sounded curiously like the word, "dork."

Blair smiled, her lips pressed together like she was trying to keep from laughing. "I'm glad you're safe now."

Haley smiled. Images of that gunman standing over her flashed through her mind. Then running through the trees. Niall getting shot. And then falling.

She squeezed her eyes shut.

"I'm sorry. I didn't mean…"

Someone moved. Probably Isaac, coming over to reassure her. Haley opened her eyes and met her brother's gaze. "You should take her for lunch. Don't worry about me."

"I told O'Caran I'd stick with you until he came back."

So she was supposed to let whoever was after her see Blair here? The last thing she wanted was for either of them to be hurt. "Go get lunch, Isaac." She added, "Please," in a whisper. He knew why.

The muscle in his jaw twitched.

"Did I—"

Haley cut Blair off. "It was nice to meet you, but you should go now."

. . .

Niall saw them come out of the room. He paced the hallway, clutching his phone to his ear. The thing hadn't stopped ringing as the team learned about what'd happened and started calling him to, "check in." Dakota was the worst. She'd left three voicemails so far. He'd only listened to one.

Despite how he'd wronged her, waylaying her when she was searching for her father, she only wanted to know if he was okay. Her dad had been an escaped prisoner—and so much more. Nightmares which forged that iron core in the woman she had become. She'd wanted to know whether he needed her and Josh, and Josh's former service dog Neema, to come and help.

But Niall already had Alvarez. He didn't need the whole team descending on the office to fix his problems. Not when he'd have to look Dakota in the eye and know she'd faced down her father. Alone. While Niall had put his family ahead of the team.

And fix his problems, she would. They were all that personality type. Every single one of them would do whatever it took to track the danger to its source, go in hard and eradicate the issue. They'd get one look at Haley and jump on that train immediately.

He hung up, pocketed his phone and picked up a second white chocolate mocha. Extra hot. He wandered toward Isaac and a nurse, who looked extremely cozy. That was interesting. Except that the nurse had tears in her eyes and Haley's brother was doing his best to reassure her.

Isaac spotted Niall headed their way.

"Get the door?"

Isaac turned the handle. "Call if you need anything."

He was leaving? Niall glanced at the woman. Yeah, he'd probably leave as well if it was a choice between his sister and a beautiful woman.

Niall was in the middle of an investigation here, so he couldn't claim the same thing. He was also headed into the hospital room of a woman who wasn't going anywhere, because she'd been hurt on his watch. Yes, she was beautiful; she also needed his help.

Niall nodded to her brother. "Will do."

He watched them go for a second, Isaac slinging his arm around the nurse's shoulder. Drawing her close to his side. Despite what he'd said, Niall wasn't going to call him.

Niall toed the door to Haley's room farther open and went in to find her fighting tears. He stopped at the end of her bed.

She held up a hand. "I don't need a bath."

"How about a white chocolate, sugar-filled coffee instead?"

The tears glistened. "That actually sounds amazing."

He handed one paper cup to her, then moved the ball cap from the chair and sat. "You okay?"

Haley rolled her eyes. She didn't answer though. Just sipped that coffee. Niall supposed it was an answer in itself. "Wanna tell me the reason there are no state police outside your door?" He'd given that order. And yet no one guarded her room now.

"I told Isaac to send them away. He called your guy, Alvarez?" Niall nodded, though Alvarez hadn't passed that on to him. She said, "I don't trust the police. He called them off for me."

"Why?"

She told him about seeing one of their officers pick up Ana's cell phone. Niall said, "Talia said that whole place is a dead zone. Satellites, GPS. Someone made it so no one knows what's going on in that valley."

He'd actually requested that the state police walk through the whole area, check it out, and see what was there. He'd have to take whatever they found with a grain of salt. But the Russians couldn't be leaning on *all* of them. Could they? Niall wondered where the source was. The state police. The local PD. Russians. Gunmen. Who was at the center of this?

There were leads to follow. And yet here he was, sitting here drinking coffee with a beautiful woman.

"How's your arm?"

He shrugged with a wrinkle of his nose. "Probably about as good as your toes."

The corner of her mouth curled up. His phone rang, cutting off what he'd been about to say. Probably would have made her laugh. Too bad someone was calling.

"Special Agent O'Caran." He grinned back at her, the phone to his ear.

"Finally." A man's thunderous voice boomed over the line. "I actually reached the right person."

Haley's brow furrowed. She lifted her hand. "Give me the phone." She looked sick. He didn't give it to her. "May I ask who this is?"

"You *may*," the man said. "But first you can tell me how my daughter is. I assume you're the NCIS agent assigned to her."

Rear Admiral Isaac Franks Sr.

Niall bit down on his molars. "That's correct, sir."

Haley motioned for the phone, the dark of a thunderstorm in her eyes.

Niall pretended he hadn't seen her. "Haley was admitted to the hospital. With some rest, she should be just fine."

"And the people shooting at her?"

"She killed one, I killed the other. The two detectives are at large."

He made a huffing sound.

"With all due respect—"

"You don't mean that, son. So don't waste my time trying to convince me."

Niall shifted in his chair. Pain shot through his bicep. "Did you want to speak with Haley, sir?"

She studied him. He couldn't tell if she was mad at him. She might've been asking for the phone with that continual wave of her fingers, but he got the feeling she didn't actually want to talk to her father.

"I'm due in a meeting with the joint chiefs," her father said. "I expect to be kept apprised, Special Agent O'Caran. Given your history, I don't suppose you'll have much of a problem recognizing organized crime. Still, I want this wrapped up quickly. With no additional injuries."

The line went dead.

Niall lowered the phone from his ear.

Haley groaned. "What did he say?"

He wanted to shake his head and play it off but it wasn't nothing, and it never would be. As much as he might wish it was. Or as much as he might've tried to convince himself that he and Patricia had left the past behind when they drove out of Boston and headed about as far west as they could get without driving through the corner of Canada to Alaska. The weather was better in Portland. Not that it was good. Just better.

"Tell me."

Niall shook his head. "It doesn't matter."

Because he wasn't going to tell her. It had taken him time to convince NCIS to take a chance on him. He'd paid his dues as a beat cop in Seattle before he applied to the federal agency. In the process of his career, he'd consulted with the FBI in Massachusetts, passing on information if he was able to help. Mostly just piecing together information they had.

Niall said, "We have more to talk about and that doesn't factor."

"He said something awful."

He shook his head. "He's just busy, and he's worried about you."

"We both know his only care is for his standing. Otherwise you'd have read a different file when you looked me up." She lifted her chin. Determined not to succumb to the grief she'd lived through. "You'd have read the truth about my mom. The fact she didn't want to deal with any of this anymore and killed herself."

Niall stared at her. Maybe Haley would find out who his family was and maybe she wouldn't. She might not care at all, but Niall just couldn't bring himself to even form the words and find out.

Fear turned cold, all the way to his soul. Fear that she would look at him like so many people had. Some of them cops and other federal agents. And they didn't even know the whole truth of his life.

He said, "Have you ever told anyone that?"

Chapter 10

She wasn't about to answer that question. He was a smart man. He'd
have figured out that no, she hadn't ever told anyone that stuff about her
mom. Instead, Haley said, "Can I ask you something?" His eyes flashed so
she added, "It isn't about my father. Or yours."

She'd meant it as a joke, something to break the tension in the room.
Instead his face changed. He shut down.

"It's about Ana."

He nodded. Still shut down. Looking at her like she was nothing more
than a stranger to him. Certainly not someone he'd been to death and back
with. Almost. She'd thought they were making progress. Finding a footing
in friendship, maybe. Not the kind of progress that Isaac seemed to have
made with Blair—definitely something interesting she wanted to know

more about. But now wasn't the time. And to make it worse, now she'd lost ground with Niall.

Because she'd mentioned his father?

She had no idea what that might mean, but figured it was a minefield she would need to tread carefully in. Evidently they both had issues with their parents. Go figure.

"What about Ana?"

She said, "Just that…if this is something. If there's a *lab* somewhere. Well, then maybe she's not the only one who went missing recently. Maybe there are more…" She hardly wanted to say the word, but forced herself to. "…victims."

He studied her, starting to nod slowly. "Not an isolated event."

"Maybe she didn't stumble across something she wasn't supposed to. Not with that app that lit up when we got close to whatever is out there in the woods."

Niall's phone buzzed against his leg. He lifted it. Frowned. Tapped the screen, then held it up between them.

From the speaker a voice said, "Tell her I'm already looking into that."

Haley frowned. "Who is..?"

Niall held down a button on the screen, speaking into the phone. "Are you listening to our conversation?" He shook his head, the beginning of an exasperated smile on his face.

Haley said, "Talia?"

That was the only answer that made sense to her. That his NSA analyst colleague was contacting them now, aiding in the search for answers.

"It's an app that acts like a walkie-talkie. She designed it."

"I'm listening to everything. How else would I know Isaac has a girlfriend? Talk about a blow. I'm not sure I'll ever recover."

Haley nearly burst out laughing. The woman had even added a mock sob in the middle. She liked Isaac? Wait. Of course she liked him. Why didn't that make perfect sense at first?

Niall shifted the phone close to his mouth. "You'll get over it."

"So heartless." Pause. "Kind of like Haley's father. Geez, what a tool."

Niall didn't glance at her. His reply to Talia was, "Mine was worse."

"Pretty sure Dakota has us all beat," the other woman said.

"True."

Talia came back. "Until she shot him."

Niall tipped his head to one side. "Can't say I was never tempted."

"Amen to that."

Haley blinked. She disliked her father. Strongly. But she couldn't say that shooting him had ever been a thought to cross her mind. Once again she was reminded that these people were in a whole different category than she'd realized. Sure, she'd had glimpses that they might be some new breed of federal agents she'd never seen before. He'd told her they were all different branches, working together. Their office was probably a model that was replicated around the country, agents fighting on new fronts. How many counter-terrorism task forces were there, anyway?

It was a mission. Something she hadn't had for a long time. Sure, she'd tried to find one in saving her mother and then by being a part of the Navy. But it had felt empty still, so she'd walked away. Now there was Isaac.

Isaac who had a girlfriend she hadn't even known about. One who had apparently been told about her. Like Haley was someone he had to warn Blair about. What was up with that? She wasn't sure she wanted to know what her brother had said about her.

Then there was Ana.

Now Niall.

Haley sighed. At least she didn't feel the need to save him. That would be a disaster. Haley didn't need any more missions. Not when they never succeeded and she just wound up feeling worse at the end than she had at the beginning. She was running seriously low on hope. Shouldn't God have shown her the way by now? Shouldn't He have provided her with answers, or a way to get them? It seemed like He was hardly even listening.

Maybe He was as disappointed in her as she was in herself.

"Anyway," Talia's next voice text began. "I'm looking into the GPS thing. And I'm sending all the information on local missing persons your way. Maybe the two of you can come up with a list of possible uh...victims."

Niall shot Haley a look of sympathy. She shook her head and said, "It's okay."

She didn't want to believe that Ana was dead—or being experimented on. But either way she wasn't going to give up until she found out.

"Thanks, Talia."

Her reply came back. "Incoming." Pause. "And you're welcome."

A knock sounded at the door, and then the handle twisted before they could even respond. Niall stood. One hand moved to his gun. Haley braced as a woman entered.

"Director." Niall remained standing.

The woman was slender, probably late forties. She wore a pencil skirt and collared blouse, a duster over her button down sweater. Hair straight and blonde. Haley couldn't see her shoes, but they were probably high heeled and fabulous. She probably left a trail of men with their tongues hanging out behind her everywhere she went.

"Special Agent O'Caran." She shook his hand, then turned to Haley. "Petty Officer Franks."

"Haley is fine." She wasn't going to pretend she had more authority than she actually did. Nor was she going to try and be more than a former petty officer who did construction with her brother. Someone who was maybe going to attend that interview on Friday. If she wasn't dead by then.

The woman rounded the bed and held out a slender hand. Haley shook it. Her grip was firm, more so than Blair's. This woman had the air of authority Haley had seen from upper echelons of the Navy and not many other places. "Director Bramlyn." She paused a split second. "Victoria is fine."

Beyond her, Niall's eyes widened.

Victoria handed an iPad to Haley. "Special delivery."

"Thank you."

A crackle sounded from Niall's phone. "You're welcome."

Victoria erupted into an incredibly distinguished giggle.

Haley doubted she'd ever be that classy in her entire life. Even if she went to like, Classy School, or wherever Victoria had learned it.

"Agent O'Caran." Victoria turned to him. "A word, in the hallway."

They stepped out. Niall left the door open so Haley could see them both. She wouldn't have minded being alone for a few minutes so they could talk, but this was nice. He was protecting her. Showing that he cared, like the way he'd brought her coffee. Professionalism didn't mean he'd had to do that. It was just Niall. Like making her breakfast.

Making sure she felt better.

Little things she could get used to but never wanted to take for granted.

Did Blair do nice things for Isaac? Haley wasn't sure she wanted every detail. Still, he'd called her "babe" and there was obviously something between them. When she'd gotten upset, he had chosen Blair over Haley. And why not? Things were moving on, so that was the way it was going to go.

She might be sad for the change, but it was for the best. Right?

. . .

Niall glanced at Haley, who was tapping and swiping on the iPad. He needed to know she was okay. It was an elemental feeling like the need to make sure his sister and niece were safe. The problem was he could never guarantee it. Which meant that for the rest of his life, Niall was going to be torn between what he couldn't do and the consequences of not having done it.

Left to pick up the pieces of what he'd been unable to prevent.

"How's the arm?"

He looked at his boss and winced.

"Thought so."

She'd asked for honesty since the first day he'd met her, even if that meant silent admittance of how much his arm smarted. When he and Victoria first ran across each other, he'd been undercover with a group using boats to sail from the Seattle area. Transporting drugs in and out of Canada and up to Alaska. Victoria had strode into a party on the arm of a powerful but nasty guy she'd killed later in the evening.

Then she'd offered him a job.

Niall had considered it interesting that she'd made him as a cop so easily, but she was just that good. No one else had been able to tell he wasn't Irish mafia. That mask was easy to slip on. But she'd seen underneath it.

"The state police reported in," Victoria said, drawing him out of that ocean of memories and back into the present. "They found nothing in the surrounding woods where you were picked up."

Niall shot her a look.

"Four of them hiked the whole area, according to them." She made a face that would've been better suited towards a bad call by a ref at the Super Bowl. "Nothing but grass and trees."

"And dirt." He needed a shower. He'd rolled around in it so much he was still covered. It was stuck to his skin, hair, and clothes, and all he'd had time to do was wash his hands.

Victoria said, "Right. The *dirt*. How could I forget about that?" She flashed him a smile. "Talia is working on the satellite images, trying to get a true picture of what's down there." She pulled a folded piece of paper from her pocket. "This is the number of the park ranger responsible for the area."

For the last year, he's been depositing cash in his bank account every two weeks."

"He's on the take?"

"Seems like most everyone is on this one," she said. "The two dead gunmen from the woods?"

Men he and Haley had killed? He nodded.

"They were state police officers. Off duty."

Niall blew out a breath. "They were dressed like guns for hire." He folded his good arm under the one in the sling. "What about the two detectives?"

"MIA, last I heard. I've got Dakota and Josh running them down, and when I leave here I'm headed to a meeting with the Internal Affairs department of Portland PD."

"That'll be fun."

"Yes." She lifted her eyebrows. "Especially when I show them the video of those two detectives that Talia found. Apparently one of the guys who chased you through the woods and tried to shoot you also thought it necessary to record their escapades at a strip club. One that's a front for the Russians. Like they were going to post it to YouTube, so they needed to video their night out?" She shook her head. "People really should be more careful with what they upload to the cloud."

"I tell Siobhan the same thing."

"How are they?"

He nodded. "They're good. Patricia is going to take some vacation time, and I bought them two tickets to spend the next couple of weeks in Maui."

"Good idea." She nodded, not that he needed her approval.

They'd already established that Niall was going to do whatever it took to keep his family safe. Including waylay two federal agents, one a fellow team member. It wasn't like he'd held a gun on them—even though he'd been instructed to go so far as to shoot them if they didn't remain with him.

Niall had been standing over a dead body at the time. One of the bad guys from that case, killed by one of his crew. Local militia types.

Dakota had known immediately that something wasn't right. Probably because he'd made it obvious, without saying as much. He'd been under duress, forced to let her know that he needed them to slow their roll going after the woman at the top of the militia food chain.

"I want Haley brought on." Okay, that wasn't how he'd wanted to broach the subject, but it was out there now. "Not as an agent. Just as a consultant. I want her under our protection."

"She isn't already under our protection?"

"Officially," Niall said. "I believe she can add value to this case because of what she knows and because of what she can get us access to."

"Because they'll let her in the front door of the 'lab?' Whenever you find it." She studied his face, not giving away anything about what she was thinking. It was incredibly frustrating.

He glanced at Haley, still bent over that iPad. He didn't want her anywhere near anyone who was bent on hurting her more than she already had been. "I want her with me. Working this case."

Yes, he was giving away where his feelings were at. But he didn't want Victoria to come to the wrong conclusion. He wanted a result *and* for Haley to be safe.

Because he was the one who was going to make sure she stayed that way.

He said, "I know I have no leverage right now." He was on probation, and that was in addition to the fact that every relationship he had with his team members was strained.

"Not because you delayed Dakota and Josh," Victoria said. "But because you didn't trust your team, Niall. You think we wouldn't have gotten to Patricia and Siobhan, kept them safe for you?"

Instead of making that call, he'd believed their captors when they'd said all his communications were being monitored. Because, duh. Talia did that literally all the time. Any attempt to ask for help would have resulted in the immediate deaths of his family.

He swallowed. "Why not fire me then?" After all, he'd ruined everything. They were never going to trust him.

Victoria shook her head. "Because I'm trying to give you reasons why you should trust *us*. Obviously we failed somehow. You didn't reach out. So now it's up to us to prove to you why you should have."

He tried to figure out how that made sense. "By benching me at the office?"

"Everyone has to take their turn at the office. You know that."

"I'm on probation."

"Technically, yes. It wasn't like I could do nothing and just let you go with a verbal reprimand. You broke procedure." She made a face. "It could've been argued as obstruction of justice."

Niall tried to process what she'd told him. Finally, he said, "That's why you're all here?"

"Because you need help."

"I know that. I have stitches in my arm." Still, he'd rather have done this alone.

She said, "You know what it's like to have to leave everything you know and go at it alone. To know that *anything* has to be better than the life you left behind."

He stared at her. Yes, he knew what that felt like.

Dakota knew what that felt like as well. Her father had been an outlaw, and she'd witnessed him shoot her stepmother when she was only a child. Niall's history wasn't much better than that.

Especially not the parts he and Patricia had vowed never to tell anyone.

Had Talia told Victoria those as well?

"I'll think about bringing on Haley." She took a step back. "But we don't want her to miss her interview on Friday."

His boss turned and walked away, leaving Niall standing in the hallway on his own.

"Niall, get in here!" Haley's voice cut through his thoughts, and he spun back to the room. Was someone in… She waved him over. "I found something."

Niall strode to the bed. She tugged him down to sit beside her. "There are seven missing people who I think are a part of this. Ana is one. There are four men and two other women, all of whom are not accounted for, and no one seems to be all that bothered that they're nowhere to be found. Five of them were affiliated with Western Oregon Research College."

Chapter 11

Niall turned the corner into the campus the next morning, Haley in the passenger seat. She had been released from the hospital that morning in a surprisingly simple and straightforward discharge. Which made her think Talia had a hand in that. If she ever met the woman, she would be sure to thank her.

He drove past lecture halls, admin buildings, and research labs. More than one.

He'd told her about his investigation into the scholarships that seemed to have been funded by the same person responsible for a modified version of VX gas getting out. How this was linked to Ana or a bunch of corrupt cops, she didn't know. What she *did* know was that there were missing people, gone like her friend, and Haley was going to find out why the cops seemed to want to cover it all up.

She said, "You think one of these buildings is the 'lab' that guy was talking about?"

Niall turned into a parking space outside the building where the dean's office was located. "Possible, I guess." He stared past her, in the direction of the buildings. "Guess we'll find out."

Haley wanted to be the one who got the answer. Not because she was determined to insert herself into this investigation. They'd had her sign paperwork that brought her on board as a consultant. It was more that she wanted to prove to them all, and probably herself as well, that she could be useful. That their confidence in her wasn't misplaced—if that was actually what it was. Maybe they were just keeping an eye on her.

Coming here was a bold move. If there really was a lab on campus being protected by the Russians and the cops because something sketchy was going on there, they wanted to find it. Either those covering it up were being paid, or they were profiting by some kind of arrangement they had with whoever was in charge here.

Did the dean know?

Not the first time that thought had occurred to her. Even considering Talia had gone through his cell phone and computer. The warrant for those had come through almost as quickly as Haley was released from the hospital and brought on with the team. So far Talia hadn't found any suspicious funds in the dean's accounts, and there hadn't been any communications between him and anyone that couldn't be accounted for.

Not completely a dead end. At least the way Niall had explained to her. It seemed like he considered it progress to rule things out—just as much as if they could confirm a lead. Scratching things off their list helped point them in the right direction.

"Okay?"

She nodded. "Thank you for this."

"Getting you out of the hospital or bringing you here?" As if both of those may not have been the best ideas.

"Yes." She shot him a smile, determined to not be a time suck. Or an emotion suck. There had been entirely too much of that so far, and she was ready to be done with it. "I appreciate you talking to Victoria about bringing me along."

"You could've gone home with your brother and laid low."

"I know." Was he really doubting his decision? "But I'd much rather be here, doing what I set out to do. Besides, there's no way my brother will let me have any peace. I'll be hearing about how I *put myself in danger* for years as it is."

Niall chuckled.

"Anyway, it's broad daylight, and there are people everywhere. Who is going to face off with us when there are so many witnesses?"

He said nothing.

"You think we're in danger here?"

Niall said, "I think we should get in there, or we're gonna be late for our meeting." He lifted the strap of the arm brace he had been wearing over his head and tossed the thing on the dash.

"Not wearing it?" He'd driven one-handed. Or one-armed, as it were. Apparently that didn't go for interrogations.

"Let's go." He cracked his door and got out.

The air was chilled. Students and some older folks—students or staff—watched them walk from the car and inside. Curious enough as to what two strangers were doing on campus to pause and stare. Was it really that unique to see people they didn't know? Maybe the college was smaller than she'd thought or at least a really close knit community.

Haley followed him up the steps of the red brick building while she tried to shake off the feeling of being watched. "I don't think my toes will ever be warm again after falling in that river."

Niall held the door open, glancing behind her. As though he felt the attention as well and wanted to take a second to stare right back.

They weren't afraid.

Okay, so Haley was kind of afraid. Her dreams had been full of tree branches, swinging in an icy breeze. Gunshots. Blood. Every time she'd awoken, Niall had been there with her.

Isaac had come by before he left for the day, to make sure she was all right. He'd even asked if she needed anything. But in the end, it was this NCIS agent who'd stayed.

She knew it was because they were collaborating information, and he was here to protect her. Which was why she was determined to pull her weight.

Haley didn't want to be a cop. Or a federal agent, for that matter. She took on other people's emotions entirely too much. There was no way she would be able to divorce herself from harrowing circumstances. Or situations where innocents were caught in the crossfire. It was why she'd thought being in the Navy, fighting on her terms—from behind a desk—

was the answer. That hadn't turned out to be the case. But she knew becoming a law officer for real wasn't it either.

Inside the building, a young guy at the reception desk looked up. The whole place was decorated in "old wood." Haley wasn't sure what she'd been expecting, but it wasn't really this. Still, what did research colleges look like? She'd kind of figured there would be more…science stuff.

The young guy was dressed in what appeared to be the student uniform of jeans and a T-shirt, at least given all the young people they'd seen so far. Along with hair that would have been clean four days ago. He glanced at them, a disinterested receptionist. "Help you?"

Hopefully he wasn't getting a communication's degree.

Niall bellied up to the counter. "We have a meeting with the dean. I'm Special Agent O'Caran, NCIS." He flashed his badge, then motioned toward Haley. "This is my associate, Ms. Franks. She's assisting on this—"

"Whatever." The kid got up. "I'll tell him you're here."

He disappeared into a back hallway.

Haley turned to Niall. "Huh."

He cracked a smile. "I get that a lot."

She wanted to laugh but also didn't want the dean to emerge from wherever his office was and find them chuckling together. Then the laugh turned to a yawn. One of those eye-watering, jaw-popping yawns that make the whole world stop turning and required a minute to regain composure.

"We'll make this fast."

"I won't say no to more coffee when we're done here."

The gleam in his eyes was swoon-worthy. "I'm thinking that it might be a while before we're done here." His voice was packed with promise. Full of everything she wanted to believe.

No doubts. No worries. No fear.

No gunmen or missing best friends. And certainly no labs experimenting like the ones in her nightmare. She still hadn't managed to shrug off the after effects of that. Was she going to be nervous all day?

"He'll see you now." The student sat back down. He motioned to the hall on the right with one finger.

Niall put his hand on the small of her back. She was authorized to be here and "assist" but not to carry a weapon. She wasn't without skills, though it did feel weird to potentially face a situation unarmed. She wanted to pray that they would be safe, but there wasn't time.

She headed inside the dean's office first. Haley stared at the man as he stood up and flattened his tie, rising to his full height. She gasped. "You."

"Excuse me?"

She took a step closer to the desk he stood behind. "You're Ana's boyfriend."

. . .

If he'd been looking for a link between Haley's missing friend and the research college, this was it. Niall watched the dean for his reaction. Surprise. Guilt. Suspicion. He quickly recovered, looking at Haley with a surprise that had to be feigned. The shift happened so fast it worried Niall. This guy didn't know her. Not like the Russians in the woods. The dean just didn't want his dirty secrets getting out.

The dean chuckled, but it sounded so fake. "Ana who?"

Haley said, "I'm guessing your wife doesn't know."

Niall had to give her credit. She had guts. Unfortunately, that bravery had made her the target of people who had no qualms about killing her.

He grabbed the back of one chair and pulled it out for Haley. "I'd like to ask you some questions. You know who we are?"

"You're some kind of fed," the dean said.

Niall nodded. "Special Agent O'Caran. Ms. Franks is consulting with me on this case."

They sat in the two chairs in front of the dean's desk. He stared at them, probably realizing they weren't going to leave until he answered, and slumped into his chair with a sigh.

"We aren't here to expose any extracurricular activities you might have," Niall looked pointedly at the dean. "What we're here for is to find out where Ana is."

His face bore almost no expression. A man used to holding his feelings close, not letting anything show on his face. "Ana…" He blew out a breath.

Haley said, "We both know she had problems." Her expression was entirely different. This guy might be to blame for Ana's disappearance, and if he was she was about to find out.

Too bad police work was usually not that cut and dry.

The dean nodded. The nameplate on his desk read, "Bartlett Manchester." A ridiculously pompous name that had probably gotten him mercilessly teased as a child. Unless he'd gone to one of those elite schools full of heirs and heiresses who all had names like that.

Niall said, "Do you know where she is now?"

"I haven't seen her." Bartlett stared at Haley, a challenge for her to disagree with him. "It's been weeks. I don't know where she is."

"When was the last time you saw her?"

Bartlett gave himself a minute. "Maybe two weeks ago."

Niall said, "Where?"

"We met." He swallowed. "At a motel. I left first, and she checked out."

"She would check in under her own name?" Niall had the notes app on his phone open but didn't write anything yet.

"How am I supposed to know?"

"But you kept yourself out of it."

"Until I found out she was scamming me. Told me it was a hundred for the room, not sixty." The first expression crossed his face. "Pocketed the rest. Like I paid her to meet me." He huffed out a breath.

Evidently that crossed the boundaries of his self-respect. Niall figured it was good he had some kind of standards. Otherwise things could get sketchy.

Haley shot him a look and he could see she felt the same, but underneath the issue of this guy's morality—or lack thereof—was the pain for her missing friend. It swamped her. Enough she could hardly speak.

Niall gave her a tiny nod and turned back to the dean. "Did she have any other dealings with this college?"

Bartlett tipped his head to one side. "How should I know?"

Perhaps he had a better handle on what was going on at his college. "And the research being conducted here, what's that about?" He'd gotten the tour of a "lab" the other day but figured mostly they'd been humoring the federal agent there on a fishing expedition.

"At any given moment there are hundreds of projects underway. Would you like me to outline each one for you?"

"Anything going on that involves a lab and the local police? Possibly something Ana was part of?"

"We have lots of labs here. Was it a particular one?"

Niall shrugged. "It's a lead we're exploring." He asked about their financials, trying to gauge where most of their funding came from. It was a privately run college. And the scholarships had been funded by a private party on their radar.

"Used to be DARPA sent us a lot of what we needed." Bartlett sat back, more at ease with this line of questioning. "That ship dried up. Now we're reliant on a handful of investors, private parties, and companies interested in what we might produce. And we fundraise. Things like that."

Sports were a big moneymaker for a lot of colleges, but this one didn't have anything like that. It was literally all science geeks and lab coats. "I see." Niall nodded like this was pertinent information. And maybe it was, but he'd have to figure out how it related later.

Money was definitely an angle to explore. There wasn't much that some people wouldn't do to get a payday. Especially considering the Russians were involved. They considered money to be synonymous with power, and in a lot of ways it was. But to what extent was money funded into this research college, only to be pocketed as cash?

"And it's mostly medical research?"

The dean nodded. "We're on the cutting edge in several of the sciences, though most of it is biological in nature. It's really exciting seeing what these young people can do." He smiled, but Niall didn't believe it.

His cell phone buzzed in his pocket, making him wish he'd gotten one of those smart watches for Christmas. As it was, he had to stand up and dig it out to find out what the notification was for.

He stood and wandered to the window, tapping the phone against his leg without looking at what the message was. They knew the Russians, the college, and the missing woman were connected. Being here was tipping their hand, if Bartlett was involved.

Haley beat him to asking the next question. "Ana had a lot of problems. I know that and you know that if you spent any time at all with her."

Bartlett said nothing.

"What I'd like to know is where you imagine she is?"

He studied her for a moment, then said, "Probably packed her stuff and left town. Went to California, or something. She talked about doing that." He smiled a pleasant smile, as though he found that answer satisfactory whether she did or not.

"And she didn't take her phone?" Haley asked. "Because I found it in the woods to the west of here."

"By the college?"

"No," she said. "A fifteen minute drive from here there's a state park."

One that was a curious dead zone, as far as technology went. Which begged the question of whether something was being hidden out there. Maybe that lab those gunmen—state police officers—had mentioned. And who was behind it? Whoever it was might even have the state police *and* the Russians in their pocket. This was too big for it to be an operation run by a few dirty cops. Multiple people were missing. Satellites had been messed with.

It basically made no sense.

"Huh," was Bartlett's only answer. "Can't say I understand why her phone was all the way out there. But I didn't know her all that well."

No, they just had a relationship that involved motel rooms and the exchange of cash.

Niall's heart squeezed, knowing Haley had to learn all this about her friend. In front of all these people. She'd cared about this missing woman. He'd know that even if he couldn't read it on her face.

Haley lifted her chin. "It's curious, though. Don't you think? Her phone being in the middle of nowhere. Her body never found." Her voice hitched a little on the word "body," but she kept it together. "I'm trying to figure out what happened to her. And you might be one of the last people to have seen her alive."

Niall flipped his phone over in his hand and looked at the screen. It was a text from Alvarez.

One of those students just put a bomb under your car.

Chapter 12

Out the corner of her eye, Haley saw Niall stiffen. Whatever had been on his phone was significant enough to cause that reaction. She turned to face the dean again. A man Haley had seen before, but only in a photo Ana had shown her of her "boyfriend." The relationship had been going on for a few weeks before her disappearance.

Now that Haley was face-to-face with the man, she was seeing their relationship for what it was. Or what he wanted to claim it had been. Ana might have believed what she wanted to, seeing in this guy what she wanted to see there. Not the reality—the cornerstone of which was the wedding ring on his left hand.

She opened her mouth to ask another question. One that would likely betray all the frustration boiling in her. She knew she looked about ready to have some kind of episode where she would go red in the face. That, along with the bandage on her nose, and she would end up looking like a crazy person recovering from plastic surgery.

Niall said, "We appreciate your time, Mr. Manchester."

No one offered to shake anyone's hand. Niall came over to her and took her elbow gently. He guided her out of the office before she could raise any objections.

In the hallway she whispered, "What's going on?"

Before they reached the reception desk he leaned close. "Alvarez said someone just put a bomb under the car."

"A *bomb*? Are you serious?"

He nodded, looking about as happy as she'd been to speak with Ana's "boyfriend." Haley didn't want to leave. She sort of wanted to pin Bartlett Manchester to a chair and make him talk. There had to be more that he wasn't saying.

"I know."

She said, "What?"

"I feel the same way you do." He shot her a small smile. "It's written all over your face. He has to know what Ana was into and if it has anything to do with that app. I mean, I don't imagine they got together at a motel in order to have long drawn-out conversations. But still."

Haley didn't want to think about that. Not when it was obviously so far from what God intended. She nodded instead. "He definitely knows what all is going on. He has to, it's part of the school."

His jaw shifted from one side to the other. They emerged from the hallway into the foyer of the dean's building. He whispered, "And then there's the whole police corruption thing."

The young man at the reception desk watched them leave. She could feel his gaze on her. At the door, Haley glanced back and made eye contact with him. These people thought they could intimidate her and Niall? He was a federal agent. She had all the personal reasons in the world to get involved with this. There was no way they were going to back down.

A tiny smile of defiance curled her lips.

He saw it. She watched the realization wash over his face. But before she could see the rest of his reaction, Niall tugged her through the door. "Haley."

She didn't react to the harsh whisper of her name. Just strode through the door like she had every right to be wherever she pleased. And that included here, asking after her friend. Or at this "lab" of theirs. Wherever it was.

In the GPS "dead zone?"

A car pulled up in front of them. She stiffened until Niall tugged her forward again, and he said, "That's Alvarez."

Niall pulled the back door wide and held it open like she was supposed to get in. She said, "We aren't calling the cops?" Wasn't it the bomb squad who dealt with stuff like this?

He didn't answer. Niall stared at something over her shoulder. "Get in."

Then he rushed around her and raced away. She turned to watch. A young man, a student probably, had taken off on foot holding a phone in his hand. That wasn't unusual, right? Why did Niall race after him like he was chasing a suspect?

"He said get in," Alvarez said.

Haley jerked back around towards the sound of the voice and bent to see a man sitting in the driver's seat. Jeans. Dark jacket. The guy could be a federal agent...or a rancher.

"That means now."

She ducked her head. Beyond where she stood, the car they had arrived in exploded. The boom split her ears. The car erupted in a flash of light. It lifted up off the ground and flipped over, metal ripping. Then the flames started.

Haley realized she was on her butt on the ground. Alvarez was out of the car. He hauled her up by her armpits and shoved her head first into the car, then lifted her feet, pushed them in and shut the door. She rolled over and sat up.

"Ouch."

He got in the front, hit the gas and swung the wheel around in an arc.

"Are we going after Niall?"

Alvarez drove the streets between college buildings. A couple of times he had to swerve to avoid a student. After a minute he slowed, muttering under his breath. "Lost him."

He held the wheel with one hand and dialed his phone using the other. "Pick up. Pick up." Then tossed the phone on the seat and bit back some choice words. He looked mad enough to say them out loud, and she was impressed he restrained himself.

"Will Niall be okay?"

"Considering he only cares that you're okay," Alvarez said, "I'd say you just need to worry about yourself."

"I'm not going to do that." She only paused half a second before she said, "Let's go ask the dean what that was."

"The bomb?"

"He has to know." Those were Niall's words, but they fit now. Maybe more than ever.

He glanced around, one last ditch effort to figure out where Niall had gone. "Fine."

Haley reached forward and grabbed his phone from the front seat. "Unlock it, and I'll call Talia. Maybe she can track Niall's phone."

Alvarez used the code 1-1-1-1.

"Really?"

"Easy to remember."

She pulled up his messages and sent a quick one to Talia. Alvarez pulled up outside the building she'd been in only a couple of minutes ago. The young man who'd been at the reception desk darted out, saw them, and pulled up short.

Haley flung herself out of the car. She grabbed him, and slammed him against the brick of the building. "A bomb?"

His gaze darted from her to something over her shoulder, kind of like Niall had done. Alvarez was probably there. He looked pretty scary, all skinny limbs and a craggy face. She thought he was a US Marshal, but couldn't remember for sure if this was who Niall had been talking about.

"You wanna talk to me, or him?" She let go of him with one hand and thumbed over her shoulder where she figured Alvarez was. "Because I'm going to get answers either way." She shoved him against the wall again, just for effect.

The young man's lips pressed into a thin line. "Fine," he said. "Let go of me."

"Not a chance." She shook her head. "Now who set off that bomb, and where would they have gone?"

She figured the young man with the phone had detonated it remotely. Right before, or right after, he took off running. A distraction—all that was left to accomplish with the bomb, considering they'd known it was there. Niall must have realized that was why he'd been around still, and so he'd chased the guy.

A man lying in wait for them to emerge from the building. He'd have stuck around for them to get close enough to the car. Or inside it. And then he'd planned to murder them.

"You wanna be an accessory to murder? Because I'm sure they can make that happen," she said. "Me? I have nothing to do with the law. But that doesn't mean I don't have my own score to settle."

His eyes flared. Good. He should be worried about what she was prepared to do.

Too bad Haley was improvising.

. . .

Niall raced after the young man. He'd noticed him right away—acting cagey when they came out. Nervous. Waiting and watching. The guy headed into an annex building. Niall caught the door before it clicked shut.

Shoes pounded up the stairs. Niall raced after him, gun in his left hand so he could grab the rail as he hauled himself up each flight of stairs. All along the walls were PerkLife posters. Apparently it was a big deal on campus, and yet Niall had never heard of it before the app came to life on Ana's phone.

On the fourth floor the guy went through another door into a hallway. Niall hit the handle and pulled his gun up as he emerged from the stairwell into an empty hall. The door clicked shut behind him.

The hallway was lined with rooms, doors all closed. Nothing indicated where the kid had gone.

Maybe he shouldn't have left Haley. He'd heard the explosion, the car going up. Was she okay? He would rather be back there, making sure she and Alvarez were all right. The team was built on their ability to work fine and, in some cases, even better solo. Still, Niall would prefer to go back to Haley than be here.

There was strength in regrouping.

But maybe that was just fear talking. Tension hardened the muscles at the base of his neck. Where had the bomber gone?

His phone buzzed. He used one hand to slide it out. Talia had sent him a text.

Franks and Alvarez are good.

He used voice-to-text to reply, "In pursuit of suspect," in a low voice. He had neither the time nor the attention to thumb text the message. He had just slid his phone back in his pocket when two doors opened, both in front of him but on opposite sides of the hallway.

A group of students emerged, moving out into the hall like lemmings. The first one to approach stopped two feet away. Shaved head. Tank top and skinny jeans, boots. "Looks like the police are here." She clocked the gun in his hand and lifted her pierced chin. "Are you going to shoot me? Because we've got cameras, and we can record that."

"Step aside."

She folded her arms. "Or what?"

The rest of the crowd were guys and gals, also pierced and tattooed. Like some kind of uniformed club. Some of his closest friends had tattoos, so it was too bad these guys were giving them a bad name.

One shoved alongside the girl who'd spoken. A bigger guy, thick biceps. Another moved to her other side. They were now completely blocking the hallway.

"Fine." Niall turned to go back to the stairs. "I'll find another route."

He remembered the bomber guy's face. If he was here, Niall would find him. Or they could come back with the FBI and a warrant and search the buildings and everyone's belongings for bomb-making material.

If there were explosives to be found, the team would find them.

More of the crowd emerged from rooms behind him. Blocking his exit to the stairs. "What is this, a flash mob?"

No one answered him, but they were basically all smirking.

"Fine," he said again. After all, he wasn't going to fight all of them. He just needed to leave.

That urge to get back to Haley rose in him again. Or was it just danger signals? Retreat to safety. Why was Haley the same thing as safety right now?

"Move aside," Niall said. "I'm leaving."

"Not so fast." A guy shook his head.

"You want to impede a federal agent?"

"When he's not wanted? Yeah," the guy said. "Maybe."

"Then you'll find yourself being handcuffed. No way to Insta-Snap whatever when you're in prison." Niall leaned forward like this was terrifying news and said, "They take your phone away."

Someone actually gasped.

"Now move."

"So you can oppress one of us? Not likely." That was the girl who'd spoken first.

"I'm conducting an investigation," Niall said. "Anyone want to tell me why a student at this college would put a bomb under my car?"

"I'm sure none of us will tell you the answer to that even if we did know." She had that pierced chin lifted. "We have the right to silent protest."

"Against a murderer? That's who you want to protect? Because all that gets you is a charge of accessory. Not to mention other things." He glanced behind him, then back at her. "I'm sure you'll have fun finishing your degree in prison. Plenty of time to study."

The first blow hit the back of his head. Had to have been a baseball bat he figured, since it was eerily similar to the time he'd been beaned during an unfortunate piñata incident at a birthday party when he was seven. He spun and fended off his attacker.

Another bat hit his right shoulder.

One swung at the left side of his head. Niall lifted his arm to block it. Pain flashed in his arm, and he cried out.

Two more blows came.

Then another against the back of his knee.

He fell to the linoleum floor. Pain burst through him with every hit until finally everything went black.

Niall didn't know what time it was when he awoke. Could have been hours later, or minutes. Or days. There were no clocks, so he didn't know.

The room was dark, and his whole body was warm. Almost like he had no arms and legs. What a freaky thought that was. And if he'd been hurt, he couldn't feel it any longer. There was nothing but floating.

He blinked to try and clear his head. Gray walls undulated around him. Whoa, that was weird. Whatever they'd given him was strong stuff.

He saw a guy in a white shirt. Or robe.

No, it was a lab coat.

Niall tracked his movement, the room around him coming into focus the more he concentrated. A row of hospital-type beds on the other side of the room. He shifted to see more. A row on this side as well. Like a hospital ward. Half the beds were occupied, the patients both men and women. Mostly young, but one had long gray hair. Victims or patients?

This could be a hospital except for the high windows. Barred, like in a prison. Niall figured then that he was in the lab the Russians had spoken of. Deep in the woods, the location kept secret through payouts and murder. Satellite hacking. Police corruption.

This was the place Ana had disappeared to.

And now Niall was their captive.

"You shouldn't have brought him here." The dean? Maybe. Niall wasn't sure that was who'd spoken. He couldn't exactly think straight.

"What was I supposed to do instead?" Another man said. "He walked right in."

Their conversation continued, but Niall's consciousness swam in and out—too much to figure out what they were talking about.

Wherever he was, he knew down to his soul that this wasn't good. And there was no way it would end well. He had to get out of here before something happened—something he wasn't going to be able to recover from.

Niall lifted his arms, then lifted his head. No. He hadn't moved. Everything swam around him.

He couldn't move.

Beeping echoed through the room. Shouts followed, and the rushing of feet. He opened his eyes again and fought to see what was happening. He needed to understand where he was and how he'd gotten from that hallway at the college, surrounded by students, to here.

The team. They would come. No way would they abandon him to this fate.

God. His thoughts dissipated. *Help.*

A crowd of white coats surrounded a bed. More orders were yelled. The beeping continued, rolling through his head until it felt like his entire brain echoed with the sound.

Low moans erupted around the room and then someone cried out. A woman. *Haley.* No. She wasn't here. She couldn't be.

"Shut that off."

A second later, the beeping quit.

"There's nothing we can do for him now." The speaker paused. "He's dead."

Chapter 13

"I know what you're gonna say." Haley gripped the phone so tightly she was surprised it hadn't snapped in two already. Talia was on the other end of the line, but she turned to look at Alvarez, who was driving. So desperate for someone to believe her.

Talia said, "I know where they took him. That giant dead zone."

He glanced over from the front seat.

She lifted the phone and told Talia, "We're already heading there."

"Well, they took a different route, but it's where they went."

"You wanna argue semantics, or do you want me and Alvarez to get Niall?"

Talia didn't have a quick reply for that. Their questioning of the young man had been fruitless. He'd claimed to know nothing about the bomb or the lab. Then local police had shown up, determined to "see to things" there.

Haley and Alvarez had basically been ushered to their car and told to clear the area. The whole thing had been so weird. In the end, Alvarez had been forced to drive on the curb to get past all the black and white cop cars. If he hadn't, she wondered if they'd have been trapped there still. Haley shuddered just thinking about the implications of the local police being a party to what was happening here.

One or two could be explained. A couple of detectives and the state police officer who'd lifted Ana's phone. They were on the take, a party to the Russians' activities. But the first responder who'd shown up had been the same one who'd responded after she crashed her car. The training officer and his rookie had immediately taken over the scene, which was fine by Alvarez. She got the feeling he didn't like paperwork anyway.

Haley just couldn't let go of this niggling feeling.

Now they were going after Niall, who Talia had spotted being hauled out of one of the annex buildings and dumped into a van. Before she'd called to tell them that Niall had been taken, things had gotten pretty heated between the Marshal and the police officer. She and Alvarez had been about to go into the building and find Niall. None of the cops wanted them walking around the campus—they'd literally all stepped in front of them to prevent it.

It was like the twilight zone. Like something was affecting them all, and they'd turned into little more than zombies. Except they seemed in total control of their faculties. Bizarre.

She'd even felt a little loopy herself.

Haley lowered the phone to her lap. "She says they used a different route."

"We don't even know if there's a building. The blind spot in the satellites covers hundreds of square miles of hills and trees."

Haley could hardly believe it was that big. It would be too difficult to hide long term if that was the case. She heard Talia say something and lifted the phone to her ear.

"Put it on speaker." Alvarez sounded as agitated as she was over his missing friend.

Haley said, "Say that again Talia."

"I can't say for sure that's where he was taken. It's a blind spot."

"So we follow the van into the dead zone," Haley suggested. "Find him that way?"

Alvarez said, "Maybe."

"Isn't that where we're headed anyway?"

Talia said, "Yes, now take the next right. I'm running a program, and I need another twelve seconds before it's complete."

"What is it?" Alvarez turned without slowing or using his blinker. Haley's body slid to the left and nearly collided with his shoulder but she managed to catch herself.

"I'm looking at power consumption in the area. They've covered their tracks, but I want a guess at how much is out there based on how much juice they're sucking from the grid."

"It's not some futuristic machine. It's a lab," Haley told her.

"Well they at least have the lights and HVAC running. I'll be able to guesstimate how many buildings, which will give me a ball park for how many people," Talia said. "Or do you not care if it's two people or two hundred?"

"Fine." But it wasn't. Haley didn't worry how many people were there. They had Niall, which meant she was going to bust the door down and take out anyone who got in the way. The urge to vent her frustration on whoever was there lit her up like a beacon.

"When we get there, you stay in the car."

She whipped around to face Alvarez. "Not happening."

"Oh, you think that was a recommendation?" He gripped the wheel with both hands while they careened down the highway faster than they should've been going. "You're staying in the car."

Haley ignored him. Instead she said, "I'll need a gun if I'm going to back you up."

She twisted to get a look at the backseat and see what they had to work with. Pain jabbed the breath from her. She hissed the air out between her teeth.

"That's what I thought."

She glared at him.

"Not arguing is a great idea. Too bad you're not up to helping out, you'll have to stay in the car. I'll be sure to handcuff you to the steering wheel. Just in case." Then he was quiet, his gaze dark on the road ahead of them. It seemed strange that such a nice day had turned out so badly. Like it should be raining or something. "And I never said I needed backup."

"Yeah? So you're the only cop who doesn't have someone hanging around, making sure he doesn't die?"

"Probably, yeah," he admitted. "But that's how this team works."

"Some team when you're all determined to fly solo." She shot him a look he paid no attention to. "Niall told me how he's on probation for trying to protect his family."

Okay, so that was only slightly less than everything he'd told her. But was that the point? Alvarez had to know she was fully aware of the score. The Cliffs Notes, anyway.

He glanced over then, not long enough for eye contact, before he focused on the road again. "Did he tell you that as soon as Victoria heard about it, she had the FBI there to protect them?"

Haley pressed her lips together. "I'm coming in there to help you get him out."

"Dakota got herself out." Talia's voice rang through the still open phone line.

Haley didn't know what to say. How was that relevant?

"Not that I think Niall will do the same thing. We can't count on that," Talia said. "He might not be in a position to get free or to find a way out."

"That doesn't make me feel better." Why were these people so determined to sideline her, and they didn't even want to give her the teeniest bit of reassurance? She needed to call Isaac, but the phone line with Talia was still open. Maybe she should just hang up on her.

"Next left."

Haley heard Talia's voice from farther away that time. The effect made her head swim, the way she'd felt when she was underwater in the river. And when she'd hit the ground after the car exploded.

"Take some breaths," Alvarez shoved her head between her knees. "And give me the phone."

She heard him talk while she tried to get a grip. When she felt like she could, Haley sat up. "Give me the phone. I want to call Isaac."

"No." Alvarez glanced at her, but he wasn't talking to her. "He was wearing it." He paused, the phone to his ear now and not on speakerphone. "If you don't have it, then there has to be another reason you're not seeing it." Another pause. "Then it's in that dead zone and it isn't just the satellite, but GPS as well." He sighed. "No, I don't know why the app would suddenly work while your tech doesn't."

"Give me the phone." She practically tackled him for it and was far more satisfied than she should have been when he let her have it. She wasn't under any illusions as to how she'd gotten it.

"Hang on." Talia's voice.

Haley put the phone to her ear. "I really need to call my brother." Seriously, she was extremely tempted to just hit the "end" button right now. "…okay. One sec," Talia said. "Because you're going to want to hear this."

"You have two seconds. That's all."

"The kid you shoved against the wall—that was awesome by the way, I was watching on their surveillance cameras—he left pretty soon after you did."

He'd been talking to the state police when they left. Being interviewed, or so she had assumed. "Are you going to tell me where he went?" Or maybe there was some other point to this. Like something she'd gotten from that surveillance footage.

"He's behind you."

Alvarez must have heard it. He hit the brakes, pulled up the emergency brake and flipped the steering wheel to the side. Haley held on for dear life while the tires screeched. Then they were facing the far side of the road, at a right angle to oncoming traffic.

He yelled. "Do the thing!"

"After you pulled that stunt," Talia said. "I should *not* do it, just to make a point. I'm not a miracle—"

"Now!"

The car approaching slowed. Its headlights blinked out. The driver looked around. Haley could see that as he closed in on them.

Moving way too fast.

She flung her door open and ran toward the bank of grass on the side of the road. The oncoming blue compact car slowed. The sound of the engine died out. At the last second, the driver hit the brake or something. Tires squealed, but the vehicle stopped just short of the marshal's car.

Alvarez stood watching, his gun pointed at the driver. As soon as it stopped, the marshal moved around to the driver's door. "Get out."

The man didn't move.

Alvarez shot his gun. Haley flinched as glass shattered the driver's window. The man inside cried out, more surprise than pain. "What the…"

Haley moved closer, but kept cover behind the marshal's car just in case the man had a gun. She didn't want to be targeted because she had no way to defend herself. Alvarez would have to save her, and that would take time away from getting to Niall.

"Haley, get in the back." Alvarez held his gun on the man in the car, lifted his foot and pulled something out of his boot. He tossed it to her—a small revolver.

She caught the weapon, no bigger than her hand. It was tiny. A backup gun only meant as a last resort. But she'd fired one of these with a friend in Colorado one time. She flipped off the safety and checked that it was loaded.

It was.

She opened the back door and held aim on the driver to make sure he wasn't going to do anything dumb. "We meet again."

She'd almost had him back at the college, had the state police not swooped in and insisted she loosen her grip on his jacket. He probably had concrete dust in the back of his hair—that, at least, gave her some satisfaction.

"Where did they take him?"

The man didn't answer. In front of the car, Alvarez fiddled with something in the driver's seat of his own vehicle. Then he stood and pushed on the frame beside where his seatbelt retracted. He walked with the car, pushing as he moved it off the road. He shoved it in one more final heave and then got out of the way.

Alvarez's vehicle rolled onto the dirt and then between two trees. It picked up a little speed before getting waylaid by a tree. Metal crunched.

He got in the front seat of the student's car.

As far as getting it out of sight, it wasn't perfect. But evidently he thought it would do. Alvarez pointed his gun at the man's temple. "Drive to the lab."

. . .

The door shut. Lab coat guy was done with his rounds. Niall shifted his hand and tugged on the IV in his left arm. The needle slid from his skin, the warmth and numbness dulling the sting. A drop of blood ran down the inside of his arm to the white blanket.

He pushed out a breath. A small measure of freedom. Life wasn't going to be fun when the aches and pains came back, particularly the stitches in his arm. But he would also be up and moving by then.

He knew getting out of here wasn't going to be all sunshine and roses. The sum of his life so far told him that and this was no exception. Small moments of joy or peace had cropped up here or there over the years. He could count them on one hand. The day they'd driven out of Boston and left that family mess behind. The day Siobhan had been born.

Niall clenched and unclenched his fingers, then shifted his feet. Anything to encourage his body to metabolize whatever was keeping him compliant. How long would it be before he could sit up? Then he'd have to make it to the door.

Down the hall.

He'd need to find an exit in a building he had absolutely no prior knowledge of. No blueprint. No clue as to the size or security measures in place. Then there was the question of what to do when he got outside. He was dressed in only his boxers, so he'd need to incapacitate someone and take their clothes. Or find a locker room. He wouldn't necessarily blend in without proper clothing.

Were there armed guards outside? He could get all the way out to the hall—even outside—only to wind up shot in the parking lot. It was a lot easier to make a dead body disappear than it was a live person.

So why hadn't they killed him yet? They could have done it while he was unconscious. Did they really need him for whatever they were doing here, or was it simply a stop-gap because he'd gone too far chasing that guy?

Niall recalled the conversation he'd overheard earlier, after he'd awoken. Someone had brought him here because they didn't know what else to do with him. They hadn't captured him on orders.

His head started to pound. That was the first clue that the drug they'd been feeding into the IV was being broken down.

He bent his elbows and planted his hands on the bed beside him. After taking a full breath, he pushed. Pain blossomed to life in his arm. Good. That was good. Pain meant he should be able to stand. That they wouldn't collapse underneath him, rendering him useless. There was no way he was staying here.

Niall's head lifted from the bed. Then his shoulders. He bent at the waist, tipped too far, and then had to catch himself before his nose hit his knees. He pushed off the bed and then untucked the covers from around him. Cold air touched his skin, the sensation was a good sign. Energy infused his muscles and the chill invigorated him.

He pulled his feet out and turned to plant them on the floor. He scooted to the edge of the bed. Someone behind him moaned. Niall would have to come back for them. Yes, someone had died earlier. That bed was empty now. He couldn't stage a breakout while carrying people, especially if he could barely walk himself. He'd carried Haley. He'd also dropped her on the ground. The most he'd be able to do to safeguard these people was bar the door somehow and wait long enough to get everyone coherent, up and moving. By that time, whoever was watching this place would be mobilized to take them down.

The door at the end of the room opened. The white-coated man strode in, followed by two others in black fatigues carrying rifles.

Niall stopped moving. So close, and yet he was still miles from possible escape. Dakota had made it all the way out of that shed before she met up with the cavalry. She'd been kicking butt, and all he could do was play it like he was subdued and not get shot. Or killed.

The men stood at the end of his bed, one on each side, their guns aimed at him.

Lab coat guy sighed. "I don't suppose I have to explain what will happen if you don't lie back down and allow me to re-insert your IV."

Chapter 14

Haley gripped the edge of the backseat as they headed for the lab. The lab. It was real. And it must have been where they'd taken Niall. Any other option meant they had no leads. The chance of getting him back would be basically zero. Or absolute zero.

"The guards won't let you guys in." The young man who'd been behind the reception desk gripped the wheel now, his knuckles white.

She said, "We're getting Niall out of there."

Did he think they would give up just because this was going to be hard? People didn't have any faith in others these days. She knew *she* wasn't going to back down and, based on what she'd seen so far from Alvarez and from her conversations with Talia and Victoria, she didn't believe they were the type to quit either.

In fact, Alvarez seemed like he was building up a serious amount of tension in the front passenger seat. The gun he had aimed at the student hadn't wavered. "You let us worry about the details."

Alvarez glanced at her. "We have no visual. There's no way to see what we're going up against."

Haley considered that. "We could get out of the car early and sneak in from close proximity." Assuming it was possible to—

"You're going to jump an electrified fence?" The student shook his head. "I'd like to see that."

"Sorry to disappoint you then," Alvarez said. "How many guards?"

The young man shot him a look. After a minute, he said, "At least two on the gate. More on the grounds. Armed guards. With *rifles*."

"We get it." She figured those guards knew her, given the gunmen from the woods might have been two of them. Out on patrol. From what they'd said, she thought they just might even want her there enough to let her inside. "I could probably walk in the door."

"Sure," Alvarez said. "If you want to be captured two seconds later. Then I'll have to get you *and* Niall out."

"They might take me right to him."

"You don't know that." He shook his head. "I'm not going with a scenario that requires the rescue of two people instead of just one."

Well, that was just unhelpful. She wasn't going to let go of the idea yet. It was still in the beginning stages, so what did he know? It might end up being a perfectly good idea once she'd fleshed it out a bit more.

The student said, "You've got about a minute if you're planning on doing something before we get there."

Haley tried to figure out why he was warning them. "You don't want to roll up as the big hero, bringing in the two of us for them?"

"That's not my job." He actually seemed kind of nervous.

"What *is* your job?"

Before he could answer, Alvarez said, "Haley, you still have that gun?"

"Yeah."

"Is there a latch behind you that flips half the back seat down?"

She twisted. "I see it. What are you thinking?"

When she turned back to the front, he was dialing on his phone. "Talia? Yeah. I need a way in." He listened for a minute, then glanced at Haley. "I already told her that wasn't an option." Then he sighed.

She didn't want to gloat, but apparently Talia was on the same page as she was. Haley didn't much care about the "how" of getting in. What she cared about was getting Niall *out*.

"Connect it to a terminal or a wall plug?" He listened for another few seconds. "Well, make up your mind."

Finally he said, "Copy that," and then hung up. "If we can get in, Talia can get eyes via my phone and lead us out."

That was a big "if" and that was in addition to the possibility of failure on Talia's part. Not through any fault of her own. It could simply be more difficult than anything she was able to overcome in the spur of the moment. Everyone had limits. Even someone as smart and capable as Talia.

"We're coming up on it," the student said. "If you guys are going to do something—preferably something that keeps me from getting into trouble—then do it now."

Alvarez said, "Will they search the car or use some kind of heat sensor to see if anyone's hiding out of sight?"

"What?" The student shook his head. "That's crazy."

Alvarez squeezed the young man's shoulder, finger and thumb close to the tendons in his neck. The student sucked in a breath and curled in on himself while Alvarez climbed over the center console into the backseat. Haley moved out of his way.

"Okay," Alvarez said. "Now you get in the front."

Haley did so.

"I'm going in the trunk. When we're inside, I'll wait a couple of minutes and then emerge." He turned to the student. "You tell them you've found Haley Franks and you're bringing her in. They'll be glad."

"I'll get killed. I'm on thin ice as it is and now she's with me?" His voice rose in pitch as he spoke. "There's no way they won't think that's suspicious."

Alvarez pressed the barrel of his gun against the spot just under the young man's ear. "Then I guess you'd better sell it. Make them believe you're bringing her in to raise your standing. If you're on thin ice, then this is your ticket to getting back in their good graces."

"You don't—"

"Or I shoot you." Alvarez's voice was ice cold. "Then I'll find your closest friends. That girl you like. I'll shoot them. Then I'll find your family. Your favorite aunt. Your dog. Everyone in this life that you care about—even your fifth grade teacher. I will kill every single one of them."

The young man swallowed.

Whether Alvarez told the truth or not, Haley believed it. Such was the level of conviction in his voice.

She had no words left, and wasn't even sure what she would've said had she had the ability. This guy was a federal marshal. Even threatening all that stuff was against the law. The only reassuring part was that he said it to get his teammate back.

Alvarez shut himself in the trunk. Haley shifted in the front seat and put her belt on. The marshal's tiny pistol would fit in her boot, or she could tuck it in her waistband.

The student turned the corner.

Something still niggled at her. She said, "Tell me why you were on your way to the lab even before we intercepted you. Especially when you say you don't want to go."

"I don't have a choice." He slowed the car as they approached the guard shack. Beyond it was a two-story white building that looked no different than an office in an industrial park, except that it was surrounded by overgrown forest.

"Why not?"

"I have to report there. If I don't…" He swallowed.

That didn't sound good. "At least tell me what your name is."

"Stan."

A wash of nerves moved through her, and she took a moment to fight back with prayer. God at work could mean the difference between failure and success here. But did He mean for her to get Niall out? Maybe whatever was about to happen wouldn't look like a win for them.

Haley prayed for justice to be done. For truth to be spoken, and things hidden in darkness to be brought out to the light.

This entire complex was blotted from existence. Hacked satellites and police cover ups abounded. So many players were involved in protecting it, and so far they'd managed to keep it under wraps.

Had God brought her here for this reason? She'd thought it was about finding out what had happened to Ana, but maybe there was more at work here. Maybe God was using her persistence to then go ahead and do even more. To enable her to solve the larger mystery, or maybe even in spite of what she'd been trying to do. Either way His will would be done, though she'd rather that He work through her than around her.

Haley closed her eyes and laid her head back. She heard Stan pull the car to a stop and tell the guard that he'd brought her. She probably looked defeated, which would help sell his story. Inside she kept praying. She asked

God to use her now, even though she had to admit she hadn't noticed His hand in this at all yet. She had to believe.

Help me get him out.

The guard got on a radio. They were waved through the gate and proceeded up the drive to the main entrance.

As Stan pulled up to the front, the doors opened. Three men in black fatigues strode out carrying automatic weapons. Haley stiffened. They were dressed like the men from the woods, the ones she and Niall had killed. More off-duty cops?

Stan moaned, muttering a few choice words under his breath. The gunmen opened the car doors from the outside. "Get out."

Haley pushed off the seat. As soon as she straightened, one of the men grabbed the underside of her arm, tearing her skin, and yanked her toward the door. Her head whipped back. *Not good.* She glanced over to see a gunman do the same with Stan. The two of them were marched through the front doors, a single gunman following behind. Probably prepared to shoot if they attempted anything against the ones holding them captive.

Inside was cold, the temperature low enough Haley's skin prickled. The lobby held almost no furniture. Two men sat behind the desk. They were dressed like the one who still had a tight grip on her arm. Their eyes tracked every step through the lobby to the back, where they turned right. Five guards so far? She didn't count the ones on the shack out front. Those guards wore white shirts and were armed with stun guns. These guys were prepared to kill.

This whole operation had to have had some serious funding. Both local and state police officers had been paid off to cover it up. Yuri had added a Russian connection. They'd been prepared to murder her as well in order to keep everything quiet.

How long had they been doing this? She couldn't tell, but it didn't seem to have been hastily assembled. It had been a while, at least, but she had no idea how long that while was. Months. Years, even. It just blew her mind. She could barely comprehend a lab hidden in the forest and no one had ever discovered their secret.

Or, if they had, they were no longer alive to tell about it.

Haley and Stan were marched down a hallway, to a door. The man holding her arm pulled her back, then got on his radio. "Open for six."

A second later, a light on the panel beside the door handle switched from red to green and the sound of a lock disengaging clicked.

He pulled the door open and shoved her through, into another hall. This one was lined with windows all the way down the left side. Beyond the windows, she could see the building was actually a square, four sides with a kind of courtyard in the middle.

Sunlight streamed in and reflected off the windows on the far side. In the center, the outdoor courtyard was little more than dirt. People, maybe twenty of them, wandered around. Listless and glassy-eyed. One stumbled. No one moved to aid her and she fell, then began to climb back to her feet.

The gunman pushed Haley forward while she stared out. Who were those people? They seemed like…patients. But the whole feel of it was entirely more like a prison yard.

Or a holding pen for animals.

She tried to look at each of them, to find her friend in the crowd. There were so many. Her breath caught and her heart filled with grief for Ana as tears spilled down her throat.

The gunman repeated the same procedure for another door. Haley stood still while the man radioed, and then the door clicked. She turned to step through and heard a thump. When she turned back, one of the people from outside pressed up against the glass. Staring at her.

The gunman bringing up the rear slammed the butt of his rifle against the glass. Apparently, double-paned reinforced glass. "Get back. Freaks."

Haley was shoved. They moved through a regular door, and the guy holding her arm called out to someone inside. "Doctor Zales?"

They moved farther inside what she realized was an office. A desk. Shelves lined with books. A desktop computer, files, and stacks of papers on the desktop. Zales wore a white lab coat. He slid a file cabinet shut and turned to them. An older man. Darker coloring, hair threaded with liberal gray.

"Ah," he said. "Yes." Then waved to the chairs.

Whether Haley wanted to sit, or not, she was deposited into the chair. Stan was shoved into the seat beside her.

"And so you are here."

Whatever that meant. Haley said, "What did you do with Ana?"

"Hmm." The doctor tipped his head to the side. "I'm not sure I recall that one. But there have been so many, I can't possibly remember all their names. It would be impractical to become first-name friendly when I have much more important things to occupy my thoughts."

Nice. That was real nice.

She figured it showed on her face. There wasn't much point in holding back now, and Doctor Zales didn't seem to care anyway. He'd turned away to rummage through some papers on his desk.

When he looked up, he seemed surprised to find them all still there. "Take her to Ward B." He glanced at the guy holding Stan. "He can go to A."

"No." Stan struggled, but it was no use. "Don't send me there. I can do better." He was dragged backward to the door, then through it. He tried to grab the frame. The gunman holding him slammed his head against the wall, then lifted Stan over his shoulder.

Haley stumbled, but the guy with a grip on her elbow hauled her back up. She hissed out a breath and forced her legs to work. Alvarez needed to get inside and do his thing. Seriously, he'd been right. This was basically the worst plan ever. She wanted to get out of here. Only the glimmer of hope that Niall could be in Ward B helped her keep it together. *God, I don't want to be here.* Wherever "here" was. She wanted nothing to do with it.

Those people…

The beep sounded. The door opened.

Haley was shoved inside, and the door clicked behind her. Locked in. Movement right behind her brought her attention around. A man tossed what was in his hand down toward her. She flung up her arms and couldn't hold back the squeal of terror.

"Haley?" He dropped it and metal clanged against the floor as it rolled away.

"Niall." Her voice came out like a breathy whimper. He pulled her to his chest and they swayed, arms wrapped around each other.

But she couldn't stay here and rest in this. "We have to get out of here."

This was supposed to be a rescue.

He nodded. "Let's go."

"How?" She motioned to the door. "These are—"

The overhead lights in the room flashed, then went out. Machinery clicked and went silent.

"Talia, I'm guessing?" Niall launched at the door and pulled it open.

A generator kicked in somewhere. Electronics came back on, the steady beep of medical machines starting up as they had been when she'd first come in.

Someone moaned.

"Come on." He tugged on her hand.

The hallway was lined with green lights that cast an eerie glow. How much worse would that be in the dark? As it was, light from the outside courtyard spilled through the windows. Speakers, high on the walls, came to life.

The chime...

Haley's steps stuttered. Stumbled. Carpet hit her knee.

No, it was other way around. She'd fallen.

"What are you..." His voice trailed off, and she couldn't hear it.

Haley gripped handfuls of hair on the sides of her head. She couldn't...

Fists pounded on the windows. *Bang. Bang. Bang.*

Niall crouched beside her. "What's wrong?"

Chapter 15

She could barely stand. The buzzing got louder. So loud she could
barely think.

The world swam around her.

"We gotta go." Niall hoisted her up. She hissed out a breath because
everything hurt. The touch of his fingers on her skin sent lightning
flickering through her nerve endings.

Haley couldn't help it. She cried out.

He let go and she swayed toward the wall, unable to keep herself
upright. She shoved her hand out and planted it flat against the wall. It felt
like all the bones in her hand shattered. She cried out again, unable to hold
it back. Tears ran down her face.

"Haley. I want to help you." His face. He looked distraught. "But we have to go. Can you walk?"

He shifted like he wanted to touch her, maybe help her. She stepped out of reach and sucked in a breath through her nose.

She had no idea if she could walk. At least not more than a few steps. She nodded anyway, determined not to be the one that let them down. Every step was like walking on shards of glass that cut up her legs. She gritted her teeth and forced herself to keep walking. Speaking would only slow them down. Not to mention emphasize her weakness. He'd been kidnapped and had who-knew-what done to him. The last thing he needed right now was for her to be helpless.

Niall was in his underpants—though she'd been ignoring that fact up until now. Blood ran in a trail from his elbow to his wrist. The bandage was still on his arm, covering a deep graze that had been stitched up. Anyone they faced would know he had been hurt—a weakness they could exploit.

She concentrated on putting one foot in front of the other despite the fact it was rapidly approaching agony. They needed to get out of here. That was the most important thing right now.

She snagged his fingers with hers and held on tight. Pain shot up to her elbow, but she wanted that connection.

People in the courtyard with their ragged clothes and stringy hair. The pounding fists on the glass penetrated the pain rippling through her brain in waves.

Beyond them, others hunched over and clutched their heads. She knew what that felt like. The buzzing. It wouldn't quit.

"...you're being affected by this." Niall looked at her, then motioned to the people behind the glass. "And I have no idea how."

She stumbled on a couple more steps while tears rolled down her face.

"Let's get you some help." His fingers gave hers not more than just a tiny squeeze.

She hunched over and cried out as nerve endings fired. Even her eyes hurt.

He dropped her hand. "Sorry. Sorry."

She shook her head, unable to look at him. How could she explain it wasn't his fault? She couldn't even form the words, let alone the questions she needed answers to. How had she been...what, infected? People had been trying to kill her. Mostly Russians—some cops—and now this? Was it just another attempt on her life that she had to fight off? She needed treatment. Would a hospital even know what to do with her?

"All…" She fought through the pain to say, "People." She motioned to the window.

"When we figure out how to treat you, we'll get the same help for them. But we can't do that until we get out of here."

She nodded.

Distant gunfire. She heard it. Niall did too. He turned toward the sound. She said, "Alvarez."

"Good. We're gonna go that way." He pointed to the door at the end. But how would they get through it when they didn't even have a…

She managed to say, "Key card."

Niall said, "If Alvarez is here, that means Talia is either already in their system or she will be soon enough. That's our way through these doors."

As if on cue, the power flickered. Everything went dark for a second, even the light on the key panel by the door. Niall ran to it, but he wasn't quick enough. The lights came back, the green glow above that was diminished by the light from outside. People in the courtyard cast shadows on the hall.

That relentless banging.

She rubbed the hair on the sides of her head. It pricked like knife points as she tugged on the strands. Every snag of hair like a cut to her scalp.

"Come on." He waved her over, standing with his attention on the red light, the one that had gone green when the gunman radioed for the door to be open. Was it true that Talia was in the system? Maybe this was nothing but power glitches. Maybe it would be fixed in a minute, and then gunmen would swarm this hallway.

Haley looked at the glass. The closest man stared back at her, drool running from his mouth. His eyes were glazed. Full of all the pain she felt running through her, even at a stand still. Movement beyond him caught her eye.

A woman on the ground. Another woman straddling her, hands wrapped around the prone woman's throat.

Choking her.

Haley turned away. More tears rolled down her face.

"Haley, come on." Before he finished, the door clicked.

Two men strode through. The first one spotted her and started to call out. Niall kicked at the back of his knee, grabbed the second man's gun and swung around to kick him with the same foot. The gun went off.

Haley clapped her hands over her ears and almost passed out. But she couldn't. Even the black of unconsciousness wasn't going to help. And then she wouldn't care, because she'd be dead and so would Niall.

The first man clambered to his feet. He was going for Niall. She raced over and kicked him in the thigh, then collapsed to the floor. The pain was like white hot lightning. He must've spotted her out the corner of his eye, because he twisted at the last second. He brought his gun butt down on her shoulder.

Haley blinked and found herself in a heap on the floor. She twisted and dry-heaved. It felt as though her shoulder had shattered like glass.

Niall had a gun now. He shot the second man, then fought with the first. Haley watched the brutal sparring from what seemed like a quarter mile away. She'd come here to save him and in the end, he was the one who was going to save her. It seemed like a bad joke. Or...something. She could barely think through it far enough to come to an actual conclusion.

Her guy brought his gun up. Before he could fire on Niall, she launched herself from the floor and ran right at him. She slammed into him at an odd angle, twisting her head painfully to the side. His back hit the door, then his head snapped back. The gun went off, a three round burst of rapid fire.

They collapsed to a heap on the floor, her on top. She grabbed the gun from him and stood, backing up a few steps. But she was moving too fast. Almost frantic. She tripped on her own two feet and landed on her butt, crying out as pain ran up like shards from the base of her spine all the way to her skull.

. . .

Niall hit the guy—again—with the butt of the gun. He couldn't think about anything or he'd get distracted. The man in front of him blinked. Niall hit him one last time, and the man dropped to the floor, halfway through the door.

He stepped back, still holding the man's rifle. Breathing hard. Pain that had been nothing but numb warmth now crept back in. The pull of stitches in his arm. Aches and bruises. His hip smarted.

The door started to shut but stopped on the man's unconscious body. Niall wanted to go to Haley but only glanced back at her. Every touch had brought her agony. Though she breathed as rapidly as he, she swayed with the pain of it. He could see it in her eyes. Read it on her expression. Too far gone to be able to hold back anything she was feeling.

"You came here to rescue me?"

She blinked but seemed unable to focus on him. His heart swelled with the idea she'd come here, like the cavalry, to save him. Niall had been incapacitated, and she'd made a move that was more like full-fledged team member than just a consultant.

Niall raided the man's pockets and the pouches in his vest. He found a protein bar, two cell phones, and a set of keys. Two twenty dollar bills. He used one of the cell phones to contact Talia via text then walked to crouch in front of Haley.

He needed to get pants and a shirt off one of these guys so he could escape this place in more than just his boxers. But he also just wanted to get out of here as fast as possible, clothes or no clothes.

Thirty seconds later, the intercom crackled.

A female voice rang through, strong and sure. "This is the feds. You are completely surrounded. Exit the building in an orderly fashion and surrender yourselves."

That was about the least official announcement he'd ever heard. This was her response to his text?

He sent another message and told her about the people in the courtyard. All of them were acting eerily similar to Haley. Clearly in discomfort over any touch. Some had gotten aggressive. Three stared through the glass at him and Haley, one banging with a fist that was now bloody.

At least one dead body lay out there. The victim of a vicious attack by another one of them. Who were they? How had the same thing happened to Haley, though with diminished effects, and not to him? Especially when he'd been the one held here?

None of this made sense. Least of all the relevance of this "lab" to the investigation.

The intercom buzzed again. "Please proceed to your nearest exit. This is for your own safety."

She wanted them to get out. The first message had been for people who worked here. This one was for them. He could hear that edge of "just do what I say" in her tone, the one reserved for him and the other team members.

Niall zipped up the pants he'd stripped off the unconscious guy. He peeled off the vest, then the man's T-shirt. Put both on himself, then zip-tied the man's hands together. He did the same with the other guy, but without stealing his clothes.

Boots on, he went to Haley. "Time to go."

She nodded and held out her hand to him.

"Sure?" He held out his palm regardless.

She clasped it and stood, crying out and dropping the rifle. He scooped it up and handed it back. "Let's make this fast."

The next door was locked as well. He pulled up the text thread Talia hadn't replied to directly, so he could ask her to open the door. There was a text there that he hadn't seen.

Get out safely.

The light turned green and the lock clicked. She apparently wasn't going to waste time telling him where Alvarez was, or what he was doing. Niall wanted to call her and find out. Coordinate their exit somehow. What if he needed help with Haley, and he had to do this by himself?

He stowed the phone in one of the pockets of the stolen cargo pants and held the gun up as they moved through the door. Haley tracked with him, but he could tell every step cost her. Soon as they got out of here, he could figure out what was wrong with her.

This hall had no windows, so no one in the courtyard could see them. Good. Haley didn't need that visual of those people anymore. Whatever had happened—or been done to them—it wasn't normal. And he had a good hunch who had the answers: the doctor who had come in the ward to see him.

The next hall was around a corner. Niall waved her to the wall and stopped. She whimpered with each step, and he prayed no one heard it. Then he peered around the corner. Two gunmen stood at the far end in the lobby. Waiting for something. Or someone.

Another called out to them. One nodded. The other got on his radio and said, "Move out now. I'll take care of everyone left inside."

Niall didn't like the sound of that.

Talia had essentially told Alvarez to leave the same time she'd announced it to them. Was he out already? If she was in the intercom, then she was also in their computer system. And their security. Full access. It was how she worked, and it had kept the team alive through every operation he'd ever been in with them.

At the end of the day, the way this team worked meant it was on him to keep himself and Haley alive. Only then could they regroup and take down the lab. Expose the corruption.

Too bad he wanted to get Haley safe first and then go back for his teammate.

He swung out from behind the corner and fired bursts, one after the other. The first man hit the ground, dead before he even realized what had happened. The second turned, gun coming up. Two bullets smacked him in the vest. The third cut through his throat.

He fell.

Noise erupted from the hallway. Niall raced down the hall, mostly hoping Haley stayed back there. Safe behind cover.

He took out the next guy as he emerged into the lobby. Another gunman—a woman this time—fired back. The bullet sang past his head. She was going to take him out.

Niall dived to the floor by the reception desk. Neither guard sat back there now.

Booted feet raced through the foyer. "Go! Go!"

But they weren't coming in his direction.

"Get him out of here!" The woman's voice rang out through the empty foyer, her voice full of authority.

Niall lifted up and put a bullet in her head.

Past where she stood, the doctor ducked his head and cried out. Two other armed guards flanked him. One fired at Niall.

He sank back down behind the desk and then crawled to the far side to get a better view.

The front doors whooshed open. They escorted the doctor outside to a waiting car. He carried a silver case. Like an oversized tackle box. He climbed in the vehicle and held the case on his lap as though it was his prized possession.

The doctor was leaving.

And he was taking his work with him.

Chapter 16

Haley fought to think past the buzzing, at least enough to figure out what was happening. The gunfire had died down. She moved forward, stumbling a few steps, and looked around the corner. In the lobby, the front doors slid shut and a car outside drove off.

Had Niall left her? A rush of fear rolled through her, causing as much torment as what was going on in her nerve endings. Her whole body was a mass of white-hot pain, like that busted outlet in England all those years ago. She shuddered just at the memory of electrocuting herself on that weekend of leave. Even that hurt.

A moan escaped her lips.

Someone called out behind her. She twisted and brought up the gun. No one was there.

"Do you read me?"

Haley realized it was the intercom. The relentless buzz in her head just would *not* quit. Except when Talia spoke through the intercom. When her announcement broke through the signal.

Why couldn't they… "Turn it off."

"Haley!" Niall raced down the hall to her.

She spun, still holding the gun up.

"Whoa." He moved to the side and used the flat of his palm to shift the gun away from his body. "Don't shoot me."

She tried to speak, but no words came out.

He looked like he wanted to ask if she was all right. Haley kind of hoped he didn't, considering it should be pretty obvious that she *wasn't*. Instead, he pulled out a cell phone and sent a text. "Talia can tell us if the way out is clear."

She nodded, then managed to say, "Those people." Only the second word came out.

"The ones in here?"

She blinked the next nod. Her strength was rapidly waning, her body about to shut down from the energy expenditure it took to fight off the pain.

"We need to get out. If we're going to be of any help to these people, then we need to bring others *in* to help. Like an entire FBI tactical team. Ambulances." He paused. "And that's just to start."

"K."

He reached out like he was going to squeeze her shoulder but then evidently thought better of it.

"Thanks." She was grateful for his forethought. And since it seemed she could speak a little, she said, "Ask Talia." She paused, taking a breath to rally her strength. "Turn off the buzzing."

He shook his head. "What buzzing?"

Haley didn't have the energy to frown. Or point to the speaker, high on the wall. She mumbled, "Intercom." Then pushed out a breath. Inhale. Exhale. Pain was good. But this kind of pain? She was ready to pass out. Maybe that was the point. Incapacitate them to the extent they couldn't function.

But why wasn't Niall feeling the effects?

He frowned but typed on the phone. It buzzed a second more. "She's turning it—"

The buzzing quieted.

"—off."

123

Haley blew out a long, slow breath. "Better." The pain eased immediately, going from five thousand on a scale of one to ten, to a solid eight and a half. "So much better."

Talia was their computer guru. She was in the intercom system, even though she was nowhere near here. Alvarez had to have snuck inside from Stan's trunk and managed to connect that phone of his to the computer system. That would have given Talia a route into what was probably a closed network. Without physical access, she probably would never have gotten into the lab's system.

Niall was still frowning. "I couldn't hear anything. Which makes no sense." He glanced around. "But we need to get reinforcements here before we can leave and figure it out."

"Can Talia call them?" The energy it took to speak a whole sentence made her slump against the wall. Even the rifle was getting heavy.

He typed again.

The intercom crackled. "Escape, party of two. Your table is ready on the lawn."

His eyes flashed with humor. "Guess not."

She started off toward the lobby. Each footstep still hurt like nothing she'd ever experienced before. It was like being touched with a hot poker *everywhere*.

"I would've suggested checking the office," he said, probably more to distract her than for any other reason. "But I figure the doctor took everything important with him in that case when he left."

"Maybe he didn't." Those people in the courtyard were still here. If he took something, could be it was just the essentials. And why had he left with his gunmen anyway? It wasn't like they couldn't take care of Haley and Niall and Alvarez as well. But instead of fighting back and taking them out—not that she wasn't grateful that hadn't happened—they had cut and run?

It made no sense.

His phone buzzed.

"Talia said Alvarez has intel and samples, and he raided the doctor's office. She got in the computer system and copied everything to her server. So we have plenty to go on."

Just in case the state police showed up and squashed it all?

Haley peered around the corner. She made sure no one was going to shoot at them as they crossed the foyer. "Clear." She headed for the door. "I don't like leaving all those people in the center courtyard."

Never mind that they would have help on the way. It just didn't sit right with her.

"And the ones in the ward," Niall said. "Most were still hooked up to their IVs. Incapacitated so they couldn't fight back or try to escape."

"Like you did."

"I only managed to get as far as the door the second time. That's when you came in."

The front doors whooshed open and a wave of cool air from outside blew her hair back off her shoulders.

Niall gazed appreciatively at her. "Sweetest sight I ever saw."

Okay, that was nice. Still.

She glanced back at him. "Is that why you tried to bean me with a pipe?"

His jaw dropped. "It isn't like I hit you!"

"I'm teasing you."

"You look mad. Not like you're making jokes."

Okay. But she had been trying to lighten the mood. Things were entirely too dour and if she was distracted by teasing him, then she wouldn't be thinking so hard about the amount of pain still moving through her body.

He'd said something sweet. Haley was so bad at that stuff she'd responded with the first thing she always used when things got too emotional. Humor. Yes, being funny was much better than getting near those walls people always said she had up.

Along with them saying she was "too intense" for them to handle. She didn't even know what that meant. How could she be too intense, when she would much rather things were the exact opposite of that?

Relationships had never made sense to her. She hadn't even succeeded with her family, and she'd had years of living with them.

Now her mom was gone. Her dad wouldn't talk to her. Isaac wanted her to go get a job instead of working with him. Was that because he didn't want her around? She'd figured she was cramping his style. But he had a romance of his own going on so how exactly was she cramping his style? He seemed to be doing fine. Or, he was determined to get her employed elsewhere—and out of his house—because of that Blair woman. Maybe *she* was why Haley suddenly needed a real job.

She shut down that train of thought fast. It wasn't going to lead anywhere good and would only distract her. They needed to get somewhere safe before her body decided that lying down was a good plan and collapsed.

He said, "You look like you need a hospital."

Now that the pain had dropped to a level that was no longer "blinding" but was now "manageable?" She peered both ways outside. "Speak for yourself."

"What is it?"

"This feels strange," she said, not actually talking about what was going on under her skin. "Did they really leave us here to just walk out the front door by ourselves?"

"I know." He moved to stand beside her. "Right?"

Haley nodded. "This is weird."

"Very weird."

"You think someone is waiting to pick us off?"

. . .

It was a good question, but he wasn't sure what the right answer was. He wanted to talk more but the phone buzzed. The intercom crackled. "Get out!"

The phone buzzed again.

Niall shoved Haley forward. The doors slid shut behind them as they stumbled outside and then turned back to face the building. Like it was going to try and grab them or something.

Shots kicked up gravel. A grouping of rapid fire bullets.

Haley grabbed for Niall as she started running toward cover. He snagged her hand and together they raced along the outside wall of the building.

Booted feet pounded behind them. Someone was in pursuit.

Niall turned as he ran, still holding her hand. He brought the barrel of the gun up between them and squeezed off a few groupings of shots.

One of the men stumbled and fell to the ground. Gunmen, guards who worked here at the lab. More off duty cops? That was going to be difficult to explain.

Niall's feet missed a step and he turned back to Haley, stumbling to follow after her. It was clear with every step that she struggled. She wasn't going to last much longer. And the only way to get free of these guys was to outrun them or fight back and win.

They needed cover. A defensible place.

And what was with the doors shutting? Talia hadn't been in control of that. If she had, she'd have given them way more notice than one second. Maybe it had been some kind of safety mechanism, and all the doors in and out of the lab were closed now. If they were locked as well, then he and Haley couldn't duck back inside to get cover in order to mount their defense. There was no cover out here. Three cars in the lot and too far away. Trees beyond them, up the hill surrounding the lab. The whole place was a huge basin.

An alcove that probably held a side door came up ahead. "Go in there." Hopefully Haley would know what he was talking about.

She slowed a fraction.

A bullet pinged off the building right beside her. But there was nothing else they could do. "In there."

She tried the handle even though he'd just meant the alcove itself. Niall pulled up short just around the corner and turned. The inset, a two-by-two concrete square, was barely big enough to hold both of them huddled together. He crowded against her, turned and peered around the corner. Gun first.

"It won't open," Haley said. "I think we're locked out." She sounded frantic, full of fear. Maybe even overwhelmed beyond her ability to think clearly.

"It's fine."

But it wasn't.

Niall aimed, then fired off two shots. He caught one guy in the leg and then missed the torso as the man fell. He hit the ground and cried out.

Niall recognized him from the woods. They'd had a run-in with him. Haley had fallen into the river before they faced off with the other two guards. Off-duty cops he now thought must have been from this very lab, maybe out in the woods patrolling the area. There certainly had been a lot of casualties…

It felt good to eliminate the threat now, even just using non-lethal force. It occurred to him that too much death had happened already. And that was just today.

The river.

Haley had fallen into the river.

While Niall thought the whole thing through, his gaze searched for the second man who'd been behind them. Not a good use of his focus, splitting it like this, but he wondered if her falling into the river had something to do with her reaction to…to…he didn't even know what. A sound—a signal?— sent through the intercom? She'd said it was buzzing. Could be they were close enough to this "lab" when she was drenched that the water had been contaminated.

That Haley had been contaminated.

He'd have to add that to the list of things for them to do; get Haley tested for some kind of substance in her blood. One that caused her pain.

And then there were those people in the courtyard, hurting each other. None of this made sense.

Movement caught his gaze. The second man was running now but not toward them. He headed for a car parked across the lot. He was leaving? The man was armed, bulletproof vest along with cargo pants and a shirt. A jacket had been pulled over his vest. He had a phone to one ear.

The guard flung open the door to his car, then paused. His gaze caught Niall's, and they stared at one another for a second.

Between them, his partner lay on the ground, clutching his leg and crying to his friend for help.

The runner got in his car, turned on the engine, and hit the gas. He blew over a concrete curb and crossed all the white lines of rows that marked out spaces as he sped toward Niall. The man on the ground rolled. The engine got louder.

The car was coming fast.

The downed man lifted a hand, as though sure his partner would stop close to him. To pick him up, so they could escape together.

But the car didn't slow. It sped up.

Niall wanted to close his eyes, but something kept them open as the driver sped toward his friend. And then drove over him. The thud was sickening.

The man Niall had injured lay dead on the ground. As the driver continued on, he lifted his phone to his ear and spoke into it, his gaze locked with Niall's.

Haley whimpered. She shifted closer to him as they both watched the man drive away.

The phone in his pocket buzzed.

Get out of there. At least half a mile.

"What is going on here?" Haley whispered the words that he couldn't make come out of his mouth.

Niall's brain kicked in. His phone buzzed again.

Run.

He snagged Haley's hand. "Come on." There was no time to tell her not to look at the dead man lying on the ground. "We have to get clear of this place."

They raced to the trees. If Talia wanted them to leave, they were going to leave. Half a mile, though? That was like some kind of blast radius. He checked around them for more cops who would try and shoot them.

"What's going on?"

He pulled her along. "Talia said go."

She puffed out a breath. Niall figured then that she needed distracting from the physical exertion. "She said half a mile, so we've gotta run. Okay?"

She wasn't okay, but he wanted her agreement nonetheless.

Haley nodded. She did a good job keeping pace with him. Every few steps, he told her as much. Kept her moving. Reassured her they were almost there. He hardly wanted to think why they were running. What it could mean.

If it was what he suspected it was, that meant Talia was not just playing it safe. They needed to get clear.

Outside that blast radius.

He wanted to text Talia back and ask about Alvarez. She'd said he was out of the building, right? He was the only person he cared made it out of there, other than Haley.

His eyes burned.

He had to believe that. Niall couldn't think about the people still inside. Patients. Victims. If he was right, there was no time. No way to help them.

A whizz in the sky overhead caught his attention. Niall slowed long enough to process what that whistle through the air meant.

Haley stopped and hung her head, breathing hard.

He saw it.

She shifted and looked up, then turned in the same direction as she tracked its flight. "That's…"

Of course, she would know what that sound indicated. Were they far enough away? They'd climbed the hill so he could see the roof of the building below them now. Four sides, open in the center for the courtyard.

"No." Haley cried out. She moved toward the building.

Niall grabbed her. She made a sound, this one was pain-filled and not just surprise. Her legs gave out. He wrapped his arms around her.

"Those people."

He nodded, his cheek against her hair, and together they watched.

A breath later, a boom tore through the air. The lab exploded. The ground beneath it gave way, and the whole thing fell into a hole in the earth.

Seconds after that, the blast rushed up the hill toward them.

Chapter 17

Haley woke up in the hospital. For a second she was back to her previous visit. Isaac had been sitting in the chair by the bed. Now it was empty.

She'd fallen in the river.

No. The lab had exploded.

Someone moaned. It grew to a shout, and she twisted the blankets to see another bed beside her. Niall sat up, blinking as he awoke from what must have been a nightmare.

"Hey." She said it louder the first time, then added, "Hey." Softer.

He glanced around, chest heaving, and looked at the window streaming light in. Then at her. "Haley."

She smiled. "Rough night?"

He laid back down. "What..." He lifted a hand and pinched the bridge of his nose. "The lab exploded."

"Yep." She slumped back onto the pillow and touched her own nose. Still swollen from the airbag.

He lowered his arm to look at the needle at his elbow. Both of them were hooked to IVs. He stared at it. Shuddered.

"You okay?"

"No."

"I know the feeling."

The door opened and Victoria stepped in. "They told me you guys woke up." She moved to stand in between both of their beds, then took off her overcoat and laid it just beyond Haley's feet. Underneath she wore a skirt and blouse in different colors, neither of which Haley would be able to pull off. She needed fall colors. Victoria was all gray and blues. Whites. Ice.

Haley brushed at her hair, figuring she looked like she'd been dragged by her feet through brush. Not too far from the truth as far as she recalled. Her hip and shoulder hurt from where she'd landed after the blast tossed them fifteen feet back.

"Where are we?" Niall motioned to the window.

Haley looked out at the buildings. What was... This wasn't Portland.

"That's part of what I wanted to talk with the two of you about," Victoria said. "So long as you're both alert enough to have this conversation."

Niall turned to her. "Haley?"

"I just want to know what happened to that building." She didn't want to believe the whole thing had exploded. Like a terrorist attack or a military drone strike. And yes, she'd been involved in those before, but this was different. She'd been standing right there when it happened. Not thousands of miles away behind a computer.

She and Niall could have been killed.

Tears clogged her throat. "Those people."

Victoria's gaze softened. Niall remained silent while his boss moved closer to Haley. She said, "There was nothing you could have done. They shut the doors so no one could get out, and they sent that drone strike to take out the whole facility." She paused a second. "The two of you were supposed to have been inside when it blew up."

Haley just kept seeing those people in the courtyard. Ana might have been one of them, and now she would never know. All that searching for nothing.

"There was complete and total destruction," Victoria said.

"So they wanted to be sure no one and nothing survived?" Niall asked.

"Including the two of you."

"And all the evidence."

Victoria nodded.

Haley looked away, not wanting their sympathy. Ana was dead. Maybe she needed to finally let go and face that fact.

Now that she knew what had been happening—and she had a whole lot of questions for Victoria about it—she had a shot to get justice for Ana. But she wasn't going to find her friend. This was far bigger than one person now. Police corruption and a secret lab.

Niall said, "Where are we, Victoria?"

She shifted to sit beside her coat on Haley's bed. "At an undisclosed location."

"Maybe, but not to *us*. Don't shut me out."

"That's not what is happening here." Victoria paused. "As far as the world is concerned, the two of you died in the terrible accident that destroyed the lab. You were probably hiking those woods and got lost."

"Forget the fact that this was not an accident at all," Niall said, "What about Patricia and Siobhan?"

Victoria said, "Dakota and Josh went to speak with them. They've been instructed to react befitting their beloved family member exploding into unrecognizable pieces. Siobhan was apparently mad she would miss the game this weekend."

Haley turned her head from the window, back to the director. "And Isaac?"

"I had a chat with him. He won't say anything." There was more there, but Victoria said nothing else.

Haley didn't know if her brother had been relieved she wasn't looking for Ana anymore or mad that she'd gotten hurt because of it. When she saw him next, she was pretty sure he wouldn't pass up the opportunity to say he'd told her so. But there was still one family member they hadn't mentioned. Haley said, "What about my father?"

Victoria said, "The Rear Admiral has demanded a full investigation into the incident. Once he told me that, Franks talked for another ten minutes about how you leaving the Navy was the biggest waste of talent he's ever seen."

That was his reaction to them telling him she was dead? Haley wasn't sure how she felt about deceiving him like that. Even if it seemed like he wasn't all that bothered by her untimely demise. Another way she'd wasted her life.

The predominant feeling that left her with was…nothing. She struggled to care about her father beyond what was expected. Most of the time, she couldn't even hit that threshold.

There was far too much water under that bridge.

She had never thought that sweeping her mother's drug problem under the rug and pretending it wasn't an issue was the right call. Haley had taken the brunt of caring for her mother through middle and high school, especially after Isaac left and joined the Marines.

The night her mother died, Haley had been at prom.

No doubt Victoria knew all the details as they'd been listed on the police report. Haley had spent nearly twenty-four hours in her prom dress talking to cops. Then NCIS agents who'd showed up at her father's behest. Then one of her father's aides got there. She'd been told what to say. What to do. How to act. While inside, she'd been screaming.

Her mom had succumbed to the ravages of her habit. An accident, they'd called it. But the truth was that Haley hadn't been there.

She hadn't saved her mom's life, because she had thought her own was more important.

"I don't want Isaac anywhere near this." If something happened and she lost him as well? Haley didn't think she would survive that, just like she knew Niall would be wrecked if anything happened to his sister or niece. "I know they're all good keeping up the ruse, but they need to be protected."

A muscle in Niall's jaw flexed.

"Right?" She glanced between them.

Victoria nodded. "I have FBI agents I trust in place to provide that protection. Though, I have to confess, the ones with your brother were eating pizza and installing bathroom cabinets."

Haley almost smiled.

Almost.

"That's good enough." So long as he had someone there to watch his back, she didn't much care what they were doing. Helping him with the house would make it look like they were just friends hanging out. Or coworkers.

"What about Alvarez?" Niall asked. "Talia said he got out. Is he okay?"

"He got physical evidence that will help, but it's not a slam dunk." It was weird hearing Victoria use a sports reference. "Talia copied their computer system. She's combing through all the data she obtained right now, but that will take a while."

"The doctor left," Niall said. "He had a case, one he held like it was everything important to him."

"We're looking for him."

Haley watched the interplay between the two. Niall was clearly the underling but Victoria didn't lord it over others, even despite the fact she was the director.

Maybe she should bench both of them. But maybe the team wasn't big enough for them to pass cases off to someone else.

Niall had told her it was the four of them, plus Victoria.

"What about Haley?"

She shifted to look at Niall. "What about me?"

He didn't look back at her but asked Victoria, "Did she get checked out?"

. . .

He had to know. After the way she'd reacted, talking about the buzzing coming out of the intercom speakers. Buzzing he hadn't even been able to hear. He didn't even know what it was, but Niall had to know she wasn't infected with something.

Victoria nodded. "A full workup was done of Ms. Franks."

Niall appreciated the fact she didn't refer to Haley by her former rank. She was a person, not just the sum of her military service. He'd met all kinds of Navy personnel—active duty and not. They all had their own ideas about how people were supposed to refer to them and their time serving this country. Niall had learned not to assume. Especially when so many left bitter and scarred.

Haley said, "And?"

Victoria turned to her. "What we've been able to piece together is this. You fell into the river, right? You were submerged downstream from the lab. When your blood was analyzed, we found a cocktail of compounds. It would take me an hour to explain to you the way they all interact." She paused, but neither of them asked her to do so.

The director continued, "The short answer is that those compounds made you susceptible to whatever the doctor was up to in the lab."

"The buzzing?" Haley asked. "That's what made them all start to go crazy?"

"It affected you to a lesser extent, yes?"

Haley nodded. Niall didn't know that there was much "less" about it. She'd seemed to be in a considerable amount of pain, if you asked him.

Victoria said, "Your exposure was much less than those people."

"Patients." Haley's face was grim.

"Or test subjects," he put in. They had to face the fact that the doctor had been conducting experiments on people right under everyone's noses. "And they had the local and state police to cover for them. Maybe the Russians as well." Though the only conclusive proof they had of a connection between the Russians and this lab were Yuri's interactions with Ana and the scholarship recipients. Who knew if that had even been a business relationship?

"It was quite the operation," Victoria said. "One we're going to have to take apart if we want to find the doctor or anyone else behind this."

"Good," Niall said. "As soon as I'm cleared, I'll help. We need evidence, and we need to find that doctor." The one who had kept Niall drugged up the whole time he'd been held captive as a patient. He'd only come in flanked by armed guards, because he knew there was a possibility Niall would be uncooperative.

He hadn't seen anything yet.

Victoria said, "I figured you'd be on board."

"Beats sitting in protective custody." Not to mention the chance to be the one who slapped the cuffs on that doctor was going to be worth the work it took to take him down.

"You will be in a safe house." She motioned at Haley. "As will Ms. Franks."

Fine. For now. Niall knew he wasn't at a hundred percent, and he wasn't going to argue otherwise. No point in doing that when it wasn't something he could fake. Victoria would see through it, and he respected her too much to try.

"Yakima or La Grande?" He knew which safe house he preferred. Close enough to his favorite restaurant he could bribe the protective detail to run out for a guacamole bacon cheeseburger.

"Neither." Victoria shook her head. "This place is entirely new. The two of you are dead, and it needs to stay that way, all right? The situation warranted something a little more…off the grid."

"Why do I not like the sound of that?" He'd never enjoyed field trips as a child.

"Whether you approve or not doesn't especially matter." She used her director's voice. "It's what is happening."

Niall pressed his lips together. Staying silent was better than arguing when she wasn't going to accept any arguments anyway. Mostly he figured she was mad they'd been hurt in the course of an investigation. That wasn't something she had ever dealt well with. But he also thought it might be more complicated than that this time.

He wanted to call his sister, or Siobhan, and make sure they were okay. He probably wasn't going to be allowed to do that, but there were ways to send a message so it wasn't trackable or able to be monitored.

First he'd have to talk to Talia.

"The two of you are 'no contact' until I say otherwise." Victoria stood. "Talia has all that data to go through, plus she's attempting to figure out how someone managed to hack NORAD and connive a drone strike on US soil. So don't bother her." She gave him a pointed look when she said that.

Then she continued, "At the point you're both cleared for travel, you'll be leaving this hospital and heading to the safe house. You'll be escorted by Dakota and Josh, who will take over for the FBI agents on the door." She pointed a finger over her shoulder. "You do whatever they say."

Haley said, "Yes, ma'am."

Victoria glanced at Haley. A smile curled up her lips at the corners. "At least one of you is thinking clearly. But the fact is the Russians, as well as the local and state police in Portland, are all kinds of tangled up in this. So you are not to make a single move without my authorization."

"You know I won't let this go," Niall said. "That lab might have been blown up, but the doctor got away. And who knows who else is involved?"

"Which is why we need to tread cautiously, Special Agent O'Caran. That means finesse, not kicking down doors and going in guns blazing."

Like that was his style? That was more Dakota. Though, since Josh came along, she seemed to have mellowed quite a lot.

He said, "Understood." Because the alternative was more probation and that wasn't okay with him. This was his case, regardless that the rest of the team was on it as well now. He was the one who had found the Russian connection. And Haley. So long as they moved forward in a way that didn't paint another round of targets on their backs, he was fine with it.

But they *were* going to be moving forward.

Haley said, "You think they'll start up the operation somewhere else?"

"I hope not." Victoria shrugged. "But the fact is, that's probably an unrealistic hope. We have to assume that the doctor fled with everything he needs to continue his work. Those people, sad to say, were liabilities they couldn't afford to take with them. As were the two of you and anyone else left in the building. They opted for scorched earth."

"Nothing left, no survivors," Niall said.

He was ready to get out of bed and go get these guys, which was probably why Victoria was here giving him her "in time" speech. There was no way she was going to risk moving slowly when it could mean they lost the doctor for good.

For all they knew, he could already be in the wind. In another country. So far underground and away from Oregon that there was no way they'd ever catch him.

There was no way Niall would let that happen.

Chapter 18

The car sped along the freeway. Near as Haley could tell, they'd been at a hospital over by the coast. Some kind of smaller town deal. Fake names. Like it wasn't completely obvious they were "someone" given the federal agents that had been present. Still, Victoria seemed competent enough to secure the situation against someone taking one or both their pictures and posting it online.

Haley wasn't sure she cared. Exposure would speed things along; instead, they had to hole up somewhere and sit around until there was some kind of break in the case.

In the driver's seat was Josh, handsome in a rough-and-ready kind of way. Which fit the picture of a former Marine with a retired service dog. The front passenger was Dakota, all Native American coloring. She was gorgeous in a way that was entirely different than Victoria, but which served to make Haley feel inferior, just like her boss did. The fact she didn't even seem to realize it did help a little bit.

Niall's teammates. Josh was DEA, and Dakota was Homeland Security Investigations. She'd told Haley like she figured that was incidental to her. Haley had noticed that with most other people, they flashed badges and then mentioned the task force before their individual agencies. With her, they'd made it personal.

Same as the fact they'd ushered Niall into the back seat with her. Josh had said it was so his fiancé could navigate, but he didn't seem to need anyone to tell him where they were going. And they'd told Haley and Niall to sit tight because this would be a long journey.

They hadn't even told Niall where they were going, despite the fact he'd asked repeatedly.

This whole thing was super awkward. And she didn't want to put Isaac in danger by breaking protocol and calling him, but who was she supposed to talk to? She barely knew Niall, let alone the rest of his team. She'd been fine on her own. Isaac was her sounding board.

Who else did she need?

Apparently God thought she needed the support of an entire task force, because He'd dropped her right in the middle of one just as she'd stepped into the line of fire. Bad guys were everywhere she turned. Most had been dressed as good guys. She would never have been able to tell the difference. They'd have killed her.

Haley prayed for a while as they sped along the freeway toward Portland, and then beyond, pouring out her thanks to God that He'd saved her butt so many times during this that she'd actually lost count.

Then there was that weird episode with the buzzing. The hallway when those people were banging on the windows, most of which was a blur. But she remembered some of what had happened. Like running outside. Trying to get back in. She'd have to talk through it all with Niall in order to get the pieces in the right order. Surely there was something to remember that she would otherwise miss.

What else were they going to talk about for however long they were at this safe house?

Niall reached over and tapped the back of her hand. "Okay?"

She turned to him. She wasn't fine and didn't plan on pretending to be. There was no way she could act like she was one hundred percent. And she was exhausted enough to know she didn't have the energy to try it either.

She shrugged, rather than betray her thoughts. Not much energy behind it, though.

He hadn't even looked at her when he'd basically insinuated she was…what, infected? Like she would suddenly turn into one of those people in the courtyard acting crazy and trying to hurt each other. She wasn't some kind of ticking time bomb about to go off at any moment. And if he thought that, why did he volunteer to be shut up in a house with her? Maybe he figured he would protect the rest of the world *from* her if she suddenly snapped. Was he planning to shoot her if she turned?

"Haley." He touched her fingers, threading his through. "You need to take a breath."

She realized she was wheezing. Like a panic attack. Ugh, how humiliating. Even Dakota turned around.

Josh said, "Do I need to pull over?"

Haley locked gazes with Dakota and tried to tell the other woman, without words, that she didn't want them to make a big deal of this. Dakota didn't look convinced, but she shook her head. "You can keep going."

"Haley," Niall said again.

Was he going to just keep repeating her name over and over? "What?" She held her breath at the top, counted to three in her head, and then let it out slowly. Like blowing through a straw.

"Wanna tell me what this is?"

She shook her head. Dakota glanced at Niall, then twisted back to face the front.

"If we're going to be in a house together, we should probably be able to talk. Or we'll have to find a board game."

Haley took another long breath and repeated the procedure for pushing it out. Then she said, "I just got overwhelmed for a second."

He gave her hand a squeeze. "It has all been pretty overwhelming. The lab. Those people." He glanced at her, but she only saw it out the corner of her eye. "I'm sorry we couldn't help them. I know you wanted to."

He didn't feel things the same way she did. Haley knew that; knew it was just a fact. He protected the people he cared about. Haley did the same, but she also felt extreme emotion for people she didn't know.

At the end of the day, people were people and all different at that. The fact he didn't feel the same emotion for everyone in the world wasn't a demerit for either of them. It was probably what made him a good federal agent, that ability to set aside his feelings and focus on the job at hand. The victory to come when justice was brought to those who had broken the law. Dakota's phone rang. She lifted it to her ear. "Special Agent Pierce." A second later, she flung her hand out and tapped her fiancé on the arm. "Turn around. Drive to the airport."

He frowned, but followed her instructions.

"Copy that." Dakota hung up. "The doctor was spotted on surveillance cameras arriving at the airport."

"What about the case?"

She turned to glance at Niall. "It was his face through the car window. Nothing about a silver case."

"He has it with him."

"As far as we know, he *had* it with him," she said. "The FBI is on their way there now, but we're closer. They want us to stall him until their tactical team gets there. They think he's hopping on a private jet." She glanced at Haley and explained, "If he gets in the air, that puts him in international airspace within an hour. We have no jurisdiction for a takedown if that happens and no idea what the extradition situation is wherever he ends up."

Niall added, "If he gets on that plane, we've lost him forever."

"I see." She kind of did. And if her brain had actually been firing on all cylinders, that would have happened faster. Still, she got the gist of the idea. They needed to catch the doctor. "Thanks."

Dakota nodded.

Niall squeezed Haley's hand and then let go. "You should stay in the car, okay?"

"Great idea." Dakota nodded. "Niall, you can keep her company."

"Wait a—"

"Thanks for volunteering."

He closed his mouth and sat back. Not happy.

Haley took a page out of his book and decided she didn't care if he wasn't happy. At least this time he wouldn't end up getting kidnapped.

. . .

Niall didn't buy it that Haley was fine, but there wasn't much he could do about that right now. Josh hit the gas and swung the wheel to the left to take the corner hard. They'd rushed through the security entrance of the airport in record time. Likely Victoria's doing.

Josh rounded the outside of a hangar. On the phone beside him, Dakota said, "Next left. It's that building up there." She pointed to a dark gray structure up ahead, the place Talia was directing her to.

They parked down the side of the building. He didn't like the fact that they were the only ones closing in on the doctor. No back-up. But if they lost him *and* that case, this was over. Never mind that in the meantime they were swinging Haley out there, putting her in a position where she could get seriously hurt. Maybe even killed.

"I can help," Niall said. Because he *had* to. Not just because they needed to get over there, and fast. He didn't want to leave Haley, but he did want to keep her safe *and* get the doc.

"Protect Haley." Dakota slammed the door, already outside.

Josh did the same on his side. They drew weapons and strode to the front corner of the building. Niall gritted his teeth.

"Sorry." Haley's voice was soft. She almost sounded sad, and the last thing he wanted was for her to get upset again. "I know you'd rather go help them."

"I just don't like anyone being in the line of fire when I should be there to protect them. Never know what's going to happen."

That was what he was going with. The line he fed himself.

But did Haley deserve that? He decided no.

Niall said, "You know what? That's part of it but not the whole truth."

"You don't want to waste time protecting me."

"What?" He shifted to angle his body so he could see her without twisting his neck. "No. That's not it at all."

She turned back from the window. Niall realized that if they were going to be on even footing, he was going to have to tell her all of it.

He took a breath. "My father is Irish mob. Back in Boston. My cousins and uncles—all of them—are connected. That was the life I was raised in. My mother died when I was really little, and my father talked about her like she was a saint." He shook his head. "I remember her like she was a red-haired angel, or something. But I doubt she was perfect."

Haley said nothing.

"All they wanted was for me to sign on. Be part of the family and everything that entailed." He shut his eyes for a second, knowing he was going to tell her things only Patricia knew. "Transporting drugs. Selling them. Weapons deals, probably explosives too. I don't doubt they sold women, maybe worse, though I never saw it back then. What I do know is that they did everything you can imagine, despite the cops trying to bring them down."

"Bribes?"

"Payoffs. Or they managed to skirt out from under convictions through different means," he said. "A couple of my extended family, or friends that are part of it, they've gone to jail. But that just expanded their reach to inside the prison. It widened the pool they could recruit from."

"But you got out." Her voice was soft but for an entirely different reason now.

He nodded. "The day I graduated high school. Patricia is a year older than me. She was engaged to marry one of my father's friends. He was forty-seven. She was barely twenty, making minimum wage at a coffee shop." He had to take a breath then, just to continue. "She had this guy she was seeing and told my father she loved him. He told her to end it because her future had been secured. Then she got pregnant. The boyfriend told her to get rid of it. She knew what dad would say. But instead, she told me."

Haley laid her hand on his. He held onto her fingers like a lifeline. It had been years since he was in Boston. How was it he could still smell his father's whiskey-laced breath and feel the sting of his palm on his cheek?

Disrespect.

But only because you weren't falling in line with his word, like it was the law. Never mind the actual law.

"We packed up her car and took off before the graduation ceremony even started. While they were waiting for me to walk across that stage, we were speeding across the state line out of Massachusetts. Neither of us has ever been back."

"And now she has Siobhan."

Niall knew what she meant, still he said, "I told her she needs a boyfriend. Siobhan is fourteen."

"And what about you, don't you need someone?"

"I've never met the right person." Until now.

He was pretty sure Haley was exactly the package that had been missing in his life. Maybe he hadn't been consciously searching for her, but he was certainly aware of what kind of person he wanted to share his life with.

Something shadowed across her eyes. He almost missed it.

Before he could ask about it, she said, "So the thing that got you on probation is all tied up in Patricia, and how you guys saved each other."

He nodded. "A few months ago, we went up against this militia who'd gotten their hands on a form of VX gas."

She winced.

"Yes, it was nasty stuff." He didn't want to tell her the rest of it, but she might as well know everything. "The person behind it threatened Patricia and Siobhan. They were going to kill them if I didn't stop Josh and Dakota from going after the woman with the gas."

"Did they…"

"They weren't hurt. Victoria had a team of FBI agents go to the house and keep an eye on them."

Haley pressed her other hand high on her chest and sighed. "I'm so glad."

"I could have pulled a gun on my teammates. Maybe I should have, because I was supposed to be protecting my family. But Dakota called me on it, like she knew. So I told her straight away."

"That's a good thing."

"It still got me put on probation." A thought occurred to him. "If I hadn't been at the office in Portland, on probation and working this case…I never would have met you."

"If my friend hadn't disappeared," she said quietly, "I never would have met *you*."

"Making the best of a bad situation?"

"More like turning things around." Haley gave him a small smile. "Working to make your life better, like you did by leaving Boston. That took serious courage. And maybe we don't always make the right choices, but that's not what life is about, right? It's about learning to be strong. And finding people you can belong to."

Niall leaned toward her. For a second he wondered if she was going to realize his intention and turn away. That was the last thing he wanted, but he would respect her choice.

When he drew close, she lifted her chin. "Are you going to kiss me?"

"Would you like me to?" He was so close he almost spoke right up against her lips.

A gunshot rang out.

Then another.

One answered it.

A thump rocked the car. Niall's head whipped to the front windshield. The doctor had run around the corner and straight into the car. He skirted the front bumper and kept going, running down the side of the car.

He was getting away.

Chapter 19

Haley watched as Niall grabbed the handle and flung the door open. Faster than she even realized what was happening, he smacked the doctor in the face and the guy fell back.

She scooted far enough she could see out, mostly by leaning over his lap a bit. The doctor lay on the ground, a red knot on his temple.

Dakota raced around the corner, gun first. She pulled up short, eyeing Niall the way one would a wayward child. She put her free hand on her hip. "Just couldn't help yourself, could you?"

Niall called out to her. "Did I get out of the car?"

Haley smothered a chuckle. Dakota couldn't argue with that.

The Homeland Security agent flipped the doctor on his stomach and cuffed his hands behind his back. When she straightened, she keyed the radio connected to an earbud in her left ear. "The doctor is secure, but we're gonna need an ambulance."

Niall shifted to get out of the car, then held out his hand to aid her. Haley scooted the rest of the way over and clasped his fingers. When she stood up, she saw a good-sized crowd gathered. FBI agents in full tactical gear, at least six of them. Two had men in suits, cuffed and in their custody. The commander strode to Dakota. "We'll take them in."

"Keep me in the loop."

The FBI agents started to dissipate. Josh rounded the corner at the end of the building leading a fourth secured man. "Pierce?"

Dakota hauled the doctor up and held him steady while he shook off the fog of unconsciousness. "I'm not hurt, but Niall smacked the doctor unconscious with the car door."

There was a serious amount of satisfaction in knowing he hadn't gotten away with that case. He couldn't continue his operation all over again somewhere else.

Haley saw Josh and Niall shared a grin. They were right to. That move had been *awesome*. Niall was barely recovered from being captured and drugged, and he'd pulled a stunt like that? Quick reflexes. He'd just flung the door out like it was no big deal. Knocked the doctor unconscious.

Haley said, "I'd still rather have gotten that kiss."

Josh and Dakota glanced over. Niall twisted to look down at her. Okay, so she hadn't exactly meant to say that out loud.

Haley opened her mouth to stick her foot in it some more.

Niall didn't wait for whatever she'd have said. "Sorry you didn't get what you wanted."

She frowned. "That wasn't—"

He spoke to his fellow agents. "Time to go?"

Dismissed. He'd just written off everything she'd been trying to say, and now he was ready to go. How had they gone from that very sweet almost-kiss to this? Just by one stupid comment he'd taken the wrong way?

Her heart was still racing—and had been since he'd asked her permission to kiss her. What kind of guy did that? Certainly none Haley had met in...forever. Mostly they just assumed that if they were prepared to give you attention, then you should be grateful for whatever they wanted to do.

Dakota stared at Niall with a funny look on her face. But she said, "Soon as we get this guy to FBI custody."

Niall nodded. The doctor wasn't even all the way conscious yet and could barely stand upright. Was she going to drag him away from here?

147

"Why give him to the FBI?" Haley shut her mouth as soon as she was done. Why couldn't she think before she said whatever dropped into her mind?

Dakota headed toward them and motioned at Haley with a tip of her head as she did so, hauling the doctor. He stumbled, but she kept him going. He looked like he didn't even know what was happening.

Haley walked with her past the end of their SUV. At the end of the building, they headed for the collection of FBI agents and their vehicles.

Dakota said, "The FBI can handle evidence collection and testing. They'll also interview the suspects we're taking into custody."

"Oh."

"You wondered why the task force isn't doing that."

Haley nodded. "You have that office in Portland, right?"

"No staff. Except for Niall."

"Because he's on probation?"

Dakota said, "We don't have a continued presence in one place. We're usually spread all over, working on cases." She paused a second. "Victoria has mentioned that we're actively looking for additional team members."

"Okay." What did that have to do with Haley?

"Which confirms what I was thinking." Dakota passed the doctor off to two FBI agents, who picked him up and carried him over to where an ambulance was waiting, beyond their vehicles. Then she turned to Haley and finished. "That buzzing thing, whatever it was the doctor was doing to those people? It messed with your head. You aren't thinking straight. Just like being there and getting drugged messed with Niall's."

"That's why he nearly kissed me?"

Dakota made a choking sound. "Uh…"

They set off, back toward the SUV. Haley figured changing the subject was a good idea. "So we don't know what's happening?"

"All I'm saying is that you need to cut each other some slack. You're both in a seriously stressful time, and you're going to say things before you think. You're going to take things the wrong way. So is he. Give it time. Don't make any major decisions until all this is over."

"We caught the doctor. Why wouldn't this be over?" Haley asked.

"We stopped him from doing this somewhere else."

Haley was pretty sure she'd heard them mention making sure the doctor didn't start up in a new place, with new victims.

Even though they hadn't saved those people in the lab, bringing the doctor in was still a victory. The loss weighed heavily on her heart, and on her sense of what she should have been able to do.

Did she need to let go of that assumption? This whole time, Haley had been so sure she would find Ana or at least find out what happened to her. Now that was in the toilet. They'd taken down the people behind it, even if they didn't understand all of what the lab had entailed.

Dakota tugged on her elbow. Haley saw that Josh and Niall seemed to be having an intense conversation. Josh said something. Niall glanced over at her with a look she couldn't decipher.

"Hopefully he'll cut you some slack, and I think you should do the same for him."

Haley frowned. Before she could ask what that was about, Dakota said, "Things are crazy. You're both under a lot of stress. When you've gotten some rest and eaten half a pizza each, then you can talk."

Now Haley had no idea what to say. She needed to process a whole lot, maybe spend some time reading her Bible and writing in a journal—if they could go to the store and get her one.

"It's hard to see the big picture when you're in the middle of it," Dakota said. "Trust me on that because I know it first hand."

"O-kay."

Dakota squeezed her shoulder. "Like I said, just trust me on that."

"Guess I should cancel that interview my brother set up," Haley said. "If I'm not supposed to make any big life decisions right now." The interview had been for Friday, and she had no idea what day it even was at this point. She only knew what time it was because they were outside.

"You'll be in protective custody for the foreseeable future."

"Yay." She made a face.

Dakota laughed. "Let's get out of here."

Haley should probably apologize to Niall. She hadn't wanted to let Ana's disappearance go, and in the end he'd been kidnapped from the college because of it. He'd been chasing the person who'd blown up his car when he was taken. If only she had thought to go with him.

Thankfully, there was no way he'd see it that way. He wouldn't blame her. No cop, or man, would think any of this had been her fault. She had to face the fact it came down to her inability to let Ana go.

Haley sighed. It was going to take forever to work through everything that'd happened, how it all related, and what it meant.

Dakota nudged her toward the car. "Pizza time."

. . .

Niall slept fourteen solid hours before he woke up, took a shower, and headed to the safe house kitchen for coffee. A lot of coffee.

Haley sat at the breakfast bar, her hand holding a pen over a notebook, writing at a speed faster than he could track. A Bible sat open on the other side, the finger of her free hand pressed against the page.

Her finger slid down the column of the text when she heard him moving. She twisted. Realized it was him. "Hey." The smile was small, but it was there.

After everything Josh had tried to tell him yesterday, Niall's head was full of things he should say, could say, would say, when he fully woke up. Instead of ruining the moment for her, he wandered over and put his arm around her back and hugged her from the side.

From her perch on the stool, she shifted partway toward him and leaned her head on his chest. He kissed the top of her head. "Hey."

Then he went to the coffee pot. Still hot. Half full, but he could make another pot after he drank all this.

"Anything new happen while I was asleep?" He'd figured updates would come to his phone, but they'd taken it away so they could make it look like Niall and Haley were somewhere else. Dead.

"I haven't been up that long, but I saw a couple of agents. They went outside when I came down." She rolled her eyes. "Said they didn't want to disturb me."

Niall leaned back against the counter and sipped his coffee while he studied her face. Namely, what that comment meant. She hadn't wanted to be alone? Would she rather have had someone with her to talk to?

Maybe. He didn't know. And Josh had specifically told him not to assume he knew what Haley was thinking—or feeling. The guy was right. Niall didn't know her all that well. They'd spent a handful of stressful hours together in the past couple of days. Niall couldn't help wondering if Josh thought Haley was somehow not the kind of person he should get close to. There was nothing Josh knew that Niall didn't, but why say it at all unless he thought that?

Haley flipped her notebook closed. "How are you feeling? Do you need anything?"

He lifted his coffee, then took another sip. Should he make breakfast? He'd done it before for her, so maybe she figured he would do it again now. Food sounded...not so good. Too much pizza still sat in his gut from yesterday. He was pretty sure that had been around lunchtime, or a really early dinner. He should probably be hungry by now, but the coffee was hitting the spot.

She smiled. "Maybe Dakota will call with an update. Or she'll come over." Haley paused, long enough to bite her lip.

"What?"

"Do you think they'll find anything at the lab?" She hesitated again. "Like DNA?"

"We can ask Talia. If you're looking for information on Ana, maybe she was listed in the database. Talia has all that, remember?"

"Right." She nodded. "So we just sit and wait here for someone to—"

The side door opened. Niall started so hard at the interruption, he worked to steady his cup. As fat drops of coffee hit the floor beside his foot, Dakota strode in. "We have a problem."

"Just one?"

She shot him a look. "You have no idea."

"Coffee?"

"Please."

She didn't shut the door. And no one else came in. Then he heard the jingle of dog tags as Neema padded along the floor behind Haley.

"This is Neema."

Haley reached down to pet the dog for a minute. Then Neema came around the counter. Niall set his cup down so he could pet her.

"Hi, dog." He rubbed her head and neck, then bent to run his hands through the fur over her shoulders and sides. "Neema. You're such a good girl."

Dakota leaned against the counter beside Haley. "Meet the world's most spoiled Marine."

Haley smiled wide.

"And the task force's unofficial mascot."

The smile turned to laughter.

"So this isn't an emergency visit?" Niall asked her. When Dakota shook her head, he patted Neema's side twice and straightened. The dog moved away to sniff everything in the kitchen.

Non-emergencies were good. He was kind of getting used to this safe-house thing.

"Don't get comfortable though." Dakota shot him a pointed look.

Niall shrugged like, *What?* But said nothing.

"Who knows what's going to happen in the next few days."

"I still don't know what's happened in the last twelve hours," he pointed out.

"Okay, that's a fair point." Dakota glanced over at Neema, in the living room rubbing herself along the couch.

"The FBI debriefed the doctor?"

She shook her head. "He never made it."

Niall pushed off the counter. "What?!"

She lifted one hand, palm facing him. "Whoa."

"He escaped?"

"No. There was an ambush en route. He was shot dead on scene by gunmen. One of the FBI agents is also dead, and another one in surgery."

"That's awful," Haley said.

"It's what we sign on for." The words rushed out of his mouth before he realized he'd barked at her. Haley's eyes filled. Before he could make it worse, he turned back to Dakota. "What about the case?"

If there had been an ambush on the federal vehicles transporting him to their office, surely they'd been thorough enough to get the vials as well.

"They never found the case," Dakota said. "We got the doctor, and they searched everything. The cars, the plane, the hangar. The case is nowhere to be found."

"So whoever shot the doctor didn't take it?"

"Nope."

"What does that mean?" Haley asked, apparently over her hurt feelings. Niall figured he should probably apologize later for being short with her anyway.

Dakota said, "It means we have to figure out what the doctor did with the case before he headed to the airport. He could have handed it off to someone or left it somewhere. We need to figure out when it left his possession."

Haley nodded. Niall recognized the fact he wasn't doing so well with whatever this was, developing between them. He had feelings for her but instead of protecting her, she kept getting hurt. Instead of kissing her, he'd done his job and stopped the doctor.

Not that it had made a difference.

Now the man was dead.

Why hadn't they questioned him themselves before they handed the guy off to the FBI? Hindsight showed a different picture. Like being on probation, knowing he would've done some things differently when his family's lives were threatened. But not that much. He'd still have done his first job—and protected them.

Like taking down the doctor, and by doing so, protecting Haley when she was in the car with him.

Keeping her safe was the most important thing. Didn't she see that?

"So now we have nothing?" he asked Dakota.

She eyed him, then said, "It's a setback. I'll give you that much. But Talia is still working on her stuff."

Like that dark web server she'd never managed to breach. The money behind the threat that had come all the way to his doorstep at home. Josh and Dakota had taken down Clare Norton and saved a lot of lives. But there were still more unanswered questions.

"I won't hold my breath," he muttered. Then louder said, "We need to find that case."

Chapter 20

Haley paced the living room. Reading her Bible and journaling was supposed to have given her some peace, but she felt just as confused as she had since the lab exploded.

What did God want for her? She'd been so convinced it was about finding Ana and getting answers. Was that just pride? Maybe she had been kidding herself. Thinking it was all about *her* and getting a result and nothing about doing what was best for her friend.

There was a really fine line between making herself feel better and doing what was right. And it was far too easy to wrap a pat on the back in with justice.

"You okay?"

Haley turned to find Dakota round the couch toward her. She shrugged. "This is a nice place."

Not the kind of work Isaac did. He made bank on his renovations, turning dumps into high-end houses. Though, not *too* high-end, or they'd be worth too much for the neighborhood and they'd never sell.

"How are you feeling," Dakota began, "after all that buzzing in the intercom stuff?"

"You mean when I went all loopy?" Haley shot her a smile. "I have no idea what that was about, but the explanation that I was contaminated when I fell in the river makes the most sense."

Especially since the doctors had tested her blood and found traces of all those chemicals. A cocktail inside her, like microscopic insects crawling through her veins.

She shuddered.

"Yeah, you're not okay." Dakota shot her a look.

Haley slumped onto the couch and tried to ignore the fact she was probably right. The Homeland Security agent sat sideways to face Haley, one knee bent on the seat in front of her. She had gorgeous dark hair and eyes, Native American features that she didn't need any makeup to enhance. Dakota wore none anyway. She was also the kind of woman who counted lip balm as makeup—and not the shiny or glittery kind.

"Would it be okay if I called my brother?"

Dakota shifted to reach into her pocket. "I figured you might want to, so I got you an untraceable phone."

"Thanks." Haley held it on her lap. "Is Talia looking into the app that was on Ana's phone?"

Dakota nodded. "She's got a ton of work on her plate right now, so she passed some of it off to a team at the NSA. Mainly the science stuff from the lab. It's not her forte as much as the rest of it. Networks and electronic information. Dark web stuff."

"Uh…"

"Yeah, so I have no idea about any of that." Dakota chuckled. "If you want an update, I'd suggest getting it direct from Talia. If you understand all that firewall, IP, server stuff."

Haley bit her lips together to keep from smiling. It didn't work for long. "Okay."

Dakota shrugged, evidently not all that concerned by the fact she didn't get the technical details of Talia's job. Haley had worked in the intelligence field and so much of that was electronic now. She had gathered intel and figured out how it tied together. If she got it wrong, military service personnel's lives were in danger. Being good at her job had meant minimizing the risk to their lives.

Not something anybody should phone in. Though, things did occasionally slip through the cracks, or wires got crossed.

It was tempting for Haley to ask for constant updates. She had to remember that she wasn't part of this team. Knowing all the information being passed back and forth wasn't going to help—it would only slow down Talia's work if she had to report in constantly. Going through it wasn't within her purview, though she wouldn't mind doing something if it helped.

No. It would take too long to loop her in. Get her up to speed. Instead, she needed to trust that these people could do their jobs equally as well as she could do hers. Probably better. Then she had to face the fact that *this* might be what God wanted to teach her.

Trust. Patience. Faith.

Didn't matter what it was, she was here and waiting was against her nature. Haley needed to die to herself and that had to be a God thing. After all, surrender was the business He was in. Yielding to Him as Lord would be a victory no matter the outcome.

"I'll let you make that call."

Dakota left her alone. Haley called Isaac's number. As it rang, she thought about asking him why he'd kept his relationship with Blair from her. No. She didn't need to get them off on the wrong footing from the first word. She wanted to know he was all right. That she'd made him safe by being here, like the men and women her intel had guarded.

"Yeah?" He sounded wary. Probably because he didn't recognize the number.

"It's me."

"Hales." His tone was soft.

Her eyes filled with tears.

"Guess you won't be going to that interview tomorrow."

"Sorry."

"Are you, really?"

"I could be," she said. "Maybe I am." Underneath everything else that had happened the past few days. All of it churned in her brain until she thought she might go crazy.

He snorted.

"Fine. But I would have gone. Maybe I'd have realized it was a good fit and ended up finding the place I'm supposed to be."

"Maybe you would have. Because it sure isn't painting walls with me."

Haley bit her lip. She didn't want to get into another discussion about how his life wasn't the life for her. Like he thought she was so much better than him. And maybe brothers were supposed to think about their sisters that way, but that wasn't the point. Instead of arguing with him, she said, "I love that you love it. And that it makes you happy." Then she dipped her toe in. "And you have Blair now as well."

She waited.

Finally, he said, "Nice. That was done well. A little poke, and you backed off."

"I have mad skills."

He chuckled. Not full laughter. He'd probably never do that again, not even for *Nacho Libre*. Which was a crying shame. "How's your guy?"

She blinked. "Uh...what?"

"What's his name...the NCIS agent?"

Isaac knew very well what his name was. "Niall."

"That's the one."

"He's fine."

"That's it?" Isaac paused. "Just fine?"

"What are you fishing for? Because I'm not gonna bite."

"Shame. You need someone to keep you from getting in trouble, and he's been doing a pretty good job."

They'd both nearly died but was that the point? She said, "You don't even know the half of it."

"What's that?" Isaac asked.

"He talked down Dad."

"Did he really." Her brother's tone had darkened. His feelings about their dad were arguably more complicated than hers. Haley wasn't sure what to say next, but he needed to know that Niall would do the right thing. Or at least, that he would do his job.

So far he'd done it in a way that made it clear he was prepared to go to bat for her. Not to mention how many times he'd saved her life since they met. Niall was basically her hero at this point.

"I'm glad for you, Hales. You need someone like you. Someone who'll go one hundred fifty percent for you because that's what you do for everyone else."

"You're gonna make me cry." She barely got the words out. Her vision blurred with tears as emotion clogged her throat.

"It was a good thing you did, trying to find out what happened to Ana," he said. "You should be proud of yourself."

"It didn't work, and we only got hurt in the process." She considered the words she was about to say. Probably wouldn't be good to give away sensitive information on a phone that was potentially unsecured. No countermeasures were ever perfect. "Now we have to sit here doing nothing, because they're out looking for what's still missing."

"He's there too, right?"

"Recovering."

"So you're not the only one."

"And I should quit whining?" she asked.

"They do say misery loves company."

"Why do you think I called you?"

Isaac laughed then. Full out. It was one of the most beautiful things she'd ever heard. Next to Niall asking her if he could kiss her. Different sounds but both equally as meaningful to her. Her brother's laughter more so, now that she was actually hearing it.

Maybe some good would come of this.

. . .

"Your description was what clinched it."

Niall bit into the apple, glad for the fruit after all that pizza yesterday. He was a big fan of balance. When he lifted his eyebrows, she said, "The car. We only found the doctor's vehicle after it left the lab, because you got the make and part of the license."

"But we only saw the doctor when he showed up at the airport."

"Talia backtracked from there. We found him after the vehicle left the GPS dead zone. She tracked it to where they stopped first. The doctor handed the case off to a group of men. The one who took it didn't look happy. She ran the photos she got of them off a traffic camera when they were driving in and found out they're Russians."

"More Russians." He took another bite.

She nodded.

They both would figure it wasn't a coincidence. The Russians were deep into this, and Niall knew enough about organized crime to conclude a few things. After all, he'd lived it for years before they drove away from Boston.

If the Russians were still in this, and not just up until Yuri's death, then they weren't just hired guns or something like that. Happy or not, whoever took possession of that case was more than just in this for the money. They had a stake in it that was bigger than getting paid. Maybe he'd known what was in there, and wouldn't be happy until he sold the case—or gave it away—to the next party.

Dakota twisted to look at the living room, where Haley sat on the couch. She was on the phone. Niall wanted to call his sister when she was done. Sitting around here doing nothing was close to sensory deprivation in the way of torture. And they would be worried about him.

Dakota said, "Are you guys doing okay?"

"With what?"

She wasn't going to ask him about "relationship" stuff, was she?

"You know...stuff."

Of course she was.

He said, "You want me to 'talk' to you?" He even used air quotes just to make sure she knew what he was getting at. This wasn't going to get all personal. Things between him and Haley were far too new to be dissected and analyzed.

Dakota rolled her eyes and hopped up on a barstool. She'd let Neema out back to do some business, and she was apparently sticking around for a while to harass him about his relationship status.

"Maybe if you left, we'd be doing better." Some alone time couldn't hurt. She had to know that, considering how she and Josh had worked things out. Namely, together. But also with guns pointed at the people trying to kill them. And he and Haley were stuck in a house?

"Hmm." She studied him. "Maybe I'll stick around. Be a chaperone."

"For grown adults?"

She actually pouted, though there was a gleam of humor in her eyes. Something Haley couldn't see from where she sat. Dakota said, "Fine."

He sighed. "I get what you're trying to do, but that's not what this is." He waved toward Haley. "At least not yet."

Dakota brightened.

"Don't get too excited," he said. "Just because that happened for you with Josh, and now you're all one happy family taking care of Neema..." He didn't know what else to say about that and so just got to the point of it. "Doesn't mean it's going to happen to the rest of us."

"I'm *praying*."

"What?" He nearly laughed at the look of pure excitement on her face. Had he ever seen that before Josh came along? She hadn't been much for spiritual things, though he knew she went to church on occasion.

Niall had gone to church as a child. Religion had been as much a part of his life as organized crime, wrapping the two up together in a tangle he was still unraveling. Now faith was more about a personal relationship, at least according to Patricia. A natural dialogue that was supposed to be ongoing all day between him and his Heavenly Father. But who had time for that?

Haley, apparently.

And Dakota.

Josh.

Siobhan and Patricia.

Niall was beginning to think he was missing out on something important.

The fact Dakota was working toward a deeper relationship with God had actually spurred him to consider doing the same. But was he going to tell her that? No way. Besides, he hadn't actually gotten around to doing it.

"About you and…" Her voice trailed off and she jabbed toward the living room with her index finger.

"Praying." He shot her a look, just because.

She grinned. "That's how I *know*."

"I'm treading carefully." He wasn't precisely sure how to finish the thought.

Dakota said, "That's fine." She lifted both hands and pushed against the air with them. "You're getting to know each other. Testing the waters, establishing trust."

Completely straight-faced, Niall said, "Is that what your shrink calls it?"

He lifted his apple like a prize, knowing he had won that round.

"I'm about to throw this at you." She picked her mug off the table. "But it'd be a waste, pouring it all over your pretty face instead of drinking it and *leaving*. Because *you're a jerk*." She said it with a smile.

He took another bite of apple then threw the core in the trash. Giving her a second to calm down. She wasn't yet at the point where he'd need to apologize to her. But it was close. "Fine," he said, all bluster and she'd know it. "Leave. See if I care being stuck here against my will."

Haley glanced over, a frown on her face. Still on her call. He didn't have time to explain that they weren't arguing.

"I will." Dakota matched his tone with hers. "And I'm taking Neema with me."

"Like I want a stinky dog?"

It was cathartic really. And later, he would make a point to explain to Haley what he and Dakota were doing—bleeding off some of the frustration from their job by being loud with each other. Firing off satisfying quips that meant nothing.

Dakota barked a laugh. "No." She dragged the word out with a sarcastic tone. "Because you're more of a cat person."

He nearly laughed aloud. Dakota was good. He said, "What's wrong with that?"

Seriously, what was wrong with cats? Siobhan had one that he'd gotten for her a few years back. It was cute, and they coexisted in harmony quite nicely.

Dakota glanced at him with a look of horror. "If you don't know, I can't explain it to you." She strode to the back door, laughing. Evidently Dakota considered herself to be extremely funny. "There's nothing I can do. You're beyond hope."

Before she pulled open the door, Neema barked. Twice. Short alerts. Dakota glanced back at him. "Get a gun. Someone's here."

Shots fired off outside.

"Haley," Niall called out. "Call it in. We're under attack."

Chapter 21

Haley spun around, not sure which to react to first. Gunshots. Niall's yell. He raced to the back door after Dakota. Gun. She needed a gun.

Her thoughts coalesced enough that she realized Isaac was still on the line. She could hear his voice through the phone in her hand, yelling at her.

She put it to her ear. "I have to go."

She hung up on him, the realization of how worried he would be wrenching at her.

Haley went to the contact list and pulled up the one saved number. It had been listed under, "Help me, Rhonda" which was just bizarre, but she didn't have time to figure out what the reference was to.

It rang once. Talia picked up before the tone finished. "Breach?"

"Yes." Haley hardly knew what to ask for or what to say. Isaac had no idea where she was. He wouldn't be able to get ahold of her, and she was in serious danger.

But her brother would pray. He'd know she was here with trained agents as protection.

"Help is on the way." Talia paused for half a second. "Dakota and Neema are there?"

"Yes," Haley said again. "And Niall went out back with her."

"Check the front."

Haley moved to the window and tugged back the curtain a tiny fraction. She looked out at the overcast afternoon. Saw no movement. Except...

"There's a man moving through the front yard." The house was in the middle of nowhere, though she was pretty sure they were in central Oregon. There was almost no cover, as all the brush and trees had been cut down and cleared away. Even the vehicles had been pulled around and stowed under the carport. There was literally nowhere for someone to hide. And no way for them to approach without being seen.

"Shooter?"

"It's one of the protective detail guys."

Haley watched the man creep around while scanning for assailants. A shot rang out. Red blossomed on his chest, and he fell to the ground.

She must have made a noise, because Talia yelled, "What is it?"

"Sniper." She nearly dropped the phone.

"Get to the basement," Talia said. "*Now.*"

They'd explained it to her. A defensible position, the stairs down to it a choke point she could use to her advantage once she was down there.

Dakota had called it a "kill box" which was a horrible idea if ever Haley had heard one. Purposely setting up a spot to take someone's life? They'd told her not to hesitate, and she'd been trained by the Navy. But she'd never actually killed anyone until the gunman in the woods. She wasn't a combat solider, and she never had been.

Haley's stomach roiled.

Talia said, "Run."

Her limbs snapped into action. As she raced for the basement door, located in the back of the master bedroom closet, she demanded into the phone, "Tell Niall and Dakota there's a sniper."

"I have. Just get yourself safe."

Haley nearly slammed into the door frame. She yanked open the closet door, then slid back the panel that led down into the basement. As soon as she told Talia she was secured in there, Talia would be able to pass that on to Niall. He and Dakota would be worried until they knew she was safe.

They'd literally told her they would worry until they knew. Not because they cared about her, but because it was their job to keep her safe. Haley's first priority was supposed to be Haley. Maybe they did care a bit. But she was their charge, and she had to remember that. And the fact Dakota didn't want to do the added paperwork if Haley was killed.

She tasted bile in her throat but forced herself to stay focused and not run through the myriad of questions in her head about how on earth they'd been discovered. This place was supposed to have been so far off the grid that they weren't in the same universe as "the grid." Whatever that meant. She'd just nodded.

Haley slammed the door shut, then closed the interior door. It sealed shut.

"I'm in."

"Copy that." Talia sounded distracted.

Then the line went dead.

Haley turned and sank into a seat on the top step of the basement stairs, breathing hard. She held the phone against her forehead and prayed harder than she'd ever prayed. Asking for protection for Dakota and Niall. Victory. Safety. All the things that rolled through her head. For her brother, and Ana—if she was even still alive.

Tears rolled down her face.

Minutes ticked by, that unseen force propelling the world onward while she sat there. Sometimes she hated time. Sometimes it went too slow or too fast. She'd never wanted to be able to alter it as badly as she did right now. To turn back the clock and warn Niall about what was going to happen.

Instead, she flipped the light switch on and climbed down the wooden staircase. The basement was small, only half the width of the house. Bathroom at the far end. Cot with a bare mattress, and no sheets. A folded blanket sat in a stack on one shelf with a pillow. MRE's lined one corner. Boxes of energy bars. Bottled water. A survival kit. First aid kit. Flashlights. A camp stove and instant coffee. A battery powered radio.

Everything she would need to survive and nothing she actually wanted.

A gun.

There it was. On the very top shelf.

She flipped the latches on a hard-sided case and loaded the first pistol she laid her hands on. There weren't even any windows for her to look out and see what was happening out there. Being trapped was the worst kind of torture. Haley had no idea how she was going to keep from going crazy, knowing Niall and Dakota were out there.

His face filled her mind. Looking down at her as they stood close to each other. Sipping his coffee across the kitchen, leaning back against the counter like he was completely relaxed and still partly waking up. In the car, when he'd leaned close. About to kiss her.

A gunshot rang out outside.

Haley's whole body flinched. She spun toward the sound but could see nothing except the breeze-block walls. *Niall.* Her mind and heart cried out for him—the man who had come to mean something to her the past few days.

They'd survived so much.

He needed to live through this as well. His family was counting on him to come home. And Haley wanted to meet his sister and his niece. She wanted to know what his personal life was like. To cross that boundary outside of "work" and get to know him better.

Would she get that chance?

Ana had disappeared from her life. Haley had to let go of her friend now. It was probably too late to find her. She needed to trust God with Ana's life, whatever that might have turned out to be in the end.

Dakota could handle herself. That much was clear from what Haley had seen of her and the dog.

Whatever happened to Niall was what would impact her the most. He was trained, and she knew Dakota would back him up. But, would he be okay? She didn't want to be swallowed up in it if something bad went down today. But she would be. She would be completely devastated. What her head knew and what her heart feared warred inside her, that push and pull between hope and reality. Between pain and truth.

Shuffling sounds on the other side of the door caught her attention. She rechecked that the weapon was loaded and ready to fire and held aim on the door.

Electronic beeps sounded. A series, like a code being entered. Then a pause. A green light illuminated above the door.

An all-clear signal.

The door cracked open an inch. "Haley?"

"Niall!"

He swung the door open and raced down the stairs. "It's clear. We're good."

Haley blew out a breath that came out more like a whimper. She strode toward him, the gun down by her side. He opened his arms, his own weapon out to the side as she moved into the hug.

Face pressed against his shirt, she blew out a breath. "You're okay."

He nodded, his chin against her hair. "But we can't stay here. We have to move."

. . .

He could still feel the imprint of her body against his, even while they raced back up the stairs. A sweet moment he'd liked to have continued, even in the midst of all this.

"Let's go!" His voice rang through the ground floor.

Dakota entered the foyer from the living room and got to the front door first. She looked mad. "Heir!"

Beside him, Haley jumped. He squeezed her hand as the dog's nails clicked on the hardwood of the hallway toward them.

Dakota opened the front door.

Neema went first. Niall followed, Haley tucked protectively behind him. He wished it was enough to keep her safe.

They had guns ready. The phone was still tucked in Haley's belt. Dakota brought up the rear, closing the front door behind her after she armed the alarm. The alarm would keep their stuff safe until they could come back to retrieve it, or have someone else do so.

As for their safety, that would be a fluid process. Neema was the one who had alerted them to intruders outside. Now they had to get to the car. Then they would head to the next location…wherever Talia told them to go.

Haley squeezed his hand. "Sniper."

"We know." He angled them both to go around a dead guy—one of the men on their protective detail. At the front corner of the house, another man lay on the ground. A young man, college age. Plain clothes, worn and dirty. Eyes open, empty as they had been when he was alive. Before the federal agent had killed him. Before the fed was subsequently shot by a sniper.

Niall had knocked out a man he'd found out back, one that Neema had taken down.

Both men's eyes were still glassy the way Haley's eyes had been at the lab, when the buzzing had been bothering her. Buzzing he'd never heard. He glanced back at her now. She seemed fine.

Was she going to stay that way?

Niall saw no one still alive, but that didn't mean it was clear. A sniper had been in play. He was pretty sure the man and his rifle that Neema had found—the third person who had been here—was the only sniper. Two foot soldiers and a man to provide cover. But he wasn't going to bet Haley's life on the assumption there was no one else here.

He opened the rear door of the SUV and said, "Get in." Then slipped in the front seat. Dakota ran around to the front passenger door while Haley and Neema both climbed inside.

Sweat slicked his hands, but he rubbed them on the legs of his jeans before he turned the key. He threw the SUV into drive and pulled out, heading toward the rear exit.

"Where to?"

Dakota was bent over her phone, typing furiously. "I don't know yet."

He found the main road and hit the gas to get them to the highway as fast as possible. Dakota's phone rang. She jabbed at the button on the SUV's dash screen and the call connected through the speakers.

"Status."

Dakota said, "The safe house was hit. Two guys, and a sniper we think might've been a cop." She glanced back at Haley, not saying more.

They'd had to improvise fast when they'd realized the two men who'd stormed weren't cops or Russians. What they appeared to be were college students, eerily similar to those he'd met in that hallway at the residence hall on campus. There was something he just couldn't let go of about the whole thing.

Plus the glassy eyes, like the people in the compound.

Their slightly slower movements. Someone prone to suggestion. Directed by the sniper? Or from another source? They'd seemed like people under the influence of something, and not in a way that made them hyped-up and aggressive. They'd been a threat, just one that was directed…like a puppet.

Niall didn't know what to make of it all. Yet. He glanced in the rearview to see if Haley was still okay, but couldn't see her face from this angle.

"Head over to…"

Dakota glanced at him. "Talia? You there?"

The line crackled. "…here." It went quiet for a second. Then he heard, "Coming in fast."

It went dead.

"What on earth?"

Niall shook his head, hardly knowing how to answer Dakota. She called Josh and asked him to meet them at the office, back in Portland. It would take two hours to get there, and that was with the lights and sirens going.

He tapped the wheel with one hand. Gripped it so hard with the other that his knuckles were white. "Haley, you okay?"

She said, "Is something happening to Talia?"

"We'll find out when we get there."

"How did they find us at the safe house?"

Dakota said, "That's a question I definitely want an answer to." She shook her head. "Nowhere is one hundred percent safe, but that house should've been close enough to it. And yet we get breached within a day of you getting there?"

"Someone is in our system." The other alternative was a leak in their organization. One of the team or Haley. And he could just about guarantee that *wasn't* the case. Mostly because he was the one who was the weak link. Historically speaking.

Niall was the one that had been targeted before. He'd put his family in danger, the pressure laid on him to act on their enemy's behalf.

None of the others. Just him.

It grated to have been assessed and concluded as the weak link. He'd taken steps to shore up his life so it never happened again. But it was like safe-house security. Not foolproof.

He chewed on the whole thing as he drove back into Portland. Exactly the place he didn't want to be when they couldn't trust the state or local police. At least, not until the person was verified by their friends at the FBI.

He attempted to skirt through traffic—which was wishful thinking mostly, considering there was no way around it—and eventually made his way to the office. He drove around the front, but saw nothing abnormal through the slow crawl past the door where Yuri had been left. The underground parking lot was clear. Few even knew it was there.

Which was what bothered him about the police officer being left at their door. Who knew about their office? Someone. And they knew about the investigation as well. Knew Niall had been at Yuri's maybe.

They headed up in the elevator to the second floor, where their office was located. Other people leased offices in the same building. They had their name tags on the directory. The task force slot was blank. The neighbors would come knocking if they knew a team of federal agents operated out of their building.

The front door was open.

"The lock has been compromised." Dakota pushed on the door. "Someone busted it in."

He glanced back at Dakota and got a nod. She used a command to send Neema in first, so the dog could sniff out any threats. Haley leaned against the wall. Fatigued. Injured. Run down and ready to drop, kind of like he felt despite the night of sleep he'd had.

When Neema came back out, giving no signal, they headed in. She hadn't found anything? No assailants. No Talia? She should have at least alerted that she'd found their computer tech.

He checked the conference room. "Clear."

"Clear." Dakota's voice called back to him. "Talia isn't here."

He met her in the main office, barely big enough for the four desks with computers. Paper files had been set up so it looked like they were utilized even though the team was on the road most of the time. The files were fake—weather reports and internal memos. Dakota stood at the open door to the hidden room where Talia worked, behind firewalls and safeguards. Layers of security that had protected them all.

Until now.

The room had several electronic pass keys, including a retina scan. It was never just left open.

Haley wandered over while Neema circled. She glanced around, like she wasn't quite sure what had happened or what the problem was. Neema shook her head, but not in the way dogs usually shook off. More like she was irritated by something.

Dakota walked to her and petted her head. "You're such a good girl."

The dog laid down.

Haley swayed. Her hip smacked a desk.

Niall moved to her. "Whoa. You okay?"

She shook her head, not a disagreement. More like she was shaking off a fog. Like Neema had just done. Haley took another step toward the room where Talia worked, her movements sluggish now. Almost to the doorway, Haley turned. Glassy eyes.

"What are…" His words trailed off.

She brought her gun up. Fear flashed in her eyes.

"Haley—"

She was going to shoot him.

Chapter 22

Haley felt the gun in her hand. She squeezed the metal and tried to anchor the rest of her consciousness—her awareness of what was happening. The buzzing in her head was like a constant ringing. She couldn't even think, it was so loud.

Niall stood in front of her.

His mouth moved, but she couldn't hear what he was saying. Nor could she figure out the look on his face. She barely had control of her body.

Haley's attention shifted.

Dakota stood over on the side. Haley didn't even know if it was left or right. A dog's relentless bark broke through her thoughts for a second. Haley blinked. "What..."

The buzzing surged. The whole world, the sum of her consciousness swam around her. Her grip on the gun. That was all she could feel. All she knew was the feel of the weapon in her hand.

That buzz in her head.

The sound surged again, louder and louder until the swell broke over her like a wave. Haley's finger moved. Her brain churned through thoughts, too fast for her to grab hold of one. What was...

The gun bucked in her hand.

Again.

Her finger twitched.

Again.

Over and over, she fired the weapon. Until the slide jammed. Bullets spent. Clip empty.

The room was vacant now, the smell of cordite strong in the air. Hanging like a cloud. It itched her nose.

Then she saw him... a foot, at least.

The buzzing swelled again. She had to get out of there. A terrible thing had happened, and she was responsible.

Haley glanced around and saw the EXIT sign.

She ran toward it and nearly tripped over the dog. It latched on to her pant leg for a second, but she kicked out in its direction and got loose.

She shoved at the bar on the door and almost fell into a stairwell. The urge to flee was strong. So strong she had trouble sucking in air as she raced down the stairs to the alley.

Haley ran into the street.

Cars honked, flying past her.

She turned and realized she stood in the middle of the street. Air stirred up by the traffic blew her hair against her face. A man on the sidewalk yelled. To her or about her? She didn't know.

What had she just done?

Her breath came fast, the rapid inhale and exhale like she'd just completed a workout interval. She lifted her hands, the empty gun still in her right palm. She dropped it on the street and stepped back.

A car whizzed past her. The driver's window was down. He yelled ugly things at her. She deserved it, after all. She'd opened fire in the office and shot everyone in there. She could see it replay in her head now, though she hadn't been aware of it at the time.

Haley looked up at the windows of the first floor.

They were dead.

She had shot all the bullets in her gun. Niall had fallen to the floor. She'd seen the blood. Dakota. Haley had hit them.

She'd killed them.

They were dead, because she had killed them.

A black and white cop car rounded the corner at the end of the street. Gratitude swelled strong in her, and she reached for it. The car pulled up and both officers climbed out. Guns drawn.

They spoke, but she couldn't make out the words.

One approached first. She tried to tell him… "Help." Haley pointed at the office windows. "There."

He grabbed her raised hand at the wrist and twisted her arm behind her back. She gasped. "Please."

"…cooperate…"

She didn't hear the rest. Couldn't make it out.

He cuffed her, then walked her to the car. The other one got her gun off the ground. Haley blinked and realized she was sitting down. The door shut. She flinched at the slam.

She was in the backseat.

The car pulled away, and she shifted on the bench with the motion. They turned a corner, and she nearly fell against the door. She tried to speak. They needed to help…

These cops needed to go back to the office, not drive away. Haley could hardly form the thoughts.

The passenger got on his phone.

She blinked. Shook her head. Tried to speak.

"Shut up!"

She flinched. She'd said something? Why couldn't she…

"Yeah, it's me," he said into the phone. "Is it still a hundred thousand for the woman?"

Haley stared at him. What was happening?

"Where do we bring her?"

. . .

Niall pressed hard against the wound in Dakota's thigh. Was it wrong to be relieved? Nah, it could have been so much worse than this. She could be dead.

Dakota said, "I should've shot her."

The dog lay beside Dakota. She hadn't stopped whining since Haley ran out of the room. *And neither had the dog.*

"But you didn't," he told her. And he was glad for it, even if things had almost come to that. "That's what counts."

"Does it?" She was mad. The fact she was in so much pain only being one of the reasons.

Niall should have gone after Haley. "Hold this."

He didn't wait for Dakota to object, just ran to the window and looked out. Cops were loading Haley into their car. A note of caution registered in him, the part that didn't trust the boys in blue since those two detectives had tried to kill them. But he couldn't think that way about every cop in the city. Just like every Russian wasn't part of their mob.

Like how Niall was no longer affiliated with the Irish Mafia in Boston.

"The ambulance just turned the corner." He went back to Dakota. "It won't be long."

"I liked her, you know."

He bit down on his molars. "I know." He pressed down on her thigh again. Dakota winced. "Sorry."

"You're not the one who should be sorry." Sweat beaded on her forehead. "Though, trying to talk her down?" Her face twisted, evidence of how she felt about that.

"Paramedics!"

"In here!" Niall yelled out to them. "It's clear!"

They entered cautiously, nonetheless.

"The shooter is gone." It hurt to say that.

Haley had shot Dakota. He wanted to sink to his backside on the floor and just let the emotion overtake him. But what would that help? They needed to find out who those cops were. Where they'd taken her. How Haley had been affected in the first place.

It seemed to have something to do with that buzzing again. He figured that was what she'd heard. What Neema had reacted to. Proximity to the room where Talia worked, behind a false wall. An office secured by countermeasures preventing anyone from breaching it. And yet, someone had. Enough to make Haley flip out and shoot at them. He was so lucky he'd seen it coming and managed to dive out of the way.

Good, but they still had plenty of problems.

For example, where was Talia?

The EMTs knelt by Dakota and cut away her pant leg. One secured a blood pressure cuff on her arm while she grumbled about how obviously she was stressed and they should know that.

Beside her on the floor, Neema never took her focus off Dakota. She didn't growl at the first responders, but she also didn't take her attention from what they were doing.

The Homeland Security agent reached over and scratched Neema's head. "You're a good dog. Yes, you are."

The EMT guy closest to her said, "The good dog isn't coming to the hospital."

"That's a shame," she said to Neema in a sing-song voice. "Yes, it is. Because you'd be the best therapy dog ever."

On the floor, a few feet away, her phone lit up and buzzed across the linoleum square.

"Get that, would you?" She looked at her smartwatch. "It's Josh."

Niall had a hundred things to get to work on. Instead, he walked to the phone and answered the call. "She's okay."

Behind him, Dakota yelled, "No, I'm not."

"One of you better tell me right now." Josh sounded furious.

Niall pinched the bridge of his nose. Before he could answer, she yelled again, "O'Caran's girlfriend shot me!"

He spun back. To say…what? That she wasn't his girlfriend? He wanted her to be. And he certainly couldn't object to the fact she had shot Dakota. She'd shot at both of them.

"I'm on my way," Josh said. "Where?"

"At the office."

"No. Where did she get shot?"

"Oh," Niall said. "In the thigh."

"And Neema?"

"She was great. I think her barking was getting through to Haley. And I think she was also affected by the buzzing even before Hayley was, like maybe she could hear it as well." The thought was only the germ of an idea, but he processed as he said it out loud. "Two uniformed cops left with her. We have no idea where Talia is, and Alvarez hasn't called me back."

"Call Victoria. I'll try Alvarez." Josh hung up.

The EMTs helped Dakota to her feet. Niall gave her phone back, and watched them walk her out to the door. She turned back at the last second. "Call Victoria."

The dog lifted from lying down to a sitting position.

"Neema, stay."

She sighed and lay back down with a grunt.

The door swished closed, and Niall jumped into action. He went to Talia's room to see if the computers were still on while he called Victoria.

When she picked up, he explained everything impatiently.

"Somewhere you need to be?"

"Finding Haley, for starters."

"I'll find out who has custody of her." If she was near her computer, she could send an email while she was on the phone with him. He'd have told her that, but she would have called him on being impatient again. "And I'll head over to you."

"What about Talia's computers?"

"Don't touch anything."

Like he was dumb enough to do that? "Where is she?"

"Check the surveillance footage."

"We don't have surveillance." It would defeat the purpose of having a secure office that couldn't be traced or tracked if they had cameras recording everything.

"Go to the reception desk computer and shake the mouse."

Niall turned and stared across the office at it. He had to squint while his brain puzzled over what she was talking about. He was starting to get a headache at the edges of his awareness. Because of whatever had affected Haley? Like it was some kind of mental suggestion that affected her because of the chemicals in her system. Chemicals that she'd gotten exposed to when she fell in the river. The suggestion had been strong enough to turn her into an unaware, unconscious murderer.

Niall didn't think she'd wanted to pull that trigger. Was it the power of the subliminal? Chemicals in her from the river, making her vulnerable. Maybe. The men at the house had been far more strongly affected, if it were that. Here she had simply been in proximity to Talia's setup.

"Did you do it yet?"

He strode over to the computer and shook the mouse. The screen came to life. Camera feeds of the office and the front and back hallways.

"You've been watching this whole time?"

Victoria's reply was, "Do you want to know what happened to Talia, or do you want to complain to me about need-to-know?"

Niall bit back what he wanted to say.

"I'm five minutes out." It was her turn to hang up on him.

Three-and-a-half minutes later she strode in the door. "Neema." Victoria went straight to the dog and knelt, stretching the limits of her slim skirt. "You're okay." She rubbed the dog's head and neck, her fingers gliding through her long, tan-colored fur. "I know."

When she turned, she stood up. "Josh is at the hospital with Dakota. Alvarez is on a stakeout, and he's not leaving. What did you find?"

Nothing good. He sighed and leaned back in the chair to run his hands down his face. "Four men. Black fatigues, automatic weapons. They moved like military. Maybe mercenaries, because they didn't walk like regular cops, or SWAT. They didn't want to kill her, they just breached the room and tied her up. Walked her out."

Victoria said, "Copy that." Then moved to Talia's room. He heard her on the phone and went to the doorway.

Niall followed, even though the surveillance tape still played. Otherwise he'd have to relive the scene where Haley fired her gun. Where he'd dived away, under the desk. Dakota had too, but not before a gunshot ripped through her thigh. Neema had tried to stall her exit, until she was commanded to release. Haley had left then.

"Okay." Victoria clicked buttons on Talia's keyboard. "It's done."

She straightened. The screen of Talia's computer flashed and text typed across it. "I see you. Keep me apprised." She tapped the screen of her phone to end the call.

"Who's that?"

"The FBI." She glanced at him. "Since 'the best' got kidnapped, we'll have to settle for the *next best* thing." She frowned, then said, "Are you getting a headache being in here?"

He nodded. "Let's move away from it."

So they weren't completely immune.

They crossed the room, almost back to the reception desk. Niall said, "It's gotta be the same thing that affected Haley. The buzzing."

Victoria's phone rang. She looked at the screen, then tapped it. "This is Director Bramlyn, you're on speaker with NCIS Special Agent O'Caran."

"This is Special Agent Ross. I'm still going through the system, but I found a subroutine planted moments before the breach. Talia saw it, but there was no time to stop it once it was in her system. You're going to want to get out of the vicinity." Ross paused a second. "Assuming she's wired to some kind of speaker system."

"It's a whole surround sound system," Niall said. "She's pretty proud of it."

"I can't be completely sure without a thorough test, but I'm mostly sure it'll give you a brain aneurysm in the next five minutes unless you get more than twenty feet away. It's localized."

Both of them walked to the hall outside the room. "Neema, heir." Victoria snapped her fingers and the dog followed.

Niall said, "That's probably what made Haley flip out. It must be the same thing they were broadcasting at the lab."

"I'll see what else I come up with," Ross said. "I've never seen this file type before."

"Copy that. Keep me posted." Victoria ended the call, then shot him a look. "So it's confirmed. This didn't stop with the doctor dead, and the lab destroyed."

"Not even with whatever was in that case, in the Russian's hands now." Assuming they didn't pass on the doctor's case from the lab to someone else.

Victoria shot him a dark look. "And they've got Talia."

Niall nodded. "Cops have custody of Haley, but I'm wondering which side they're working for—if they even are working for whoever is behind this"

"That would be a serious level of corruption."

"And it goes all the way to the state level," Niall said. "The satellite feed, GPS stuff takes it further. That's some serious power." He paused a second and thought it through, voicing his thoughts out loud. "What about whoever funded the scholarships? If they also had a hand in what was going on at the lab, and however it was connected to the college…plus they paid off all those cops to keep it quiet…" He trailed off.

She nodded. "They could have figured out that Talia got a copy of the system at the lab. She might've triggered something."

"Like when she was trying to hack that server, and she kept finding nothing. This person knows how to cover their tracks." Niall tried to tamp down the frustration. "Whoever they are, they had a modified VX gas. Now they're involved in experiments."

"Looks like we've got ourselves a little conspiracy. Or at least someone with a horrifying agenda."

Niall did not like the sound of that. "We're an agent down, and we need to find Talia *and* Haley."

Victoria said, "Yes, we do." She tapped her phone against the palm of her other hand. "I'll call my contacts at the FBI. They'll be motivated to help because their guys were killed at the safe house."

Niall wondered if her thinking that way wasn't a little messed up, considering it played on the emotions of federal agents. But Victoria had done stuff like this in the past. She had her own way of solving problems and if it got Talia and Haley back, then Niall didn't mind so much.

Niall fought through the crushing sense of having lost too much this time. "Do it. Call them."

The sooner they got the two women back and figured this out, the better.

He strode toward the door.

"Somewhere you need to be, Special Agent O'Caran?"

He nearly winced. Sore subject, considering he was on probation for abandoning the team to safeguard his family. He jabbed at the button for the elevator. She had her ways of solving problems.

And he had his.

"I'll be back working in the office when this is done."

Chapter 23

The back door of the police car opened. Haley didn't bother looking. The cop reached in and grabbed her elbow. "Let's go."

They'd driven across Portland. This was an industrial complex with offices laid out along the main street. Like a strip mall, with a dentist and an employment recruitment office.

Not the police station.

He tugged on her elbow. She stumbled and nearly fell, then decided it was safer to stick with him as they moved forward. Her head had cleared. That was good, but it was also bad. She needed to play along and figure out how to get out of this. Now that she'd gotten some distance from the task force office, the details of the last hour came rushing in.

She'd heard Dakota scream, hit by one of her bullets. And Niall had to have been hit, otherwise he would have stopped her. Right?

Bile rose in her throat. The officer hauled her toward an empty storefront with a FOR LEASE sign in the window. "This isn't jail."

He said nothing. The second guy moved in front of her and tugged the door open.

"I killed someone." They should be taking her to jail but they weren't. "Are you guys working for the Russians?" That mafia organization had been there at every step.

She'd thought that cop, Yuri, had done something to her friend. Maybe abducted her, or killed her. Now she knew it was so much more than that. It had also been about bizarre goings-on at a college—though how that related, she still didn't know. The lab. Cops covering things up. Russians running around like any of it was their business.

The cop made a sound, like she was crazy. "You think the Russians are in charge here?"

It was like falling out of a boat upside down, and then realizing you are the wrong way up. Or maybe that had something to do with the bleed off from whatever had made her flip out and start shooting. She had no idea, but either way it felt like she was the wrong way up. No equilibrium. No way to tell where the surface was.

No air to breathe.

A sob welled up. Haley tried to stuff it back down. What if Dakota was dead? What if they were *both* dead? She would be a murderer. Branded. Jailed. She would have to live the rest of her life knowing it was her fault. She had shot that gun and taken them from their families—the people who loved them. Including her.

Because Haley had begun to love them both.

And now she didn't even deserve to feel that loss.

Tears rolled down her cheeks as she was shoved into the building. Bare floors. Cardboard boxes. Paint cans. An old wood ladder.

Niall.

She couldn't even pray. God shouldn't listen to her, not if she had killed him or Dakota. Either. Both.

The fact He might listen wasn't the point. She didn't want Him to give her any of His time. Otherwise things would never be fair. She didn't deserve to have God's ear. Not if she'd done what she feared she had.

The officer walked her to a chair and shoved her into it. He shot his partner a look. "The Russians." He did this combo snort-laugh thing.

The other one said, "She got whammied, remember?"

They took off the cuffs, but only long enough to secure them to the leg of the chair. Haley shivered. She tried to wipe the tears from her cheeks with her shoulder, but it was too painful to twist like that.

The officers shifted their weight. One on either side of her, but behind so she couldn't see them. Like she was being…presented to whoever was waiting here.

The rear door opened. A woman strode through. Slender legs encased in skinny jeans. Boots. A green pea coat. Long red hair in a shade Haley had always thought was gorgeous.

Pale face. Dark circles. Slightly blood-shot eyes.

"Ana."

She could barely choke out the word. Her friend was here. Alive. Not a victim of the lab destruction. *She was here.*

"Haley. Yay." Her scratchy voice was threaded with sarcasm. She even lifted her hands and wiggled her fingers. Any interest in her eyes at seeing Haley here dissipated then, and there was nothing left but cold in her expression. "Where's the case?"

"I thought you were dead."

"Blah. Blah. I'm here, you're here," she said, void of any inflection. "Great. Now tell me where the case is." Coupled with the look in her eyes, Ana seemed…dead. Maybe she felt that way.

Haley frowned. Ana was part of it all. The case? That was what she wanted?

She tried to figure it out but her brain struggled to process what was happening. Sluggish and confused, the residue of whatever it was that had taken over her brain and caused her to shoot at people who were her friends. Or that was just an excuse. Maybe she was too wracked with guilt to be able to consider helping someone who had a hand in all this. Even if that someone was her friend.

"I looked for you," Haley said. "I tried to help you." And in the end she'd wound up hurting people who should've been the ones taking care of her.

More tears fell. The wet itched her cheeks. It was done. She had destroyed whatever was between her and Niall. The friendship she might've had with Dakota. None of it was real now. Not after what Haley had done.

Ana sighed. She glanced at the ceiling for a second, then looked at the officer over Haley's left shoulder. She nodded.

The blow hit Haley in the back of the head, whipping her face forward. The rear chair legs lifted off the floor. So far that she nearly tipped onto her knees. Pain slammed through her skull.

The officer grabbed her shoulder and pulled her back. The chair hit the ground, jarring her whole body. Haley grunted.

"The case." Ana spoke slowly and loudly, as though Haley had a hard time understanding. "Where. Is. It."

"The doctor…"

"He's dead. Does the FBI have the case?"

Haley shook her head. "I don't understand." Her brain refused to combine thoughts into ideas. She sucked in a couple of full breaths, her chest heaving. "That buzzing. I killed…" She could hardly speak the words out loud.

"Are we going to have to shoot *you*? Because they will." Ana waved at the two men with a dismissive sweep of her hand.

"You're in charge." Whether it was a question or a statement, she didn't know.

Ana said, "I have my role." She stepped closer. "And you have yours. So tell me where the case is now, or you're of no use to me."

Would they kill her?

Maybe they should. Maybe that was Haley's *role* in all this. To aid the feds up to a certain point—*God, please don't let them be dead*—and then wind up getting killed. Like Yuri had.

"Officer Kartov. I went to see him." He'd been killed later that night.

"Kicked his butt." Ana almost smiled. "It was great. Everything since then has been completely screwed up, but that? That was good. I almost appreciated having to kill him."

"Why?"

"Because the Russians needed to learn to back off," Ana said, like that was obvious. "Trying to get a piece of this thing. As if."

One of the cops snorted.

More tears burned hot in her eyes. She'd thought she was done crying, but this came from a well deep within her. A soul-deep grief.

For her friend.

For Dakota.

For Niall.

Help me, Lord.

Even if she knew where the case was, she would cease being useful if she gave them the information. Every piece of this had been covered up.

Extensively. For years. That meant she would be, too. The cops would suppress evidence of her murder.

Niall might even think that she'd killed herself to escape the guilt of what she had done.

And he might be right.

Haley lifted her chin and played the only card she had left. It was going to get her killed for sure, but she would be dead no matter what. She said, "I know where the case is. But I'm not talking to you. I want to speak to whoever is actually in charge."

Ana stared at her for a second. And then she laughed.

. . .

"Did you do it?" Niall gripped the phone as he crossed the street.

His cousin, on the other end of the line, sighed. "It's done."

Niall hung up. There was zero point saying thank you. They both understood the cost if this went wrong, but Niall had explained about Haley and Talia both being in danger. That this could be a nationwide terrorist threat. What had convinced Iain wasn't the potential for imminent danger. If it didn't make him money, Iain normally wasn't interested. What clinched it was the promise that Niall would talk to the assistant US attorney on his cousin's behalf. To "see what he could do" about Iain's legal troubles.

Mostly Niall had figured this was exactly what Victoria would have done; utilized every avenue available in order to get the result. Maybe that wasn't the honorable thing to do. Victoria tended to burn bridges. There were also a serious amount of people in the world of federal law enforcement who owed Director Bramlyn more than they could ever repay. She collected favors like they were pennies in a jar, left on the shelf for a rainy day.

He stowed his phone out of sight and pulled open the door to an Eastern European restaurant that was supposed to have the best sausage soup on the west coast. Too bad it was also a front. A way for the Russian mob to launder money.

Maybe they paid off all those online reviewers to say great things about their food. Niall would never know, because he wasn't here for the soup.

The man he was here to see sat at the very back table, facing the front door. The two suited, armed men stood flanking his table. Both clocked

Niall the second he came in. On a mission. Here to see the boss. He figured they could tell he was a cop, even if he was technically a federal agent for the Navy.

The Russian mob boss lifted his napkin and wiped his mouth. He took his time placing it back beside his plate, then reached over to squeeze the knee of the woman who sat beside him. Tiny dress, big hair. Heavy makeup. The boss said, "Get lost."

She didn't hang around to be asked a second time. Just slid the gold chain of her purse over her shoulder and eyed Niall as she made her way to the bar.

"They said an O'Sullivan was coming to see me." The boss paused half a second. "They did not say cop."

"It's complicated," Niall said. Kind of like having to change his name. He'd stuck with his heritage, just switched out Sullivan for Caran.

The Russian laughed. "It always is. When men come to me with hat in hand, asking for favor."

"I don't have a hat."

"But you do need a favor, *da?*"

Niall nodded.

"Which means you owe me." He eyed Niall. "But I have no need of your allegiance."

He thought he was untouchable? That kind of arrogance always preceded destruction.

"Maybe you're the one who owes me," Niall suggested. "After all, Yuri Kartov was left on my doorstep. How many guys do you have in the police force?"

However big this guy's operation was, it had been established by cops and Russians working together. That was bizarre. There had to be one person in charge, or there could never be cooperation at this level. But who was on top, and who was the underling? He just couldn't figure out the Russians-scholarship-college-lab-police connection. Not a puzzle. More like one of those kid toys where all the pieces had to be assembled in a row.

In precisely the right order.

The Russian eyed Niall while he took a sip of his drink. He swished it like mouthwash and then swallowed.

"Some of your men took possession of a silver case recently. It came from a doctor, who was associated with a lab hidden in the woods. One that might have been Portland's biggest secret. Until it was destroyed."

"And if I was to know about this case, what then?"

Niall had used his family history to get in—the boss would never have agreed to speak with a cop. Now he was going to use his federal career to complete whatever deal they could come up with.

He said, "That case is material evidence in an ongoing investigation. It also represents a threat. Possession of that case will only bring a world of hurt down on whoever is holding it when it's found."

"So it's good thing I already sell case to highest bidder."

"You…" That was the worst possible news. "Cashing in on your work with the lab?"

"I know nothing about a lab."

He looked like he was telling the truth, but Niall wasn't sure what to believe. "So Yuri had no connection to it?"

"I'm afraid I do not know this man."

Yeah, that was just him covering his own butt. Niall said, "Have you ever, at any time, been contracted by an employee of the Portland Police Department, or the State Police, to protect anyone or anything associated with the lab that was destroyed?"

"I know nothing about science experiments."

"But you knew enough to get the case."

"What can I say?" The Russian smiled. "I am resourceful man."

Niall shifted his jaw side to side. "I need to know who you sold it to."

"I tell nothing."

Of course. Niall wanted to stomp his foot like Siobhan had as a toddler. "Who is the person behind the lab?" Someone had employed the doctor to work there and also managed to get the police to aid in keeping it all under the radar. That person was either connected, extremely wealthy, or blackmailing everyone involved. Maybe all three.

The Russian said, "Go ask around at that college. You find answers."

Or he would get cornered in a hallway, drugged and nearly experimented on like the last time. Niall said, "I'm missing a friend and a coworker. One was taken by two cops, the other one—a valuable asset to the right person—was kidnapped from my office. You know anything about either of those women?"

"I deal in product. Not women."

A mafia boss with standards? Niall hardly believed it. That certainly wasn't true of his father.

He said, "Thanks." *For nothing.*

Niall turned to leave. The Russian said, "O'Sullivan will hear about this. You use his name to get in here, he won't be happy."

Niall figured the only reason this guy hadn't ordered him shot was because the restaurant was half full of witnesses. Maybe they would follow him and take him out later.

"I'm sure my father will hardly care what I've done." Niall gave the Russian a second to realize his connection. Then he drew a business card from his wallet. "I apologize for interrupting your meal. If you can provide the information for whoever purchased the case from you, that will be the end of your involvement in this business." He laid the card down on the table and strode out of the restaurant.

He climbed in his car and looked at the building. One of the gunmen, bodyguards—whatever he employed them to do—stood at the front door, watching Niall leave.

Thirty seconds later he got an email on his work account. An account number the funds received from the sale of the case had been paid to. And an email address for the person who bought the case.

The second he realized who it pointed him to, Niall's eyebrows rose.

Maybe the Russian was right.

Chapter 24

Ana looked up from her phone. "He's on his way."

Haley stared at her. "You were going off the rails, drugs had their grip on you."

Was she using now? Haley couldn't tell if she was still under that cloud. She was nothing like those people in the courtyard at the lab had been—zombies under the influence of something. The buzzing. Even more chemicals in their systems than Haley had been exposed to by falling in the river. And yet they'd managed to get her to shoot her friends.

The man she cared about.

"Then you disappeared," Haley said. Ana didn't even look at her. Or just flat-out refused to acknowledge her existence, now that the person in charge was on his way. Who was it? Someone from law enforcement or another party entirely? Haley couldn't quite let go of the idea of some kind of connection to the college. Though, she didn't know why she felt that way. Ana had been dating the dean. Was he the one in charge?

She'd been convinced Ana needed saving, when the reality was Ana had been party to this whole thing. Haley didn't even know what it was yet, not in full. Maybe she would die before she got all the answers.

She'd thought Ana was dead.

"I tried to save you. Get answers, ready to avenge you if someone had hurt you."

Ana snorted. "I don't need saving."

"Maybe you think that."

"And you don't?"

Haley only shrugged. Her former friend probably didn't want to know what she thought. Ana was doing…whatever she wanted to do. Haley had been swept into it, just trying to get to the truth.

"You could have let me know you were all right. Then I wouldn't have looked for you. People wouldn't have died."

Ana made a face. "What people?"

"Everyone in the lab." For starters. That Russian cop had been killed after she talked to him, but now she knew that was Ana's doing and not Haley's fault. The doctor, though. And those federal agents at the safe house.

"The people we tested on? They were dead already."

Haley wanted to vomit. "I thought you were one of them."

"I took steps," Ana said. "I made sure I came out of this on top. Something you should have done. Could've saved yourself from being cuffed to that chair."

And yet she was here because Ana needed to know where the case was.

Haley decided to turn the tables. "I'm not the one who lost the case."

They thought she knew where it was. The whole exchange with the person in charge was predicated on the notion they thought she was going to hand over the information.

When they got the information, they were going to have no more use for her.

At that point, she would be dead.

"Why sign on with them?" Haley asked.

What could Ana have gained by it? Someone whose only thought was where their next fix would come from hardly had the foresight to jump on an investment opportunity—or at least they'd struggle to put aside their needs for a longer term result. It made no sense.

Between the last time Haley had seen her—when Ana had told her about her relationship with the dean—and today, some serious changes had occurred in Ana's life.

Ana shrugged. "They gave me something better."

"Like drugs?"

Her friend sighed. "Do you have to sound so high and mighty? *Drugs.*" She over-exaggerated the word. "I'm not 'ill.' And what they gave me set me free. This is so far beyond the help those idiots get at those recovery meetings. Thinking it's all about having the will power to deny yourself. This is so much better."

Okay, she was crazy.

"Is it what the doctor was making at the—"

The door opened. The dean strode in, a gun held in his hand like he figured he'd need it the minute he walked in the door. As though flashing it around meant he was strong. Or that he'd be perceived that way. Given the kind of man he was, she wondered if he knew how to use it. She couldn't be sure until he lifted it. Training was ingrained. Lack of it was all too obvious when it came to handling weapons. But that didn't make a person anything but even more deadly with a gun in their hand.

She swallowed, wanting to wince. He was going to shoot someone's eye out.

He waved his empty hand in a flourish, then glanced at the officers. "You guys can go."

"We get paid, right?"

The dean turned to Ana, handing her a smartphone. "Make the transfer. Fifty thousand."

One started to argue. "Fif—"

The dean swung his gun up and shot the man. Haley shut her eyes and heard him fall to the floor. He said, "Fifty?"

The other officer said, "Sounds good."

"Make the transfer so our friend can leave."

Haley opened her eyes to see Ana on her phone. When Ana lifted her head, she said, "It's done." There was no trace of the effects of drugs in her eyes beyond some redness. For all intents and purposes she really did seem to be free of that life. What had they given her?

A cure, maybe. Something else to get people hooked on—another revenue source. If it worked in one dose like it seemed to be doing with

Ana, then addicts would be lucid. They would be productive. They would never need any more of it. No more petty crime to get money to buy more and get their fix. The wider effects were significant. But why make something that made people better?

She couldn't figure out how that would make money. Which was cynical, but why else did people make new products? No one was altruistic enough to do it for the betterment of humanity.

"Now," the dean said over the sound of the front door closing. "Where is that case?"

"You have no doctor. Why do you need it?"

He studied her. "You think I'm going to explain myself to you?" As though she was an antibody under his microscope.

She wasn't bacteria, something he'd find distasteful. No. Haley was the good one in this situation—the one that could start the healing process.

She lifted her chin. "You're gonna kill me, anyway. Why not assuage my curiosity in the meantime? Like a last request."

"It really is too bad you won't be here to see it, considering it will be spectacular." Bartlett really seemed to believe his own press release. "Phase two has been completed. We have nowhere to go from here, but up."

Ana laid a hand on his arm, entreating. "Honey—"

He whipped around to her. "Did I ask for your input?"

Ana sank into herself, losing a good inch of her height in the process. Slumped shoulders. Eyes to the ground.

Haley's grieving heart swelled with yet more sadness. This was what her friend had chosen? She needed to get his attention off Ana. Haley said, "What's phase three?"

"When we roll out the next update of the app." He actually grinned, flashing straight white teeth as fake as the rest of him. "One of those annoying games that's totally addicting, and it gives you rewards. Like real cash back. We've had hundreds of downloads across campus already."

"What does that have to do with—"

He let out a frustrated noise. Like she was beneath him, and he couldn't believe he was forced to explain it to her. "It's all *part of the app*."

"I thought it was medicine?" Weren't there chemicals in her blood, ones she'd gotten from falling in the river?

"Everyone in Portland already has the right chemicals in their system by now. We've been contaminating the water for months. It's literally in their brain chemistry. Once we go wide with the app, everyone will be ours."

Everyone? Haley couldn't make sense of this. It was the buzzing. She didn't have an app.

Niall hadn't reacted to it. And Dakota. Victoria. They didn't live here. She'd been the only one...

The lab. The room at their office. Her thoughts coalesced. She'd heard it. Because those were localized instances of exposure. She remembered Niall and his team say they traveled extensively. They hadn't been exposed to the drinking water.

"What..." She could hardly—Haley fought through the screaming in her mind. "What app?"

"Perklife." Those white teeth flashed again. "And phase three is ready to roll out."

. . .

Niall strode into the FBI office and spotted Victoria immediately. "Where's Alvarez?"

Her eyebrows lifted, but she said, "Still running that surveillance job."

"And it's relevant?" He had to ask if what Alvarez was doing actually related to the case they were on right now. Because Victoria was, well, Victoria, and so he felt the need to be reassured that all hands were on deck.

"He's been at the college for days setting up bugs and cameras. Getting information and feeding it to Talia." Her voice hitched saying their teammate's name. "And now the information is coming here."

He didn't like the idea the FBI was being looped in on something that involved his team and no one else. But the reality was that they needed all the help they could get.

"She was on to something," Victoria continued. "We think that's why they breached her system and then took her. The subroutine left behind was a booby trap. For you and Haley."

A voice from behind Niall said, "Okay."

He spun to find a gray-suited man with a badge on his belt. Red tie—a bold choice. But it was high quality. "I'm sorry. I had to take that call."

Victoria said, "Assistant Director Mark Welvern, this is NCIS Special Agent Niall O'Caran."

His eyebrows rose, and he glanced between them. "The Irish connection?" When Niall started to argue, he said, "I've read the files of each and every person on your team. It was part of my agreement with Victoria to provide support." He paused a second. "I don't work with people I don't know. Especially a team as unique as yours."

Victoria smiled, like that was a compliment.

Niall wanted to get defensive about the fact this guy knew he'd left Boston and changed his name.

She said, "O'Caran, would you like to update us as to what you learned while meeting with the head of the Russian Mafia in Portland?"

He explained about the case and gave them everything else the guy had said as well.

Victoria's brightness dimmed. "So we don't have any leads on either Talia or Haley?"

"If I had to surmise a theory," Welvern said, "I'd say the Russians sold the case to a third party to pay off that debt." He glanced at Niall. "We've been watching them closely. They're up to their eyebrows in issues, and the whole empire is about to come crashing down."

"That fits what he said about not being part of the cover up," Niall said. "In fact, if the Russians knew about it, and wanted a piece of the pie, then they might have been sniffing around to find out more. Then when the doctor passed off the case, they got in the middle of that deal and sold it for a profit."

"Whoever has the case now, it doesn't get us Talia or Haley." Niall had to point it out, even though they knew it. He just needed to say it. "And how can we be sure you guys didn't know about this cover-up as well. You could have either been paid off to look the other way or had some part in it?"

He glanced at Victoria, expecting her to object. She lifted her chin. "My agent has a point."

Welvern studied him, then Niall's boss. Finally, he said, "As insulting as that accusation is, I do see your point."

"I've been shot at by police detectives and brushed off by state police. None of you noticed a drone strike in your backyard the other day?"

Welvern shifted his stance. "We're looking into it, but there isn't much at the site to go on."

"I know," Niall said. "I was there when it exploded."

Victoria set her slender fingers on his forearm and squeezed. "Go check in with Alvarez. See if he's learned anything from his—"

"Sir!" A tech in a lab coat raced out of the elevator and across the room, holding a tablet above his head.

Welvern spun to meet him. "What is it?"

"We got a ping in the database." He had to stop and catch his breath, his dark head of hair hanging forward. After a second of deep breaths, he swept his long hair back as he straightened. "It looks like Talia Matrice is—" He noticed Niall and Victoria. "Oh."

"Please finish what you were saying," Victoria said.

The tech swallowed. "Yes. It's just…we got a hit from the dark web. Talia Matrice is famous in my circles. She's basically a legend."

"Do you know where she is?" Welvern asked.

"She's being sold." He turned the tablet around. On screen was a live video of Talia, gagged and chained to a brick wall. The tech said, "They're auctioning her off to the highest bidder."

"We have to win—"

"—that auction."

Niall turned to Victoria. They both nodded. That was how they were going to get the NSA analyst back. She'd only been doing her job and this had happened. She wasn't a frontline agent. Not the way they were. But even if she was, they'd still do whatever it took to get her back.

"It had to have been the state police or the person behind the lab," he said. "Someone with money and power, and the insight, to know who we all are. He realized what a prize Talia is."

"It was mercenaries who took her out of the office. Not locals. Taking her and *selling* her." Victoria's voice choked a bit. "It's the best way to slow us down, so we have a smaller chance of finding him."

"Try no chance." And how did that information affect Haley? Mercenaries? That wasn't who'd taken Haley from the street.

Niall's history had gotten him a sit down with the Russians. It wasn't going to help him find Haley. That was his NCIS training. His investigative skills—which kept bringing the college back to mind. Why, he wasn't sure. Only that there had to be something with those kids in the hallway and the fact he'd been abducted from there.

That meant a connection between it and the lab, regardless of who was in charge.

Victoria twisted her body a fraction toward Niall. "I'll get Talia back."

"I'll team up with Alvarez, go to the college and find Haley." The college had to be the answer. It was the only thing they had left. Anything else, and he would have no chance of finding her.

"Good." She nodded. "You get her safe. And call her brother if you need additional backup. We can't trust any of the locals."

"Hey now," Welvern said. Like he was attempting to make a joke out of being offended but knew the timing was awful.

Niall couldn't give him anything. He had to get out of there.

"Barnes!" He shouted so loud it made Niall flinch. At Welvern's call, a young agent raced over. Welvern said, "Get this man outfitted in full gear. Whatever he wants."

"Yes, sir."

Niall said, "Thank you."

He went with the agent and got a protective vest, along with a radio to call the FBI if he needed anything. A shotgun and two pistols. Extra ammo.

He bypassed the elevator and went for the stairs, too antsy to stand still in the car as it descended. He called Alvarez as he drove out of the parking lot onto the street.

"I need an update."

"Copy that," Alvarez said. "And you have good timing. I'm sitting on Bartlett Manchester. That other woman is with him, Haley's missing friend." He pushed out a breath, like he was running. Or just moving fast. "I'm headed around the back of the building they're in."

Alvarez paused. "They just loaded something in the trunk of his car."

"What?"

He was silent long enough Niall asked again.

"It looked like a body."

Chapter 25

Haley came awake. She could feel scratchy carpet under her bound hands. She was bent at an odd angle into this small, dark space. Beyond the boundaries of it, she heard the hum of the road. They were moving.

She was in the trunk of a car.

Think. Wasn't there a way to escape from a trunk? Too bad she had *no idea what it was.* Haley tried to roll. Her hands were behind her back. She heard the clink of handcuffs, felt the cold metal digging into her wrists. Instead of pushing against the trunk lid, she lifted her feet. Her knees hit the lid of the trunk. Ouch.

She slumped back down.

The car turned a corner and she rolled to one side. Her face mushed against something hard and she fought to breathe for a second before the road straightened and she rolled back. All the tears she'd expended had dried up. She needed to use the bathroom. Badly.

Would she be stuck in this trunk until they pulled her out and killed her?

That's exactly what they would do when they arrived at the airport and realized she had no idea where the case was.

Instead of telling them the case was held in evidence lockup with the FBI, she'd settled for telling them that the doctor had hidden it before he was arrested.

Haley had no idea if that were even true. For all she knew, it totally could be. The last she'd heard was that the feds never found the case when they arrested the doctor at the airport. Dakota had informed her of that on the way to the safe house. Talia had been looking for it.

The doctor might have hidden it. What did she know?

That tiny gem of possibility was enough to convince them she'd been genuine; that the case was stashed somewhere they could get to. Even Ana, who knew her well, had believed her. She'd assumed her *former* friend could tell if she was lying. Though, maybe not. Ana had so assumed she was telling the truth that she'd convinced Bartlett that Haley was credible. To be honest, that had pricked her conscience.

She didn't like lying. Ana knew that and trusted it.

That one untruth would hopefully keep her alive long enough for—

The car swerved. Tires squealed, and she rolled again as they hurtled around a corner. Were they being chased, trying to get away from someone? The police could be right behind them. But that wasn't a reassuring thing, given the amount of corruption she had seen the last few days. It was more terrifying than the dean and Ana being in control.

Bartlett only wanted the case so he could, "continue the work." New phases.

The cops would probably just kill her this time. Or turn her over to someone worse.

The car swerved. She rolled so far she was pressed against the inside corner of the trunk. Someone screamed.

Then metal screeched and the car went airborne.

It flipped over and landed upside down.

She regained consciousness hearing gunshots outside. The trunk was open, spilling daylight onto her. Haley didn't care if the gap wasn't big enough. She wormed her way between the open trunk lid and the frame of the car. It was tight. Metal scraped her side and she cried out, but she managed to get out onto the gritty road where she landed in a wet puddle.

Another shot rang out.

She rolled onto her side, cuffed hands pinned under her and looked around. Ana ran over. She hauled Haley to her feet and pressed a gun to her side. "I'll shoot her!"

Across from them, behind the cover of a silver car, Alvarez crouched with his gun pointed at her. And Ana. His mouth was set in a line. "Let her go!" The low command made *her* want to comply, even though she wasn't the one holding the weapon.

Shame filled her. Under the influence of the audio buzzing and the chemicals in her system, she'd destroyed his team. He probably hated her. "It wasn't my fault."

"Shut up." Ana shook her.

Where was the dean?

The sun made her squint. Haley couldn't see Alvarez's expression now, and she wanted to be able to. She needed to know if Niall and Dakota were okay. To know what she had done.

God, You have to take care of that. I can't do it.

Admitting where her control left off and His began was probably the first step to getting this right. Though she figured she needed to be in that place where she had zero control. Where God had *all* of it, and she just trusted in Him completely.

Haley wanted to get to that place. She couldn't rely on herself. Not when she failed so much and had chemicals in her that could turn her at any moment. She wasn't trustworthy right now. And with her heart skewed the way it had been, convincing her that she had to save everyone, she wondered if she was trustworthy even without chemicals flowing through her brain.

"Ana, put the gun down now." Alvarez came out from behind the cover of the door. He walked slowly toward them. "Before someone gets hurt and you go so far you can't come back from it."

"Come back?" Ana's grip on her arm shook her again.

Haley shifted. The gun glanced off a rib. She winced. "Ana, don't do this." Her friend had to know that facing off against a federal agent wasn't going to end up anywhere good.

"I don't care what happens to me," Ana said, "as long as Bartlett gets away. His work is important."

Was it worth dying for?

Alvarez took another step. He could probably shoot Ana from this range without it hitting Haley. But Haley didn't especially want to test that theory right now. He said, "There's no chance my colleague will allow him to get away. He'll pursue Bartlett until this is done."

Who? Haley stared at him. He had to say who it was. She didn't care about the gun pressed against her side. She needed to know who he was talking about before the next thing happened. She could die never knowing whether Niall and Dakota were okay.

Or she would live and go to jail for shooting them.

Haley's breath hitched in her throat and she moaned. *What did I do?*

Alvarez's gaze snagged on hers. He glanced to her left, a slight movement. Haley moved immediately. She ducked left.

His gun went off.

Ana was dead before she hit the ground. Haley spun around to see her flat on her back, her eyes vacant and wide open. Alvarez kicked the gun away regardless.

She took two steps back, unable to take her gaze from the woman. Her friend. Her assailant. Haley blew out a breath that emerged more like a whimper.

"Turn around."

She did as he asked. He was probably going to arrest—

The cuffs fell away.

He said, "I have to go after Niall. He needs backup." Alvarez frowned, not leaving yet. "I don't like leaving your friend on the street, but the police are probably on their way. I don't have the time it's going to take to figure out if the ones who show up are on our side or not."

Haley said, "He's okay?" It came out breathy and desperate.

"Niall?"

She nodded.

"He's fine, but you shot Dakota in the leg." He lifted Ana's gun and slid it into the back of his pants. "You can come with me. If you stay where I can see you—and no sudden movements."

. . .

Niall raced after the dean. The man had a gun, and he lifted it and fired. Niall ducked behind a line of dumpsters to escape the wild bullets.

The knock-on effect of the past few days, physical stress and all the other stuff, meant he was quickly hitting a wall. The dean seemed to be in really good shape—or Niall was even worse off than he believed.

Either way there was nothing else he could do. Niall prayed, and he ran after the dean all the way through streets and past buildings. They were close enough to the college; he figured that was where the man was heading.

He could do this, with God's help. But he also knew that if He didn't ordain it, then Niall would have to be okay with whatever God deemed necessary. Niall didn't even know if he had the right to ask for help. Either way, Niall would be content knowing he'd done everything he could. He needed to capture the dean and figure out what Bartlett Manchester—most stuck up name he'd ever heard—knew about the lab and the doctor's work.

Up ahead, Bartlett turned a corner.

Niall did the same, gun first, onto a street full of college students. A note of fear rang through him. Students had cornered him in one of the residence halls before. They'd beaten him and taken him, unconscious, to the lab. He wasn't going to let that happen again.

"Out of the way," he yelled. Loud and commanding. There was no reason any of them should not comply—at least that's what his tone implied. "Police!"

A couple moved into his path. Niall glanced off the guy. "Sorry." He ran on, hearing a muttered exclamation. Whether they considered the police to be oppressive militants or not, that wasn't the point right now. He was bringing down a threat that put all their lives in jeopardy.

Up ahead, he saw Bartlett run into a building.

That note of fear rang louder now, but he pushed it aside and raced on. The last time he'd felt like this was a night when his father had gone up against an old friend. Eleven-year-old Niall had known something wasn't right. That his dad was going out into danger, maybe never to come back.

He'd been scared for him. Now he was scared for himself. For Alvarez and Haley. She could be dead in the trunk. Loaded in at least—maybe already dead. The car had flipped—that might have killed her. More than one chance for the worst to have happened. Was she alive? If she was still with them, then it was an act of God. And Niall had full faith that He could do that.

I trust You.

That wasn't the problem.

He slammed the handle down and flew into the lobby of a building he hadn't been in before. The Cerium Center for Technology, according to a giant plaque on the wall. "Where did he go?"

The young woman at the desk screamed and rolled backward in her chair.

"Where?" He barked the word at her.

"That way." She pointed to her right.

"What's in there?"

"The computer lab, where they're developing the app."

Like Niall cared about what these students were working on. Maybe it was interesting, but it scored really low on the scale of relevance to this case. He ran on. People gave up all kinds of information to the police without realizing that was what they had done. He figured it had been nothing but a nervous reaction to his presence.

Niall ran down the hall and pushed through a set of double doors.

Inside, the dean was right up in one of the student's faces. It was the man Niall had interviewed most recently about his scholarship. Hassim Bukhari. That was his name.

Now Hassim had a gun pointed at his face, and the dean was yelling.

"Manchester!" Niall yelled the guy's name as loud as he could. "Stand down," he ordered, equally as loud.

The dean swung around. He brought the weapon up, already firing.

Niall reacted, diving for the ground before the sound even registered—the heavy click of a weapon that was empty of bullets. He clambered to his feet and ran to the dean, tackled him to the floor and stuck his knee in Manchester's back.

Niall pushed out a long breath and tried to slow his heart rate. He pulled both of the man's arms behind his back and looked at Hassim. "Give me something to tie his hands with."

"Dude." Hassim blinked. "That was O.P."

Whatever that meant. Niall said, "Now, Hassim."

The young man handed over a cable and Niall tied the dean's hands. He stood, hauling Bartlett to his feet.

The dean groaned. "Do it now." But he wasn't talking to Niall, he was talking to Hassim. "Do it," he repeated. "Send out the update or it's all over. Everything we've worked for is done, and we won't be needed anymore."

"What update?" Hassim shook his head.

"Where's Haley?" That was really…okay so it was not *all* Niall cared about. But it was first on the list.

Bartlett said, "She was supposed to get the case. So we could start over with the next testing pool."

"Am I meant to understand what you're talking about?"

"Portland is ready to roll out." Bartlett turned to Hassim again. "So send the update." He yelled that last part so loudly it hurt Niall's ears. Spit landed on Hassim's shoulder.

The student shook his head. "What update?"

"Phase three. Send it *now.*"

Niall shoved the dean into a chair, then asked Hassim, "What is phase three?"

"It's a theory." Hassim glanced at Bartlett, then at Niall. "Nothing but an intellectual exercise."

When Niall made a face, Hassim said, "Like when you search for a product on one website, and then all of a sudden all your social media ads are that exact thing."

"Okay."

Hassim continued, "Underneath Perklife, there are subroutines that allow for an update, one that was only theory."

"Send it!"

They both ignored Bartlett. Hassim said, "Taking those algorithms a step further. Making suggestions, that when coupled with certain environmental factors, can make people…choose things they wouldn't otherwise choose."

The way the buzzing had with Haley? How would that, as part of an update, ever wind up controlling people to the extent Haley had been controlled? He was definitely missing pieces of this puzzle. But for right now, what mattered was that it wasn't going out. No way. Not if he could help it. At least it appeared Hassim understood enough to know it was wrong.

Niall said, "Like it's able to control people?"

"It's nothing but a theor—" Hassim's eyes glazed over. He didn't finish what he was saying. Instead, he clutched his ears and groaned.

Niall didn't hear anything, but he knew what this was. He looked high on the walls for speakers. Nothing. The computers then? Or someone's phone was broadcasting. Whatever affected Haley, had just been turned on in here.

Why wasn't he hearing it?

Bartlett started to laugh. "Send the update!"

Niall grabbed Hassim's shirt and shoved him back. His chair rolled two feet and hit the back of another student's chair. Their heads slammed together, knocking both unconscious.

Across the room someone else laughed. Another student Niall had only been partly aware of.

"Send it!"

Niall ran to the student and shoved her back away from her computer. But it was too late. The young woman burst into drowsy laughter and slumped in her chair.

He looked at the screen.

Update published.

Chapter 26

Haley ran beside Alvarez, down the middle of the street. The students were all acting weird. Some had started fighting a second ago. One guy shoved another right in her path so that she had to jump over him. The downed man tried to grab her leg. Haley stumbled out of the way and raced after the marshal.

She glanced back. The man who'd done the shoving jumped on the downed man and started beating him. His movements were sluggish, but he was strong.

"Come on!"

She glanced forward again. Two girls stepped in her path, swaying as though they were intoxicated. Haley brushed past them. "Where is he?"

Alvarez lifted his hand to look at his phone. Then said, "That building up ahead."

They ran to it.

The thirty or so students on the street collided in different ways, hurting each other. Falling down. What on earth was going on?

The door to the building opened and a young man ran out, blood streaming down from a wound on his temple. Something had happened here. It was eerily similar to the effect that buzzing had on her, back at the office. But there was no buzzing right now that she could hear, anyway.

They needed to get to Niall. "Are you sure he's okay?"

"You shot Dakota." Alvarez stopped at the door. He didn't seem to be partial to sympathy. Or striving to make others comfortable by reassuring them. His personality was too abrasive for that, making him more of a put-up-or-shut-up type of guy. And he still hadn't given her a gun.

"In the leg," Alvarez added, then pulled the door open.

How was she supposed to defend herself?

She said, "That doesn't answer my question of whether Niall is okay."

A blonde woman screamed and ran at them. Alvarez shot her in the forehead. "Don't expect Dakota to want to be your friend. At least not anytime in the next ten years."

Haley swallowed the squeal at seeing the woman fall down. Dead. Reacting like that wouldn't make Alvarez more inclined to try and make her feel better. At least Dakota wasn't dead as well. And Niall was okay, right? Both of them had been protected when she'd flipped out and shot at them. *Thank You, God.*

That made her feel better. Something she thanked God for on top of the first prayer. Whatever was happening here, it was insane. But God was good, and they would be okay. She had federal protection.

"O'Caran!" He continued on, walking in like they were out for a stroll. Chatting about Dakota being mad at her for shooting her in the thigh, like they'd had a mere spat in their friendship—not that she'd been shot after Haley had been whammied by that buzzing.

Niall answered Alvarez's bellow. She heard him yell but couldn't make out the words. "That way." She pointed to the hallway.

Alvarez nodded. He went first, her protection leaving her side to make his way into the lab. She followed. Every step she took, she wanted to collapse. Fall to the ground and just give up. But she didn't. She pushed herself forward despite having almost no strength left.

Then she felt a surge of energy.

Niall was pinned under a Middle Eastern man, a student. The dean was lying on the man's back, and it looked like he was trying to bite the student. His hands were tied behind him. The closer she got to them, the more her energy came back.

Alvarez kicked the dean off the man on top of Niall.

"Took you long enough." Niall wrestled with the student.

Haley ran over and pulled the student off him. She punched him in the nose, then shoved him aside. He tripped over Bartlett and landed on his backside. Haley dived after him. She was going to cause him so much pain that he...

Alvarez's arm snaked around her waist. He dragged her back. Haley kicked out with her legs. Her head pounded, that relentless buzzing.

In the lobby, he threw her to the floor. She cried out, landing in a heap.

"Easy." Niall knelt beside her, running his fingers down her hair.

That felt nice. And the buzzing had eased.

"They sent something out through the app," Niall said, glancing back at Alvarez. "It's making them all go crazy."

Alvarez frowned. "But Haley is only affected by proximity? And us not at all? This is nuts."

"It was the buzzing that made the student send the update. That's what is also affecting Haley. The app is getting the rest of them." Niall glanced at her again. "We have to turn it off. Make them stop acting like this. At this point, does it matter how it's all happening?"

Haley blew out a breath. She wanted to know. Someone was controlling her. It had nothing to do with an app, considering she didn't even have a phone on her.

Niall said, "You okay?"

She stared at him. "Are you?"

She'd thought he was dead. Now he was here, and she was all right. But she should *not* be going into that lab again anytime soon.

"We don't have time for emotional reunions," Alvarez said. "We aren't affected, so we need to stop it." He motioned to Niall, then back at himself.

Niall nodded. Inside the lab, the student was rallying. Alvarez strode in and kicked him in the face. The man fell back to the ground, unconscious.

Haley didn't know what to do. She couldn't help, or she would end up trying to kill someone again.

"So let me get this straight. The app is supposed to make suggestions. But how could it possibly do all this?" Niall gestured to them.

She shook her head. Then she called out, "Alvarez, find a computer!" She couldn't go in there, but maybe he could do something. Anything. Haley watched him move to a computer. Maybe he could figure out how to turn the buzzing off before this got any worse.

He called back, "It just says 'update published.'" He hit a few keys. "I can't get this window to go away."

She told him the shortcut to the task manager. Then said, "Click 'End Task.'"

"Done."

But nothing changed. She could hear the buzzing, though it was quiet from this distance. The update had been sent. Was the damage done already? The men in the room, lying on the floor, moaned. The dean snapped his teeth together. She could hear the click-click. It made her shiver.

"Are you okay?"

She nodded. "You should go help him."

What could she do? If she went into the lab, she would go crazy. She never wanted to feel like that again. But the reality? God was ultimately in control. Haley just didn't want to hurt anyone. Let alone get her hands on another gun. She might fire it again at someone she cared about.

Niall ran his thumb over the home button on his cell, then handed it to her. "Call Victoria." He kissed the top of her head, then headed into the lab.

Haley dialed the number, gripping the phone.

Victoria answered. "Make it fast."

"The dean set off the app. Everyone at the college has gone crazy."

She was quiet for a second, then said, "Here, talk to the FBI. I'm close to winning back Talia."

Before Haley could ask what "winning Talia back" meant, a man said, "This is Assistant Director Welvern."

She explained who she was and what Alvarez and Niall were doing.

"I've already dispatched agents to your location. Emergency services are getting a flood of calls from your area. Students saying their friends and professors are going crazy. Cops are inbound, but who knows if we can trust them?"

"Okay." That didn't sound good at all.

"Sit tight. Get yourself safe."

Relief flooded through her. Help was on the way. "Thank you."

In the lab, someone cried out. Gunshots echoed down the hall.

She said, "Please hurry." But he had already hung up.

. . .

Niall didn't like leaving Haley out in the hallway now that he had her back. He glanced around the lab. There had to be... He moved around the computers, looking at the screen of each one. At the far end was a door. He walked toward it after he'd exhausted this room, left Alvarez to secure the dean and Hassim, and opened the door.

Inside was what he thought might be a server room.

As soon as he got the door all the way open another man ran at him, a tablet in one hand. Niall dipped one shoulder. When the man was close enough, he pushed off the guy's center and straightened at the same time to flip the man over his shoulder. The device smashed to the floor.

Niall spun to watch the guy land on his back and hit his head on the floor. He left him there and checked the room. It was clear.

He picked up the tablet, wincing as his fingers encountered the cracked screen. It illuminated.

Hurt them all.

The command had been entered in a thread. Instructions. Ways to hurt people, to influence them to do some of the worst things humans could do to each other. Had this guy controlled the message sent out through the app, the one that influenced everyone? Niall wanted to smash the thing on the ground, but that probably wouldn't cut off a connection like this. It had gone out.

He typed on the screen. Cracked glass sliced at the pads of his thumbs.

Stop.

He tapped SEND. Blood smeared the screen. Then he figured he'd aim higher.

Kneel down. Hands on your head.

It was worth a try.

"Whatever you're doing," Alvarez called out, "it's working."

Niall tried to figure out how on earth this was even possible, controlling people through an app. It couldn't be this easy, could it? As though these people had checked their brains at the door. Handed over control of their lives to an electronic device.

He'd known some of what Hassim had explained. Social media and online stores used algorithms to show customers things they thought the person wanted to see, based on their history. Social media especially held back notifications until a certain time and then strategized on the best time to alert people of likes and comments in order to maximize people's usage of their apps and websites.

It was a game, and most people didn't read the terms and conditions. They didn't know they were playing. Or that apps themselves were designed to be addictive.

Niall headed back to Alvarez. He dropped the tablet on the first clear desk he came to. Hassim and Manchester were both out cold. "Good?"

He was ready to get back to Haley.

Alvarez nodded. "What just happened?"

"I hardly understand myself, let alone possess the ability to explain it to you." Niall sighed. "Maybe Hassim can clear it up, but he seemed to think it was an intellectual exercise. Not something he thought would—or should—be used."

"And the lab that was destroyed?" Alvarez paused. "They were testing it on people. A compound in the water. The audio-whatever that kept affecting Haley. Then this app, controlling people."

"Pieces of a plan."

Alvarez nodded.

"Did we stop it?"

"Time will tell, once we get the FBI in here."

"They're on their way," Haley said.

He headed for her. "You shouldn't be—"

She lifted a hand. "It turned off."

"Sure?"

"I don't want to be close enough that it ever happens again, so yes. I'm sure it's off."

Niall was so relieved, he pulled her into his arms. Haley sighed and pressed close to him. Calmed. Safe.

"I thought you were dead." Her voice was barely above a whisper, but he heard the relief and hope loudly enough.

"I know." He felt the same relief surge in him. "I thought the same about you when I heard you'd been loaded into that trunk."

Haley pulled back, tears in her eyes now. "I need to call Isaac. Let him know I'm all right."

He nodded, because that was a good idea. Her brother had been on the phone with her at the safe house when the breach happened. She hadn't had the chance to call him since then, so he was probably worried sick about her. Not knowing if his sister was alive—or dead.

She said, "The FBI should be here soon."

"Good." He gave her a squeeze, thinking he should make sure his family was all right as well. They'd all come so close to having their lives taken from them over the past few days. Now that he thought it might finally be done, he was hesitant to believe it.

"Ana would've killed me," she said. "She was part of it, along with the dean. She even killed Yuri, because the Russians wanted in on the operation, and she wanted to warn them to back off." Haley shook her head. "I still can't believe all this. She was...so different than the last time I saw her. Better. Not strung out. But she was also completely sold out to whatever they were doing." She motioned to the room. "An app experiment?"

He shrugged. Whatever it was, they'd put a stop to it. The damage was done and there would hopefully be no more craziness now.

She blew out a breath. "I don't know what to make of it. What would Ana have to do with the work done here? Except that Bartlett was her boyfriend. It was like she'd sold out to an ideology. They gave her something that was better than drugs, and then she signed on to their cause."

"Maybe they altered her brain as well, just in a different way?"

When she shrugged as he'd done, he continued, "Seemed like Manchester thought he was in charge."

She nodded. "They wanted the case, Ana and Bartlett did. The one the doctor had when he left the lab."

"The Russians got it. They sold it off. That's all I managed to learn from them. Yuri was fishing," he said. "The Russians knew something was going on, they just didn't know what. They were definitely trying to figure it out."

Haley shook her head.

"That means we need to track down the case and get it out of circulation before anyone else gets their hands on it. Or worse, figures out what it is and what someone might be able to do with it. When Talia gets back." And she *would* be back.

"Earlier, when I was on the phone with her, Victoria said she was close to 'winning her.'"

"Good." He glanced back at Alvarez, who'd heard it. His teammate nodded.

"Good."

Haley gave him a small smile. Niall pulled her in for a hug again. He found in her a kind of calm in the middle of choppy seas. A place to call his own, after years spent proving to himself and everyone else that he deserved it. Searching for what his life was going to be. Trying to convince himself that his past didn't matter. And now he could clearly see that history had forged who he was now.

Thank You, God.

Victoria seemed to have had faith in him, despite putting him on probation. She had even commended him for the fact he'd put his family first. Even over the team. She'd said that level of commitment was a good thing.

He knew the team could take care of themselves, but still he wanted them to be more than just a group of agents working their own angles. Would that ever change? Or would God do a work that brought them all together finally?

"Helicopter." Alvarez strode to the window and looked out. "State police, according to the decal."

Niall said, "Is that going to be a good thing?"

"It's not the FBI?"

He squeezed Haley's arm. "They're on the way, right? So we don't have to worry. Everything is going to be—"

Automatic gunfire broke through his comment.

Windows shattered.

Niall watched Alvarez's body jerk and fall, as if in slow motion.

Chapter 27

Haley landed on the ground, tossed there by Niall. Broken glass shattered across the floor. Automatic gunfire popped and cracked like fireworks. The sound of a helicopter's rotors grew louder.

His breath on her cheek wouldn't have been bad except for the circumstances. "Alvarez."

The gunfire ceased.

Niall lifted off her. "Stay here. Do not move."

Her head swam. Alvarez had said it was the state police. More bad guys, determined to harm people? Had they targeted these windows because they knew she and two federal agents were in here?

She watched him run out of sight and sat up, still tucked behind a desk. A tied-up man three feet away moaned. The dean was regaining consciousness.

She wanted him behind bars for what he'd done. Mind controlling all these college students into hurting each other? It was unthinkable. What did it prove, but that he had power over them? Some kind of social experiment. Or another reason.

Haley backed up. When he came fully around, she didn't want to be within arm's reach. She called out around the desk. "Is he all right?"

There was a fraction of a second's pause, then Niall called back in a choked voice, "We need an ambulance or he's not going to make it."

Haley ran for the phone she'd dropped and called 9-1-1.

"It's giving me a busy signal." She hung up.

They had to be overwhelmed with calls. Were they all from the college, or was this more widespread than that? She crawled over to Niall. Alvarez's chest was covered in blood. She didn't even know where the wound was, but for the fact Niall had removed his jacket and now pressed it against his friend's body.

Niall glanced at her, teeth gritted.

"The feds are on their way, right?"

He nodded. "But we don't know if they'll get here in time." Then he glanced at the window.

Haley crawled over there, trying not to get cut on broken glass. She lifted up. "The helicopter landed. There are state police, they're dressed like SWAT. They're going toward—"

Those kids. They were on their knees on the street. Hands on their heads. Most looked around at each other. A few tried to call out to the state police.

Four officers—whoever these cops were—lifted their weapons and sprayed bullets at the crowd.

Haley cried out. She scrambled around and got Alvarez's weapon from where she'd dropped it.

She swung it up, out the broken window, and pulled the trigger.

Niall yelled something. She couldn't hear it over the *bang bang bang* of the pistol in her hands. The state police guys scrambled. One dropped and didn't get up. Haley kept her aim high so she didn't hit one of the students by accident.

They were scrambling.

People ran all directions. One state police officer slammed a young woman with the butt of his rifle.

Haley shot the cop. She hit his vest, which only made him mad. He twisted to aim in her direction.

Haley ducked behind the wall under the window and covered her ears. Bullets peppered the wall and flew in the window.

"I think you pissed him off."

She glanced at Niall. "No kidding."

"And if he comes in here?" He shot her a look.

Ah. She hadn't thought of that. "What if it's a she?"

"Is it?"

"No, but—"

He cut her off. "See how much time we have."

She lifted up and looked—fired. Missed. Haley ducked back down as more bullets flew. He was going to breach the window and kill her if she didn't figure out how to get the upper hand.

Then there was nothing but the approaching sound of rubber tires meeting asphalt.

She moved to the side, just in case.

A second later, a man's face appeared in the window. But he thought she'd be in the same spot from where she'd just looked up.

Haley squeezed the trigger—

It was Niall's shot that killed him, hitting that vulnerable spot between his shoulder and helmet. The bullet blew through his neck. Haley squeezed her eyes shut for a second. He fell forward, over the window frame.

A car door slammed.

"Haley!"

She blinked and glanced at Niall.

"Who just got here?"

"I—" She tried to form more words than that.

"Look again."

Before she did so, he felt for a pulse on his teammate's neck. The clock on his life was ticking. It was winding down as his body succumbed to the trauma.

Haley pulled on the window with one hand, ignoring the sharp pain. She had to get close to the dead man. With a tight grip on the gun in her hand, she lifted to stand beside the window and then looked around the frame.

Two different groups. Bulletproof vests with FBI on them in big yellow letters. Around them, other agents swarmed in between people, moving with purpose. Guns were pointed in her direction.

Haley yelled, "We need help!"

There was nothing she could do but watch as agents made their way in, sprinting down the hall to where Niall sat beside Alvarez, trying to keep him alive. Medics were waved in. Then an ambulance that had been close by was called to the building.

Minutes later, what seemed like an eternity, Alvarez was hauled away.

The college campus was a mess. Like a massacre. Dead bodies littered the ground outside. Agents wandered between, taking pictures and laying evidence markers.

Niall didn't get up. As soon as they shifted Alvarez to a gurney, he'd sat back on the floor. He looked drained. Sad.

He lifted his hands. They were covered with blood. He let them fall back to his lap.

Haley didn't know what to say. What to do.

A federal agent walked her to a chair and sat her down. The woman agent asked her questions, and Haley had to try to think clearly enough to explain everything. Cops trying to kill them. The buzzing at the lab. The doctor and his case. The app. Her friend.

Was Ana's body still on the street?

Niall glanced at her, exhaustion and grief in his gaze, and then walked to the door. He started speaking to an agent. The one who seemed to be in charge. The agent nodded, and they both moved into the hallway where she couldn't see them anymore.

The female agent asked more questions. Then she got Haley's information, as well as her brother's address.

"I missed my interview." She didn't know why that was important. Haley wasn't even sure she cared what she did next.

The female agent frowned. "Is there someone I can call for you? Someone who can pick you up?"

Haley opened her mouth to say Niall's name. She shook her head. He was busy and worried about his friend. He had plenty of special agent things to do, which had nothing to do with her. She'd looked for Ana. Found her.

Now things were so far off the rails, she didn't know where to start. Or if it was even possible to fix any of it.

Alvarez could die. Dakota was in the hospital, Josh there with her. Victoria was getting Talia back, and there was absolutely nothing Haley could do to help. Except pray.

She needed to go somewhere and pray.

Get out of the way of these federal agents doing their jobs.

Haley said, "I'd like to call my brother."

. . .

Niall wanted to rub his hands down his face. He glanced once at where Haley sat talking with an FBI agent and then headed for a bathroom. He scrubbed twice with cheap soap to try and get Alvarez's blood off his hands, watching the red-stained water swirl down the drain.

His hands shook as he turned off the tap. The bleed off of adrenaline. Alvarez was being treated. He'd probably need surgery, and it was questionable if he'd even survive the ordeal. There was nothing Niall could do about that.

They'd brought down all the players here at the college. The FBI would take over now and tell everyone how they stopped a terrorist attack, before it could go from awful and horrific to full-out devastating. As it was, there were at least a dozen students dead.

Niall hadn't gotten to the dean before he set the app off.

No, that wasn't true. It might feel like he failed. It might feel in his soul like once again he'd come up short. But the reality was that he had done everything he could. It was the signal coming through the speakers— the one that affected Haley as well—that had driven the student to send that update.

An intellectual exercise that had resulted in so many deaths?

Niall grabbed two paper towels and held them against his face for a moment. How could such intelligent people—people who were supposed to be smarter than the rest of them—be so clueless? Where were the safeguards that protected everyone else, or consideration for the risks involved? Such an exercise should never have been connected to a real app.

But that kind of debate would be for the media, bloggers and talk shows to all pick apart and analyze in the aftermath. It didn't change what had happened. It didn't restore life where it had been taken.

Niall pushed out of the bathroom and looked for Haley first. Maybe that shouldn't have been his first instinct, given he was working, but it was where they'd come to. He needed to know she was all right—that the agent was taking care of her.

Outside was a mess. People. Blood. Smoke hung in the air. And the fuel from the state police helicopter. It looked odd parked in the middle of a walkway.

An ambulance pulled out. Probably transporting injured students. The dead were being seen to, the living aided. The trauma was never going to go away, though it would lessen some with time. Niall had known federal agents who'd worked scenes like this. The memories they lived with were almost as hard to endure as the experiences of the victims.

Someone called his name.

Niall turned, aware that to anyone who knew the signs, he looked shell-shocked.

Welvern trotted over. "O'Caran."

Niall nodded. "Have you heard from Victoria?"

"No." Welvern knew she was going after Talia.

Niall wanted an update as soon as anyone heard anything. But Welvern was the assistant director here, which meant Niall couldn't start making demands. He just about itched to go help her. If things at the college hadn't blown up the way they did, he'd have been right there alongside Victoria, getting Talia back. And who had taken her, anyway? They were going to regret doing that. All of them would make sure the consequences were serious. No doubt.

"I'll get you a phone," Welvern said. "And I'll get you an update on that as soon as there's one to have."

Niall said, "Thanks."

"No problem." Then Welvern asked him to run down everything that had happened.

Niall told him exactly what had gone down. He figured he would be reciting the same events for days, as well as filing multiple sets of reports. Later, when the dean came to trial, he would have to go over it all again.

When he was done, he said, "There's just one thing I'm not clicking on."

Welvern looked like he had a hunch as to what that was, but just said, "Tell me."

Niall gave himself a second for his thoughts to coalesce. Then he said, "The lab blew up because it was hit by a drone strike, right?"

Welvern nodded.

"Was that the state police maintaining their cover up?" It seemed out of reach for state police to use a method so destructive. He could see them burning it down. Or setting a bomb and leaving. The drone felt like…more.

Niall turned. The Cerium Center for Technology. The money behind the lab? "Talia was working on finding out who hacked NORAD when she was taken."

"Maybe that's *why* she was taken."

Niall nodded. "Then she caught their attention, trying to figure out who they are."

He couldn't help remembering the person who'd sold Clare Norton a modified version of VX gas. Someone behind a dark web server there was now no trace of.

The same person behind this research center?

Cerium.

He said, "I also think whoever sent the drone managed to set off the signal in the office that incapacitated Haley *and* the one here that caused the update to be sent."

"I can still hardly believe it." Welvern blew out a breath. "Mind control?"

Niall agreed. "Sounds like it was a combination of biological contaminants and suggestion through electronics." Given the buzzing sound Haley had heard and the app's functionality. Neither of which he really understood. "Not my forte, I'm afraid."

"Yeah, me neither." Welvern shot him a look, amused at himself. "But I have people for that."

"You'll copy us when the investigation is complete?"

Welvern nodded.

Niall said, "The case is still at large."

"Correct. But the latest word I got was that agents were closing in on its location. So I'm confident it will be recovered and in bureau hands soon."

Niall wanted to believe this was all over, but part of him just couldn't trust it. The fallout would take weeks to wade through. "Is there anything I can do here?"

"Sure," Welvern said. "We'll put you to work."

He glanced around to try and find Haley. "Any idea where Ms. Franks ended up?"

"I'll find out." Welvern wandered off.

He'd like to talk to her. Continue the conversation they'd been having in the car before the doctor slammed into the hood.

Niall wasn't all that comfortable with these unfamiliar feelings. He'd never felt this way about anyone before. He wasn't quite sure what to do with it, given it had all happened right in the middle of an investigation. He'd been trying to regain his standing with the team and rebuild some of that trust.

He'd like some time where work wasn't a factor to maybe take Haley out to coffee or dinner. There was so much to do here that his chance would likely be a few days away, and Niall didn't want to wait that long.

They hadn't had the opportunity to say much to each other that was personal through all of this, but he thought that maybe she felt the same. Attraction. Respect. Care. He wanted to be certain it was mutual. That maybe she wanted to see where this might go. The way he was sure that he did.

"My agent said she called her brother," Welvern said as he jogged back over. "He picked her up a few minutes ago."

Haley had left?

Chapter 28

Two days later

Haley pulled into the driveway of the house her brother was renovating. He pulled the front door open before she even turned off the engine. *Shoot.* He was going to see.

Isaac shook his head.

Haley climbed out and slammed her door, praying the tall box on her front seat didn't fall over onto the driver's side. There had been nowhere else to put it. The car was packed to bursting with her stuff.

"That's it?"

Haley strode toward him, keys in hand. "I can't be here." That was the crux of it. "I don't feel safe in Portland. The police…" She shivered just thinking about coming face-to-face with someone in uniform.

It had been all over the news the last couple of days. The feds had arrested so many police officers. It was crazy to think corruption had been so widespread. The National Guard had wound up having to send in men and women to help with basic police duties so there wasn't a lapse in emergency services.

The police that were left, both local and state, were honorable men and women. Those who wanted to do the right thing in their jobs. They would uphold the law and hadn't sold out to the cover up.

Haley knew that.

But it was so hard to fight the fear every time she saw a uniform. Or a badge. And that wasn't their fault. It was entirely her issue, which meant she needed time and space. She needed to get away from Portland and figure out what she was going to do next.

Isaac opened his arms. Haley nearly burst into tears. Instead she buried her face against her brother's strong chest. He held her for a moment and then let go. "Need some company?"

"I thought you'd want to stay with Blair. You would really do that for me?"

He shot her a look. "You're an idiot."

Haley smacked her fist against his shoulder. "Then no, I don't want company."

But they both knew she could use it. Haley didn't want him to give up his life and the business he'd built. Having to start over from scratch somewhere else wasn't an easy task. She could figure it out—she had some savings and time. He needed something to do.

"Don't go too far," he said. "It'll be a killer in gas money for the bike."

She nodded. So grateful he intended to come see her that she could hardly speak. "I love you."

"Whatever, dweeb." But he pulled her into his arms for another quick hug. "Love you, too." She could feel him shake his head against hers. Haley chuckled. When he let her go, he said, "You're not going to even call him and tell him you're leaving town?"

This was the part she didn't want to go over.

Haley took a step back.

"Coward."

"He's busy." It was a lame defense. "There's so much clean up, he'll probably be working for weeks."

"Plus you shot that woman."

"In the leg."

Isaac snorted. "You're trying to convince me it wasn't that bad? How about going to the hospital and talking to her? She knows you didn't do it on purpose. It's not like she's going to hold a grudge for the rest of eternity."

That was assuming Haley wanted to feel the grudge right now. Or that she had any interest in being part of their group, which of course she seriously did. She blew out a breath trying not to acknowledge the fact she was too chicken. She wanted them to be her friends. She wanted to know if Talia was back. How Dakota and Alvarez were doing. If Niall was off probation.

All of it. Any of it.

Haley wanted to be part of their lives and being apart from them hurt more than she let on. But the reality was that if she got to know them, then she would care about them more than she already did. And then she would need to save them.

"Cutting yourself off from everyone—except me—isn't the right way to move on."

"I just need—"

"Space." He sighed. "I know."

"Who's cutting people off now?"

He didn't laugh. Even though she was funny, and she had a point. Isaac just looked disappointed in her.

"Don't do that." She waved him off and took another step back.

"What?"

"That 'big brother' thing."

He said, "It's the truth. You care about these people. You care about that Navy cop. And it seems like they care about you as well, considering how many times your phone has rung the last two days." He pulled her cell from his pocket. "Texts asking if you're okay. Checking in. *Just making sure you're all right.* This is not the behavior of people who don't want you in their lives."

Haley glanced at the street, trying to figure out what she was supposed to do. She wanted to call Niall, and that was exactly what she would do if she hadn't given her phone to Isaac so that she didn't weaken her resolve and reach out in desperation. She wanted to connect. She needed to feel like she was part of something. But first, Haley had to be all right by herself. She had to find what she wanted. What she needed.

She had to find peace.

"Maybe, for once," he said softly, "you should let somebody save *you*."

. . .

Niall lifted the phone from the base and put it to his ear. Across the glass was Hassim, and the scholarship student didn't look happy to see him. Hassim just stared. Niall waved the phone, then motioned with his head for him to pick up the one on his side.

The young man did, but with reluctance.

"Thank you for speaking to me."

"My lawyer said it would look positive for me to cooperate with the authorities." Given the set of his jaw, Niall figured he didn't want to.

"I'd like to ask you about the work you were doing at the college. Specifically, who was the money behind it?" Their funding had to have come from somewhere. And the Northwest Counter-Terrorism Task Force was moving forward on the theory that the money had originated from an independent source.

Someone was funding research, and they were going to use it for ongoing acts of terrorism.

The person who was behind the server Clare Norton had accessed in order to purchase modified VX gas?

Whoever discovered Talia breaching their system and had her abducted and almost sold on the dark web?

Victoria had gotten her back, but Talia was far from all right. She just refused to speak to any of them about it. She had retreated into herself. And all of them were beyond frustrated. They were the kind of people who "fixed" problems. And this one meant more than any other had before. Yet Talia wouldn't allow them to even try.

She didn't want to be anywhere near a computer right now.

Niall wanted answers.

The scholarship student said, "Maybe you should ask *Bartlett* that question." Then rolled his eyes. "Why would I know?"

"Just humor me," Niall said. "Because it'll look good."

Hassim sighed. "The name on the building. At least that was what everyone said." He shrugged one shoulder. "They're telling me there was this other lab, out in the woods."

Cerium. That was who was behind this? Niall had never even heard of it.

Niall said, "You didn't know?"

"No, I didn't know about another lab. We did work at the school. We ran simulations. There were rats." He paused. "My part was only the programming of the app. They told me what tweaks to make, and I did those. Whether that was to try and make the rats more placid, or more aggressive, didn't matter much to me. It was science."

Niall had his own opinions of what science should or should not be doing. He'd seen too much hurt and couldn't let the idea of manipulating people go. Not completely. No one should have control of another person that way. Making them act against their will? That was what traffickers did. That was what abusers did. The idea that the college was essentially abusing all those students who were supposed to be under their "care"? It was horrifying.

Hassim might not be ultimately responsible. Though tell that to the media, because he was quickly becoming the face of it. The young man still held some culpability. He'd been a party to it, even unknowingly. There would be consequences for that. Worse for the dead and the police officers who'd covered it up.

"What can you tell me about Bartlett?" Niall asked. Everyone wanted to know what extent he was a party to everything that'd happened. It still seemed crazy to think he'd masterminded the whole thing.

Which was why he tended to go with the task force theory that someone else set everything in motion.

"He was always working some angle," Hassim said. "He'll do the same thing in trial. He'll probably go free."

"That won't happen."

Hassim's face indicated how he felt about that. "It was his idea. Everything was."

"As an intellectual exercise?"

Hassim nodded.

"And then the money had come from that outside source?"

"The other lab in the woods? I have no idea."

"Okay." Niall nodded. "Thanks."

Whatever the lab had been about, it was far more than what had gone on at the college. More than students doing experiments. Had it been the testing ground for what took place on campus? That was possible. Or it was an extension of it.

Field tests.

A new way to control people.

Some considered that the ultimate goal. Humans were unpredictable. They had a nasty habit of doing whatever they wanted. A method for controlling choices and actions would go a long way for some. Terrorists who thought everyone should believe as they did.

Freedom was under attack. And they might have fought this battle to a positive end—not the best outcome considering how many people were dead—but he wondered if there wasn't more on the horizon.

Was a war coming?

Niall drove home and let himself in the front door. Siobhan was on the couch. She didn't even look up from her phone. He stood at the entrance to the living room. "So I should change the Wi-Fi password again?"

She gasped and looked up. "You wouldn't!"

Niall chuckled. "Then get over here and say 'hi' to me."

She didn't get up. "Hi."

Niall let her go with that. He wasn't going to force her to hug him, even if he could use one right now.

His sister trotted down the stairs in jeans and a slim-fit T-shirt. "Got a date?"

She laughed. "We went shopping while we were on vacation."

"Ah." New clothes.

"When you see your credit card bill, don't hate me. Okay?"

Niall said nothing.

Patricia hugged him. "Everything okay with you?" When he nodded she lifted her brows, a tiny frown crinkling her forehead. "Liar."

"Siobhan, get in here."

When his niece wandered in to join them, he took a breath. Where was he supposed to start?

Siobhan said, "I'm not moving."

Patricia nodded. "I agree with her."

Niall said, "The team is relocating. To Seattle."

"Good." Relief washed over Patricia's face. "We'll be able to drive up and see you for the weekend sometimes."

The idea they'd stay here in Portland and he wouldn't be able to see them every day didn't sit well. It wasn't a huge issue, but he also wasn't great with the idea of leaving them. "You want to stay?"

"Yes." Siobhan hugged him and then went back to the couch and her phone.

Patricia shook her head. "She's right. We're settled here now."

"You do have a date."

She chuckled. "No, but I have a life. And I want to see what I can make of it. Something you should seriously consider doing."

"You haven't held me back. That isn't what—"

"I know." She shook her head, like she thought his discomfort was adorable. "I know you care about us. I know you like being here with us. But all of our lives move on, and they don't always go in the same direction. You were there for me when I had no one. We discovered life together and supported each other. You gave me what I desperately needed, being Siobhan's uncle and my right-hand guy." She grinned. "Don't get a big head or anything, but you're basically the best brother *ever*."

He nodded. "I know." Then took a breath. "You're really okay with me leaving?"

"You're old enough," she said. "It's time to kick you out of the nest. So go fly, little birdie."

"Dork."

She laughed. Niall hugged her, so happy that she was all right with it. That Siobhan—the teenager—didn't apparently care where he was. Whatever. Niall would still see them often, and he wouldn't have to worry so much that they were vulnerable because of his job.

Still, there was a tiny part of him that wanted to call Haley again. For the thirtieth time, or however many he was up to. Texts included.

She'd dropped off the radar since the college and he was okay with giving her space, but it would be nice to know she was all right.

Niall decided then that he would give it a week, tops. Then he would find out where she was, and go talk to her. There was too much feeling for this not to be *something*. They just had to figure out what that something was.

Epilogue

Two weeks later. Seattle, Washington

Haley was pretty sure this was a setup, but she went with it anyway. It was time to reconnect. And if this was the way they were going to do it, then that was all right with her. Neutral ground. That would be easier.

She'd been basically on vacation for the last two weeks. Sequestered in a tiny house she'd rented on a small island close to Seattle. No people. No stress. It had rained the entire time, and she'd enjoyed watching it out the window while she read.

Okay, so she was all right...but she was also completely bored.

Isaac had been plotting for the past two weeks. This was his answer.

Haley pushed open the front door, purse under her arm. Her heels clacked the tile of the foyer as she crossed to a security door. She entered the code Isaac had passed on in the email where he'd listed the time for her interview. He hadn't *said* what the company was, but she was pretty sure she had a good idea.

The door buzzed, and she pulled it open.

Inside was an open-plan office. Six desks with a couple of closed doors at the far end. The whole right side was a wall of windows with a killer view of downtown Seattle and the cloudy sky above.

Cardboard boxes littered the whole room, and there were five people here among them.

Alvarez—sitting and looking pale. Dakota, on crutches. Josh stood close to her, pulling stuff from a box. Talia was in the corner, on the floor, organizing books by the look of it. Victoria had a dusting rag in one hand, and wore "work clothes" which were everyone else's regular clothes of jeans and a shirt.

Nerves washed over her. Now that she was face-to-face with them, she couldn't deny how much she wanted to be part of this. To be part of them. Even if Niall wasn't here to talk to her.

She took a step back.

Alvarez yelled, "Don't do it. Don't run." He looked about as happy as a kid who'd just been told they were due for shots.

Haley froze. She wanted to bolt, though.

One of the doors at the far end opened, and Niall stepped into the office. "What is…" He saw her then. "Ah."

Was that good or bad? Haley had no idea. Maybe he didn't want to see her. Maybe—

"Did you guys start yet?" He looked at Victoria, then everyone else.

"No." Victoria set her dusting rag on a desk. "The place is a mess, as you can tell."

Haley stared at her.

"We have cases piling up. We need an office manager who can keep everything running, as well as someone with the training to safeguard our…assets."

Talia glanced over at Victoria's back. The director didn't see, because Talia was behind her. The NSA analyst frowned. She looked markedly more subdued than the impression Haley had gotten of her from their exchanges over the phone. Because of what had happened to her?

"So," the director said. "Do you want a job, Petty Officer Franks?"

Haley glanced at each of them. Then she settled her gaze on Dakota. "What do you think?"

"I think I'll kill you if you ever shoot me again."

Josh glanced at her but said nothing.

Dakota continued, "But I'm fine with it."

One down, one to go.

Haley said, "Niall?"

She needed to know.

Instead of answering her, he turned to Victoria. "What's your policy on dating coworkers?"

She lifted an eyebrow. "The same as my policy regarding them marrying each other." She waved in the direction of Josh and Dakota, who were both grinning.

Alvarez made a moaning sound. Haley thought she saw a tiny smile on Talia's face, but she couldn't be sure.

Niall turned to her. "Take the job. And go to dinner with me."

"And if I say no to dinner?" She wasn't going to, but things could get complicated here fast.

"Then you should take the job. So I have time to convince you about dinner."

Haley smiled. "Okay." She shifted her gaze to Victoria. "The answer is yes." Then back to Niall. "And…is seven o'clock okay?"

Did you enjoy this book?

Please consider leaving a review on your favorite book retailer.
You could also share about the book on Facebook. Your review will help other book buyers decide what to read next.

Visit www.authorlisaphillips.com where you can sign up for my NEWSLETTER.

Be the first to hear about new releases.

Also by Lisa Phillips

About the author

A British ex-pat who grew up an hour outside of London, Lisa attended Calvary Chapel Bible College
where she met her husband. He's from California, but nobody's perfect. It wasn't until her Bible College graduation that she figured out she was a writer (someone told her). Since then she's discovered a penchant for high-stakes stories of mayhem and disaster where you can find made-for-each-other love that always ends in happily ever after.
Lisa can be found in Idaho wearing either flip-flops or cowgirl boots, depending on the season. She leads worship with her husband at their local church. Together they have two children and an all-black Airedale known as The Dark Lord Elevator.

Lisa is the author of the bestselling Sanctuary (WITSEC town series), the Double Down series, and more than a dozen Love Inspired Suspense novels.

Find out more at www.authorlisaphillips.com

Made in the USA
San Bernardino, CA
21 July 2019